"YOU HAVE A CHOICE."

"You mentioned that you might need a favor, but marriage is out of the question." Monique studied Nick's handsome face. She'd never seen him look so worried.

"You will marry me for six months, or I will send you a bill."

"But Nick. . . ." Monique mulled over her choices. How could Nick force her into marrying him? But she couldn't lose her salon. "Okay. But I'm only doing this because I can't pay you."

"I understand. We'll pretend to be in love."

Monique didn't like what she was hearing. "I think we should reconsider the romantic gestures."

"If we don't show affection for each other, we might as well not bother."

Unable to deny Nick almost anything, she said, "Okay."

"I think we can pull this off," Nick said, as if aware of her indecision.

"You mean act as if we're in love," Monique said. At that moment, clear visions of Nick's passionate kisses crept out of the deep recesses of her mind where she had carefully buried them the night she had ended their love.

Nick reached out and pulled her into his arms. His lips grazed her, sending hungry sensations spiraling through her. He pulled away, lifting his head. His gaze burned deep into her soul. Nick kissed her again. Suddenly, he dropped his hands, walked to the door and stepped out onto the porch.

"Good night."

Monique closed the door. She had finally settled one disaster, only to find herself in another disaster worse than the first.

REAL LOVE

MARCELLA SANDERS

BET Publications, LLC
www.msbet.com
www.arabesquebooks.com

ARABESQUE BOOKS are published by

BET Publications, LLC
c/o BET BOOKS
One BET Plaza
1900 W Place NE
Washington, D.C. 20018-1211

First Printing: February, 2000
10 9 8 7 6 5 4 3 2 1

Printed in the United States of America

ONE

Monique McRay's ringing phone sent her hurrying from the closet to her bedroom to answer the call.

"Monique."

Nick Parker's warm voice sent a ripple through her, arousing memories from the past summer.

"Nick," she said, hoping he hadn't changed his mind about assisting her with her disastrous financial problem.

"Are we still on for this morning?" Monique stilled her subconscious that threatened to surface memories, reminding her of the love that she and Nick had shared that past summer.

"Yes, we are." Nick paused. "But there's a change in location."

"What do you mean, a change in location," Monique questioned her lawyer.

"I had an important meeting at the hotel this morning, so I . . ."

"Are you saying that my business is unimportant?"

"I didn't say that."

"So, what exactly are you saying?"

Nick chuckled. "Our meeting is just as important as the meeting I had this morning with the Young Men of Tomorrow club."

"Good, I wouldn't want you to grant me any special favors."

"I thought it would work out if I met with you here, instead of driving to the office." For a moment, Nick was silent. "We could have breakfast and discuss your problem."

"Are you assuming that I didn't have breakfast?"

"Did you?"

"No, I didn't."

"Then what's the problem?"

The problem was clear, Monique considered. In Nick's office, she knew he would be all business. She wouldn't have to answer any of his questions on why she broke off their summer romance. With this thought in mind, Monique considered the restaurant too casual for a meeting. "I . . . the office would be better."

"What are you afraid of?"

"Nothing," Monique said, wanting to end the phone conversation.

Nick's husky laughter reached out to her over the telephone line.

"I don't see the humor in this."

"Look, you asked for my assistance and I agreed to give it to you. Where we meet shouldn't be a problem."

"And that makes you laugh."

Nick's laughter rang out to her. "Why are you so cranky this morning?"

"I'm not cranky."

"Listen, I'm not going to fight with you. Do you want my help?"

"Yes," Monique finally said. Not only did she want his help, she needed it.

Unlike her, Nick Parker was a man who kept his word. She had consciously promised to love him, until the past reared its ugly head, leaving her no choice but to wrap her feelings in her mental cocoon until she was certain it was safe to love again.

"...'ll be waiting for you," Nick said, cutting into her thoughts.

"I'm on my way," Monique heard herself say in a strained voice.

Nick's good-bye seemed to hold the same final ring as it had the night she had told him their romance was over.

For a moment after Nick hung up, Monique held the phone to her breast, wishing that her meeting with the man she loved could be more than a business meeting, discussing her unpaid debts and phone calls to a company that threatened to destroy her business.

That alone had kept her busy and her mind free from thinking about the love that she was unable to share with Nick Parker.

Monique took the gray wool angora pullover from the plump, sugary-white comforter that covered her bed. She stroked the soft wool material with one manicured finger before slipping into the sweater.

As Monique stroked the soft material, she remembered how just a few months ago her life had been almost as warm and cozy. All of that had changed when she bought her second skin salon, Shagreen II.

Monique picked up and opened the folder that held her future. She read one of the threatening letters. Apprehension coursed through her. She laid the folder back on the nightstand and went to her closet.

She chose a pair of black heels from the shoe rack and stuck her feet into them as her thoughts wavered.

Her financial problems seemed to have been growing by leaps and bounds since the manager of Shagreen II had run off without leaving the expected two weeks' notice. The young woman gave up her position at Shagreen II to work with her boyfriend in a cruise ship beauty salon.

Regarding the fact that her business was on a downhill slope, her nonexistent love life offered small promise of

fruition. This consideration brought back memori
Nick Parker for the second time that morning.

All summer, Monique and Nick were lovers. It wa
Monique who insisted that they end their romance.

Nick wanted them to share more than hot smothering
kisses that made her body sizzle, turning her blood into
scalding liquid that inched through her, scorching her
body and mind. It was as if the passionate imprints on her
soul were a permanent stencil that promised never to fade.

For Monique, taking their relationship to another level
was impossible. She had issues in her life that needed to be
solved and questions that needed to be answered. She
would not give all of herself until the scattered puzzle of
her life had been connected and laid out for her to see and
accept.

Therefore, a love affair with Nick Parker was off limits.
With Nick's demanding kisses, it was all she could do to
smother the fiery passion that threatened to ignite.

Monique dismissed her deliberation quickly. Too
quickly. Just thinking about Nick Parker gave her unabashed thrills and passion that tempted her to dismiss
her promise to search for the misplaced pieces of her life.
She wanted to succumb to his world, and share his linger-
ing, soul-shivering intimacy.

Monique turned on her high heels, went to her bedroom and stuck a pair of diamond earrings in her ears.
She banished any musings about Nick Parker, sending the
thoughts back to the deep recesses of her mind.

The clock on her nightstand indicated she had twenty
minutes to get to her meeting with Nick. Monique took
her purse and folder that held the creditors' threatening
letters, and hurried downstairs.

She was confident that Nick would help her solve her
problem as she stepped out of her house into the cool fall
airy morning. She walked through crimson, brown and
yellow leaves that had floated from the tall oak tree at the

edge of her yard, on to the brown and green patched lawn like colorful confetti. Monique made a mental note to call the lawn service.

"Hey girl," Monique smiled and spoke to her neighbor and best friend Colleen Jones, who was going to her car.

Colleen walked across the lawn to where Monique was standing by her car. She waved her hand at a leaf that flew from the tree and over her short haircut.

"Did you take care of that problem you're having with the equipment company?" Colleen asked as she shifted her petite body on her black heels.

"I'm on my way to meet with Nick now," Monique said. A slight shiver crawled up her spine as she considered seeing his handsome face again.

"Monique, why don't you tell Nick the reason that you broke up with him?"

"Because . . ." Monique started, but Colleen stopped her.

"Because you don't think he'll understand?"

Silently, Monique agreed. The fear of being rejected was too painful.

"I'd rather wait and see what the outcome will be," Monique said, not wanting to involve herself in a serious relationship until she was sure that there weren't skeletons in her closet that would ruin her love life and turn the man she loved away from her forever.

"While you're worrying over something that probably doesn't matter to Nick, you could be dating that man, girl."

"Colleen, you don't understand."

"No Monique, I do understand." Colleen shifted her work bag onto her shoulder. "I told George that what happened in my past was going to stay there. If he couldn't live with it, fine. I was moving on."

"But George is different. He seems so understanding," Monique said, remembering how she had been rejected by the man she was supposed to marry. He had seemed understanding, too. Once his family had learned about her past, the wedding was off.

"Of course George is different. But you didn't give Nick a chance to make a decision."

"I know that, Colleen." Monique checked her watch. "I have to go."

"Me, too," Colleen said. "We'll talk later."

"Sure," Monique replied. Any discussion concerning Nick Parker was off limits. Monique wanted to forget what she and Nick had once shared.

Monique unlocked her car door and got in, with the memories of her and Nick's love affair surfacing from the corner in her mind.

As she prepared to drive to the hotel for her breakfast meeting with the man she knew might never be a part of her life, she wished she had never asked him to help her. Seeing Nick again meant smothering old flames that hid behind her heart. But she had asked for his assistance. Now, she was forced to be in his presence, taking care of business problems, instead of relishing in an unabashed love affair.

Tailing that unpleasant reality was the undeniable truth. She was sorry their romance had dissolved into nothing more than a business relationship.

Once again, Monique pushed her musings to the back of her mind. She started her car, eased the gear into reverse and backed out into the street. She waited for a passing car before slipping the gear into drive and turning on the radio.

A love song that she and Nick had danced to at a party on the lake reeled her back to the warm summer night. Nick had held her close and whispered sweet nothings in her ear. Unable to forget, she softly hummed the tune of the sensual love song while the radio played.

In the meantime, Monique drove across town, lost in

her pondering. She could almost feel Nick's strong arms around her waist, pressing her against his hard, strong body as she inhaled the heady cologne. That night, she knew that she wanted him.

Monique pressed on the gas pedal and drove to the hotel, passing rows of houses in her tree-lined neighborhood until she reached the thick traffic that led to the hotel. She slowed her speed and turned her attention to the wedding shop in the strip mall across the street.

Tall slender mannequins dressed in long flowing white gowns, with pink bouquets pasted to their hands, slowly rotated on movable stands. The display reminded Monique that her chances to have a wedding were slim and none.

She drove past the wedding shop and moved in to the slow thick traffic on the narrow street. She crossed the bridge that led to the hotel where Nick was waiting for her.

Minutes later, free from any smoldering thoughts about Nick Parker, Monique got out of her car and stepped out into the cool fall morning, squinting against the bright sun rays that peeked out from behind fluffy white clouds.

Monique took brisk steps across the parking lot and through the hotel's glass doors. She smiled and nodded to the desk clerk as she passed, moving down the corridor to the hotel's dining room.

Low-volume contemporary music piped from wall speakers in the dining room. Monique's black heels sank into the thick plush blue carpet as she took measured steps, passing rows of round tables covered with white linen cloths and centered with dried scarlet and small bouquets.

While Monique searched the room for Nick, she tuned out the soft rumbling voices and the crinkling sounds the morning's newspaper made while being turned and folded by the breakfast diners.

Monique saw Nick sitting near the back of the room. His dark wavy head bent as if he was in deep concentration studying the paper in his hands. She moved toward him, feeling the familiar fluttering around her heart.

Seeing Nick again for the first time since she had dissolved their relationship shouldn't have posed a problem for her. But it had. She knew that the choice she had made to stop dating him would never allow her to look into his soft brown eyes again or feel his lips against hers, capturing hers with his drugging kisses. Monique banished her musing, remembering her and Nick's love affair was much too hard to bear.

"Good morning Nick," Monique interrupted him from his reading.

Nick looked from the paper he was reading, and Monique could've sworn that she detected a sparkle in his dark eyes.

"Monique." Nick flashed her a pearl-white smile. He laid the paper down in front of him and rose to his full six-feet three-inch height.

Nick walked around the table and pulled out a chair for her.

"Are you feeling better?"

"What do you mean, am I feeling better?" Monique answered him with a question while sitting in the chair he had pulled back for her.

"You sounded as if you were upset this morning," Nick reminded her while walking around the table to his chair. He sat and lifted his briefcase from the floor, put the papers he had been studying inside the case, and snapped it shut.

"I was not upset." Monique placed her purse and the folder on the table before she looked into his soft, dark eyes. Monique turned her attention to the waitress that walked over to their table.

"Are you ready to place your order?" The waitress poised her pen over the pad she was holding, her glance switching from Nick to Monique.

"Coffee for me," Monique said, smiling up at the woman.

"Same here," Nick said to the waitress. He turned his attention back to Monique.

"You want to talk about it?" Nick asked, holding her gaze.

"There's nothing to talk about except the business that I need you to take care of for me," she stated in a firm, confident voice.

Any other discussion is not necessary, she considered, realizing that Nick had never accepted her explanation for breaking off the budding affair.

"You know what I mean," he said, holding her gaze while the waitress set the coffeepot on the table.

"Nick, it's over. Put a period behind it and move on." Monique forced herself to lower her gaze. She poured herself a cup of coffee and reached for the sugar. She stirred the hot liquid slowly before sipping it.

"When you give me a reason that I can accept, maybe I will. But right now, nothing makes sense." Nick's voice was edged with steel. He filled his cup with coffee, not bothering to sweeten it.

"There are no other explanations," Monique said, wanting to change the subject. She glanced at him and his eyes seemed to brim with fire.

"What's the problem with Shagreen II?" Nick leaned back in his chair, resting his arms on the chair handles.

Thankful that Nick had decided to get down to business and not continue his interrogation for the true reasons she had ended their relationship, Monique handed him the folder.

She had mentioned some of the details of her problem relating to her business when she called to ask for his assistance. However, in the middle of their phone conversation, there had been a small crisis in the salon. Monique had told Nick that she would discuss the details in full at their meeting.

She explained to him how Faceology Equipment was planning to bring a lawsuit against her if she didn't pay or come up with a plan to clear her debt.

Nick opened the folder and read the information.

"I'll take care of it," Nick said, reaching down to get his briefcase. He opened it and put Monique's folder inside.

"There's one other thing," Monique said.

Nick pushed his chair away from the table. "I'm listening."

"I need to know how you are going to bill me for your services."

Nick reached down and lifted his briefcase, setting it on the table.

"Don't worry about it. I might need a favor from you."

"I want to pay you."

"We'll work something out." Nick stood up and walked around to Monique. He reached out and covered her hand with his free hand, slowly and seductively pulling her up to stand beside him.

Standing close to him with his hand covering hers, inhaling his masculine cologne, was enough to make her give up on her reasons not to date Nick Parker, and take a blind chance on being with the man she totally desired. Suddenly, her good senses returned. Monique believed that it would be in her best interest to stick to her plan.

Nick freed Monique's hand from his and took his suede brown jacket from the back of his chair, and pulled it on.

With slow, even steps, Monique walked with Nick out of the hotel's dining room, stopping at the register so that Nick could pay and tip the waitress for the coffee.

Visions of scattering her cares to the wind and allowing handsome Nick Parker to make sizzling sweet love to her returned and skidded across her mind.

"Thanks Nick," Monique said once she was outside standing on the curb next to him, preparing to go to her car. She silently hoped that Nick would be successful in helping her solve her problems with her creditors.

Nick slipped his strong arm around her waist and walked with her to her car.

Relishing in the comfort of his closeness and the effects of his arms around her waist, Monique didn't resist. She allowed herself to enjoy the moment and dream of what might have been. If, however, her findings from her past were acceptable she would be free to love Nick without fear. A scary thought winged its way across her mind. *If he's still free for you to love.* The small voice warned her.

They reached her car. Nick pulled Monique around to face him. He pressed her against him with his free hand, while still holding on to his briefcase with the other. Lowering his head, his lips brushed hers like soft feathers, sending tingling sensations through her. Still she didn't resist.

"We need to talk." Nick's voice was low and smooth. He kissed her again.

Speechless, Monique allowed herself to sink against his rock-hard chest and enjoy the moment that she thirsted for, as the desire to change her mind played with her heart.

Nick gathered Monique closer, crushing her to him, and he parted her lips with the tip of his tongue, smothering her lips with a masterful kiss.

Unable to walk out of his embrace, Monique slipped her arms around his neck, savoring the sweetness of Nick's kiss and ignoring her instincts that silently warned her to run.

Nick held Monique at arm's length. "I'm serious," he said, releasing her.

"Nick, I need time," Monique said, retrieving her car

keys from her purse. She unlocked and opened her car door.

"I'm willing to give you all the time you need, Monique." He placed one hand on the door, opening it wider. "But you know how I feel about you."

Monique sank down on the seat. She couldn't give Nick a response or an answer, because she wasn't sure how long Nick would have to wait.

Nick closed the car door. Monique watched him take long strides across the parking lot to his car. To Monique, everything about Nick was right; the way his short brown suede jacket hugged his narrow waist; his jeans fit just perfectly, hugging his slim hips; the sensation that weaved its way through her body and settled around her heart when his hand touched her; his kiss. Monique closed her eyes and leaned her head against the headrest on her car seat, her lips still burning from Nick's hot tantalizing kiss.

Monique sat in her car longer than she intended, savoring the moments and replaying the intimacy that she and Nick had shared. Finally, she inserted the key into the ignition and drove to work.

She knew that she had followed her heart instead of her level head. But resisting Nick Parker wasn't easy. She drove out of the parking lot and onto the street, promising herself that she would take heed of the red flags that waved a danger warning when it came to Nick. There were no spaces in her life for love and romance.

TWO

The rich aroma from the perfume greeted Monique as she made her entrance into Shagreen aesthetician salon. Several clients were seated on the mauve leather sofa and matching pink winged-back chairs, reading magazines in front of the stone fireplace while they waited for their appointments.

A thick glass tabletop rested on an unstained oak branch which served as a coffee table. Lamps with wide-brim shades sat on matching end tables standing on each side of the sofa. Behind the sofa stood four thick corn plants, their long green shiny leaves barely touching the gold vertical blinds.

"Good morning," Monique spoke to her patrons as she slipped past them and headed behind the glass counter. Her receptionist, Tamika, was kneeled down behind the counter arranging the gold necklaces around the velvet statues.

"Hi, Tamika," Monique spoke to the twenty-year-old woman as she went over to check the appointments on the computer. As usual Shagreen's appointment file was booked for the week. It was Shagreen II that kept Monique awake nights and in a tizzy.

"These are for you." Tamika rose from her kneeling position, reaching into the pile of messages that she'd taken that morning.

Monique read one pink sheet after another. When she came to the message from Elaine, the manager at Shagreen II, she set it aside and went to the next. Her last message was from Roger Cummings. He was in town and wanted to talk to her.

A twinge of curiosity settled over Monique. If Roger was prepared to continue working on the project, she simply wasn't ready. What if he had worked on the project and found out the information that she needed to know? Monique dismissed that idea, and lifted a flyer from the fax tray.

MEN, PAMPER YOURSELF AT SHAGREEN II

Monique had played with the idea for weeks before making a final decision whether or not to advertise for a male clientele. After giving the matter careful consideration, she asked Elaine to put together a flyer for her approval.

Monique held the advertisement out in front of her, reading the bold heading. She wondered if Nick was interested in being pampered.

He was well groomed. His square fingernails were clean and buffed to a shine, even though his hobby was working on old cars. His olive face was clean shaven except for his neatly trimmed black mustache. If it weren't for the small scar at the edge of his jaw line, his skin would be flawless.

With those considerations, Monique wasn't sure if Nick would patronize her establishment. Maybe, maybe not, she mused, pressing the flyer against her breast, savoring the taste of Nick's sweet burning kiss that seemed to have etched a place in her that she knew only he could fill.

Banishing the memories of her early morning passion, she checked the appointment book before she went in to her office. The appointment book was almost filled except for thefour o'clock time slot for the next day.

Hoping that the four o'clock appointment would be filled before the day was over, Monique went to her office to call Roger.

Monique unlocked her office door and stood in the doorway for a moment before seating herself behind her desk to call Roger, who was nothing but trouble. He had a tendency to stir up trouble, constantly reminding her of her past and her childhood.

She dialed Roger's cellular phone number. On the second ring Roger answered her call.

"Roger, what's this message you have for me?" Monique got up from her chair, paced around to the front of the desk, and sat on the edge while waiting for Roger's reply.

"I have the information that you want, except for one small detail."

Monique drew in her breath and let it out slowly. "Roger, I asked you not to continue the search until I settled the salon business."

Roger couldn't resist reminding her that if Nick knew her secret he would disavow that he ever knew her.

"Monique, you can always pay me later. Besides, that's what friends are for."

"I wish you hadn't continued without my permission," Monique said, annoyed that Roger had taken the liberty to help her.

"All right, all right. I'll ask for your permission before I gather the other information."

"Good Roger, you do that." Monique hung up. She didn't know what drastic or pleasant news Roger had for her. If the news was good, she would be free to love Nick. If it wasn't . . . Monique let the unfinished thought slip from her mind. Like magic, her mind replaced the horrible thoughts that had begun to rise with images of her and Nick loving each other.

Again, Monique banished her musings, as anxiety swept through her. *Please let Roger's findings be good.*

While contemplating Roger, Monique went over and straightened a plaque on the wall near her desk. She had never considered her life a secret. She just hadn't gotten around to telling Nick her past history. Besides, the timing was not right.

Monique understood her situation clearly. She had no intention of settling down into happy matrimony with the few dates she'd had over the years after her first romantic misfortune. Therefore she had no reason to disclose information concerning her life to Nick, other than current information.

But Nick . . . he was different. Why hadn't she told him when Roger proceeded to remind her. She hadn't. Instead, she had hired Roger to find the information she needed.

The phone buzzed, drawing Monique back to the moment at hand.

"Monique speaking."

"I have a client that needs the works . . . facial, pedicure," Colleen said. "Can you fit her in?"

"We're booked for the day," Monique said. "But I can give her an appointment for tomorrow afternoon at four o'clock."

"I'll let her know," Colleen said. "How did the meeting go?"

"It went well. I think things will be taken care of," Monique replied, leaving out the intimate details that took place between her and Nick after the meeting.

"You're not considering taking him back?"

Monique was quiet. She had considered the possibilities all morning.

"Colleen, you are a nosy woman."

"How am I going to know if I don't ask?"

"I never asked you about your and George's business," Monique said.

"True. But you did ask me to take George back when we broke up."

"That's because you kept pestering me. Telling me how much you loved him."

"I took your suggestion and now we're happy."

"As I said before, my meeting with Nick went well."

"That's all right, keep your little business to yourself," Colleen chuckled.

"Good-bye, Colleen." Monique hung up.

Determined to keep her mind free from thinking about Nick, Monique swiveled her chair back to the computer and made out checks to her suppliers. While the checks printed, memories of Nick cradling her in his arms floundered across her mind.

Quickly, Monique banished the thought and called the linen supply company. About two dozen towels were fraying around the edges. Monique placed the order.

When the checks were finished printing, she took them from the tray and began signing them. She had to keep busy. Seeing Nick had refreshed too many old memories.

With determination to keep her mind clear of Nick, Monique signed the last check and carried them out to the reception area. She dropped the checks in the tray and hurried back to her office.

It was almost impossible to wipe the memories of Nick from her mind. A flash of anxiety wavered through her as she considered what would happen to her business if Nick was unsuccessful in solving her financial problem.

Worrying about her financial predicament replaced the memories of her earlier unabashed trifling. She had shamelessly allowed herself to enjoy Nick's tantalizing affection.

She didn't know what was worse, thinking about Nick or fretting over her money problems and the final results of both situations.

No matter how hard she tried, one delicious passionate thought after another surfaced, bringing Nick Parker to mind, astonishing her with the fulfillment she allowed herself to relish in. It was as if he had touched the vacant space that lay between her heart and her soul, that only he could fill and satisfy.

Stop it, she told herself, leaving her office. Monique headed up front to assist Tamika with the clients.

THREE

Nick slowed the speed on his hunter green BMW as he approached his grandmother's land. White fence posts stood alongside the brown pasture, serving as a guard for the two or three black and white cattle that grazed on a haystack.

Nick neared a clump of oak trees that towered over the lane, marking the trail up to the faded white mini-mansion.

The faded black sign etched in white letters clearly read, "Morgan Estate." Nick could almost smell the dry hay as he turned into the dirt trail that led to the house. He drove closer to the house, noticing the horse stable that sat further back against the trees. The scent of the stable's fresh red paint penetrated the cool fall air.

He parked his car, got out and walked across the field, the heels of his boots crunching against the hard dirt. Carefully he surveyed the land, considering the possibility that one day he would own it. Nick's dream was to build a camp for the inner-city children, especially the children who were members of the community center.

The way things were going now, he had serious doubts that the camp would ever materialize. He moved closer toward the faded barn that was more gray than white. The building was old, but the structure was good.

Nick pulled the latch and opened the squeaking door.

A slit of the morning's sunlight streamed through a crack in a wall on the far side of the barn. Nick adjusted his eyes to the partially dark room, allowing himself to ponder the idea of how he was going to own this property.

In his deliberations, Monique McRay came to mind. Nick moved farther into the barn, wondering what pressing problems Monique had that were keeping them apart. *Was Monique married and getting a divorce? Did she have other problems, in addition to owing Faceology for equipment.*

And what was this project she worried and fretted over? One unanswered question after another trekked across his mind. He decided to take a look at the house. Maybe the house would take his mind off her. Nonetheless, thoughts of Monique stayed with him.

He had caught a glimpse of her when she made her entrance at the hotel and walked to his table that morning. The gray outfit she wore was sexy, capturing the roundness of her hips and showing off her narrow waist. Her long black hair bounced, lifting slightly, showing off the tiny diamond earrings she wore.

If anyone would have told him he was capable of feeling passion after his divorce, he would have told them they were lying. He had been careful, staying in control of his emotions, until he met Monique McRay. Only to have her discard him as if he was an old magazine to be picked up later and read.

Somehow, when he wasn't paying attention, Monique had slipped into his heart, then quickly slipped out. Now she was back. She needed him. He would move mountains for her if he could.

Nick walked out of the barn and back into full sunlight, dismissing his thoughts about Monique, while climbing the steps to the thirteen-room house.

Taking long steps, he crossed the porch to the front door and jiggled the knob. Locked. Nick looked around to see if the caretaker was nearby.

"Hey!" Nick heard a voice.

Nick turned around to face Wallace, the caretaker.

"I need to get in," Nick said, watching as Wallace straightened the western brim on his gray head.

Wallace pulled a ring of keys from his overalls pocket. He unlocked the door and stood back for Nick to walk inside. "Your grandmother is finally getting rid of this place, uh?" Wallace asked, following Nick into the living room, which was filled with boxes and old chairs, a few tables and worn lamps with faded pink and light blue shades.

"It seems like she has made up her mind," Nick said, remembering that his grandmother had decided to give what would have been his share of the property to her granddaughter, if and when Sharmain ever married.

When Nick married, a portion of the land was to be given to him for a wedding gift. For some reason, his grandmother did not like the woman he was marrying.

Lucy Morgan had a few choice words to say about Nick's bride-to-be. His grandmother thought Debra was spoiled rotten and someone who thought that the sun didn't shine until she got out of bed the next day.

As the result of his grandmother's evaluation, Nick and Debra did not get the land for a wedding gift.

Nick stood in the center of the living room where he, Brant and Sharmain spent many summers. He realized that his grandmother saw something in his ex-wife that he hadn't seen. Nick moved through the room, appreciating his grandmother's sound judgment.

"I think we'll have this place fixed up before a wedding takes place," the caretaker said as he followed Nick into the study.

So, Nick thought, *Sharmain is planning to marry soon.*

"Needs a little paint, a few walls patched," Wallace said, scratching his fingernail against the chipped beige wall, drawing Nick out of his musing.

"Yeah." Nick acknowledged the caretaker with staid calmness. He remembered when Brant got married, their grandmother's wedding gift was several acres of land.

However, Nick's grandmother didn't hesitate to let it be known that if Nick married again before Sharmain did, and she approved of his bride, she would gladly give him the house and the surrounding acres.

Nick moved over to the dusty blond bookcase that stood against the wall. He wiped one finger across the case and realized that the coloring underneath all the dust and cobwebs held a glossy shine.

A few books sat in the corner on the middle shelf. Nick opened the century-old dictionary. Dust flew from the pages and up his nostrils, activating his hay fever and sending him into a sneezing frenzy.

"I'll be outside if you need anything," Wallace said, heading out through the back, as if Nick's sneezing was contagious.

"I'll speak with you later, Wallace," Nick said, between sneezes.

A terrifying realization inched across his mind, promising to pose a problem almost as discomforting as his hay fever. Before he could build the camp on his grandmother's land for the inner city children, he had to get married.

Nick walked outside and stood on the front porch. He needed a wife, which would serve as a master plan to keep his cousin from receiving the land. He wondered if Monique would marry him. She was the sweetest woman he had ever known.

It was as if a picture of Monique was forever frozen in his mind. Her soft full lips were, to say the least, a compliment to her lemon complexion. Her slender waist and round hips . . . Nick dismissed his vision and quickly drew himself back to the present, facing the dreadful truth.

Monique had ended their relationship. She didn't want him. He knew that, and he had kissed her anyway.

Nick went to his car. He sat behind the wheel and looked out over the land that could be his if only . . . Nick started the engine. He had work to do.

It wasn't long before Nick had made the trip back into town. He was undecided on how he was going to own the property that had been in the family longer than he had been on this earth.

He walked into his office. The only light that lit his office was the blue, yellow and green circles that rolled lazily across the screen saver on his computer.

Nick moved past the leather-bound law books on the bookshelf that covered an entire wall. Before seating himself behind his desk, he opened the vertical blinds, exposing the smoky tinted windows that displayed a bird's-eye view of Forest, New Jersey. He pulled off his jacket and laid it on the sofa.

He sat at his desk and opened the folder with information on his next case. He couldn't concentrate. He tried. All he could think of was how good Monique had felt in his arms this morning.

Nick pulled his thoughts together and began working on Amelia Wakefield's case. She had breezed into town a few months ago and had chosen his firm to handle her legal matters.

Nick studied the documents carefully. A large sum of Amelia's late husband's finances were tied up in probate. There wasn't anything he could do with the report until he received the doctor's evaluation.

Nick laid the folder aside and swiveled his chair to face the window. He got up, walked over to the window and looked down at the street, trying to keep his mind from wavering to Monique. It was useless. He could almost smell her perfume.

He made his way to the conference table and dropped down in one of the chairs. He stretched his legs out, locked his fingers behind his head, and closed his eyes.

He had two problems. One. He wanted Monique. Two. He wanted his grandmother's property. Could he have both? He quieted his thoughts as if by doing that, he would receive an answer to his question.

Instead, he thought of his divorce. For several moments he allowed the bad memories to reel across his mind like a bad movie. He made the choice for all the wrong reasons when he married.

The door to his office opened. Nick's best friend and partner Stone Johnson walked in wearing one of his usual expensive suits. Stone sat across from Nick.

"Looks like you got problems, Parker." Stone crossed one leg over his thigh, folded his arms across his chest and waited for an answer.

Stone was almost forty, tall and lean, with black hair and eyes the color of onyx.

"I'm not sure," Nick said, opening his eyes.

"Let me see," Stone said, tilting his head, looking at the ceiling as if he was thinking. "You met with Monique McRay this morning." He looked at Nick as if checking his buddy's reactions.

Nick straightened. Stone understood him most of the time. But he didn't understand this problem. What if Monique was just like his ex-wife? Nick quickly pushed the question out of his mind.

"What's she up to?" Stone asked, referring to the information that Nick had told him after Monique broke off their relationship.

"She's still working on her project, and believe me, I'd like to know what the project is about."

Stone reached into his jacket pocket and pulled out two tickets.

"While you're worrying, have fun." Stone slid the tickets toward Nick.

Nick smiled. Amelia Wakefield was having a bachelorette's auction to raise money for the local orphans and foster children.

"Well?" Stone questioned.

"I . . . it's not a bad idea," Nick said, wondering if Monique would like to attend the auction with him. "No," Nick said after rolling the thought around in his head.

"What do you mean, no?" Stone asked his friend.

Nick rested his chin between his forefinger and thumb. "I was thinking about asking Monique to go with me, but . . ." his voice trailed.

Nick didn't want to give Monique any indication that going to Amelia's party meant she had repaid his favor.

"I'm not going."

"Nick, if you keep this up, you'll be older and grayer before you learn to have fun." Stone tapped his fingers against the table. "You need to take a vacation and meet some women in another state."

"I don't want to meet women from other states. And what do you mean . . . older and grayer?" Nick touched the gray strands that edged his temple.

Stone let out an easy laugh. "Remember, all women are not carbon copies of your ex-wife."

"Stone, man, I thought you knew me."

"Are you trying to tell me that you're not having women problems?"

Nick leaned further back in his chair. "Stop analyzing me."

"I . . . knew it," Stone said, slamming his fist against the table.

"Stone, get out of my business, man."

"Now let me see, ahhh, I know you're not losing it over that little puny-looking woman."

Nick raised up long enough to give Stone a half-masked look.

Stone laughed. "It has to be that fine woman . . . you know, the one with those salons. Tell me I'm right."

Nick smothered a smile. "Don't you have someplace to go?" Nick asked in a desperate firm tone. How was he going to forget Monique if Stone continued to remind him.

Stone checked his watch. "Matter of fact I do. I need to settle a score with Brant." Stone stood up. "Oh yeah, I bought a car. You will help me fix it right?" he asked Nick.

"When are you going to the garage?"

"We can go by the garage tonight."

"I'll be there."

"Hey Nick, remember what I said about those women, buddy."

"Will you go to lunch."

Nick knew Stone was right. He also knew all women weren't alike. Or at least he hoped every woman wasn't a replica of his ex-wife. What didn't fit was that he knew he cared for Monique more than he'd ever wanted to.

He went to the computer and pulled up Faceology Equipment. After studying the company's payment plans and options, he went to his desk and called Faceology.

He spoke to the credit manager on Monique's behalf. Nick decided that the best way to solve Monique's problem was to ask for the special program that Faceology Equipment had recently established. The manager was willing to work with this payment plan for Monique. However, Monique would have to pay on time. Any late payments would void the contract.

Nick made a mental note to speak to Monique about these matters and receive a dollar figure on what she would be prepared to pay monthly.

A tap on his office door interrupted his reflections concerning the woman he wanted in his life.

Thinking it was his secretary, he allowed the person to enter.

"Come in," Nick said, putting Amelia Wakefield's folder inside the file in his desk, without looking up to see who was in his office.

Detecting the familiar scent of perfume that floated out to him, Nick looked up from the files.

"Jacqueline." Nick said, surprise ringing in his voice. "What can I do for you?"

"You can have lunch with me," Jacqueline cooed as she sauntered across the office floor. Her off-white dress was a little too sexy for lunch, Nick considered as he closed the drawer to his desk file and sat back in his chair.

"And don't tell me that you're working through lunch. It is not acceptable," she smiled, sitting across from him.

"No, I hadn't planned to work on my break," Nick assured her. He studied Jacqueline's heart-shaped face for a moment. Her makeup was expertly applied. Her hands and nails seemed as if they had been freshly manicured.

"What are you looking at?" Jacqueline asked Nick.

Nick moved his mouth to speak, only the words didn't come. He shook his head. "Nothing. I mean. I can't look at you?" Nick said, measuring his words.

"Well, I must go back to Shagreen II more often if I'm going to get attention like this," she said, leaning over so her cleavage showed more.

"Maybe you should do that," Nick said, turning his attention to a letter that he wanted his secretary to file.

"I understand that the salon will be serving men soon. You should check it out."

"I might," Nick said, avoiding looking at Jacqueline's bosom.

"Are you in a bad mood or something?" she asked Nick.

"No," Nick said, not liking the way she was going out

of her way to show herself off to him. It wasn't that he was a control freak, at least he didn't think he was. Sometimes, he wanted to be the first to approach.

In this case, he and Jacqueline had close contact once. She seemed to think that a certain kind of closeness signified love.

"What's wrong?" Jacqueline inquired.

Nick pushed away from his desk and stood up. He walked over to the sofa, picked up his jacket and put it on.

Jacqueline rose from the leather chair she had been sitting in. "Are you trying to tell me something?"

Nick pulled his jacket up around his shoulders and straightened.

"Jacqueline, let's just be friends."

"I want more than a minor friendship, Nick. You know that."

"I'm not ready for a serious relationship with you, and I don't think you are either," Nick said.

"Oh, you're ready for a serious relationship." She stopped and brushed one hand over her new hairdo. "It's just me that you're not ready to have a serious relationship with."

"I don't understand."

"Then let me enlighten you."

"You see, my apartment is being repaired. So, I had to get a hotel room last night. And who did I see this morning having breakfast with that witch who owns Shagreen or Shagreen II, but you."

"Wait a minute Jacqueline, I don't have to explain myself to you."

"Of course not," she said.

It sounded to Nick that Jacqueline's words would choke her as she lashed out at him.

"Then what's the problem?" Nick asked sharply, trying to control the fury that was rising in him. Jacqueline was acting if she was his wife and he had been unfaithful to her. He understood that an explanation would have clarified the heated argument that he and Jacqueline were having. It was a matter of telling her that his meeting with Monique was business. Nick chose not to explain. His professional or his personal life was not Jacqueline's business.

"Did you sleep with her last night?" An icy frost hung on the edge of her question.

Nick hadn't expected that his involvement with Jacqueline would lead to this. He swallowed hard, and again he tried to suppress his anger.

"I think that we should end this conversation," Nick replied with contempt.

Jacqueline walked over to the chair where she had sat earlier and leaned against it. "I went to Shagreen II this morning just to see this woman. But I guess she was with you."

Nick started moving toward the door, as Jacqueline's accusing words floated out and stabbed at him. There was no room in his life for her. He had many women clients. He could imagine that Jacqueline's bristling indignation would send his clients running to his competition. But Monique wasn't just a client, she was the woman that he would love to spend the rest of his life with, if only she would allow him to do so.

Jacqueline blocked his path. "If you're interested in that woman why don't you just say it."

"Keep your voice down." Shades of anger tinged Nick's voice as he measured Jacqueline's actions. *Not only is she a spoiled brat, the woman is crazy,* Nick concluded.

He watched as Jacqueline's lips trembled. Her rage seemed to mount with each word she spoke.

"You and that little witch are going to regret the day you knew each other."

Nick felt his insides heat to a higher degree. To refrain from saying anything that might injure her, himself or Monique, he opened the door and ushered Jacqueline out.

In his office, Nick waited until he thought Jacqueline was in her car and out of sight. Jacqueline was too exhausting. He didn't have the energy or the time.

The tantrum scene was one of the reasons he didn't like her. It seemed to Nick that she thought her scenes and tantrums would bring them closer.

"Are you all right Mr. Parker?" Nick's secretary, who had obviously heard the argument that had taken place between him and Jacqueline, walked through the adjoining door that connected their offices.

Nick looked at his secretary and nodded.

"Are you sure?" The middle-aged woman seemed concerned about her boss.

Nick nodded again, attempting to hold his angry emotions in check.

"I'm fine, Doris," he finally said.

"You know, I stepped out of my office for a few minutes to speak to the receptionist. We're planning a baby shower for one of the girls." Doris rambled nervously. "And I guess while we were in the lounge that woman just walked right in."

"Don't worry about it," Nick said to Doris in a discontented voice. He wasn't upset with his secretary. He was upset at himself for getting involved with Jacqueline in the first place. The game she intended to play was not working. She had undoubtedly chosen the wrong opponent if she thought she could threaten Monique and remain his friend.

As far as he was concerned, the very idea of Jacqueline making threats on anyone was a crime within itself. Nick hoped she was not foolish enough to carry out her threat. Jacqueline did not want to make him her enemy. Nick walked out into the corridor and took the elevator down to the ground floor.

FOUR

Monique walked briskly into Shagreen II. The salon was the exact image of her original Shagreen. A mauve sofa and matching wingback chairs sat in front of the gas fireplace. Silk green plants sat on each side of the mantel, and above those hung a picture of her newest advertisement, a male and female model with flawless honey and lemon complexions.

"Hi," Monique spoke to one of her regular clients that was lifting her cup from the coffee table, sipping the mocha flavored coffee.

"Oh, hello," the woman spoke and smiled once she had positioned her cup back on the table. "I saw you this morning." She gave Monique a knowing look.

"Really," Monique said, recognizing the eye contact the client made with her. "I had a few things to take care of this morning," Monique said, hoping to end the conversation.

"You were taking care of business, girlfriend."

Monique smiled and, without any other response, walked out of the waiting area, to the far side of the room next to the receptionist area. She passed the makeup counter, which displayed pearl, blaze, wine, beet red and crimson nail polishes and gold and floral tubes of lipsticks in matching hues set on glass shelves. Underneath those colors were black and white eye shadows and face creams in white jars capped with golden tops.

"How're things going?" Monique asked Elaine, who was busy cutting into a box that overnight delivery had dropped off earlier that morning.

Elaine looked up from the box she had just cut open that held bottles of rich, heady, male colognes.

As she rose up, the overhead light glinted against her skin, which appeared to be as clear and flawless as the pictures of the models that hung on the wall in both Shagreen skin salons.

Elaine's fire engine red lipstick and thick black lashes complimented her nut brown complexion.

"Things are fine around here," Elaine said, reaching inside the box and taking out a bottle of men's cologne, handing the bottle of rich, heady aroma to Monique.

Monique cupped the black bottle with the black glossy cap in her palm. Adding another product to Shagreen II was just what she needed to bail her out of her crisis. Elaine had ordered the colognes the day she and Monique came up with the idea to capture a male clientele.

Monique removed the top from the bottle and sniffed the manly scent.

"Hummm, sexy," Monique said, chuckling at the thought that slid uncontrollably across her mind. She wondered if Nick would be interested in purchasing her newest items. She'd enjoyed the fragrances he'd worn while they dated.

For a little while longer, Monique took the liberty and let thoughts of Nick run freely over her mind. God could not have blessed a man with prettier teeth. And he smelled so good. Monique assessed the handsome Nick Parker, who had the power to make her go weak with shameless desire.

"Monique," Elaine called out to her, interfering with her contemplations of the man she wanted and didn't have the nerve to love.

Monique composed herself, while ignoring Elaine's laughter.

"Come back to earth."

"I was thinking," Monique answered, half smiling.

"Apparently," Elaine said. "It must've been nice."

Monique shrugged. "It was nothing."

"My instincts tells me it was a powerful thought."

Monique didn't respond. She'd never discussed her private life with her employees. That line of conversation was open only to her best friend, Colleen Jones.

"Ummm," Monique groaned as she set the bottle on the counter and opened a letter.

"Anything interesting?" Elaine wanted to know, taking another bottle of cologne from the box.

"I'm not sure," Monique unfolded the letter and read. "It looks like we're going to a seminar."

"Where're we going?" Elaine asked, removing the top and inhaling the aroma of another cologne.

"Florida. The second weekend in October," Monique said. Getting away from the state of New Jersey was what she needed. For one weekend, she wouldn't have to think about her debts and the fact that she was unable to pay Roger to continue her search for her past. And most of all the realization that she wouldn't sit home another weekend night watching television or reading another book to smother the lonely threads of her life.

"That's next month," Elaine said, setting the bottle down.

"It's short notice, but I think we can go."

"Do you think the others will attend?" Elaine asked with concern. The last two nail technicians Monique had hired hadn't attended a seminar in years.

"If they want to," Monique stated firmly. Before her finance problems begun, she had paid for her employees to attend seminars. She couldn't afford this luxury anymore. "I'll mention it and maybe you can post this letter on the bulletin board."

While Monique was reading the letter, Elaine opened an invitation from Amelia Wakefield. She smiled. "Darling, we're invited to a bachelorette auction," Elaine read, changing her voice to the tone of Amelia's silky voice. "We're invited to participate," Elaine teased.

"We are?" Monique asked, wondering if Nick would attend the party. She fanned the thought away. He probably would, since he volunteered on a few committees in town.

Amelia Wakefield didn't joke when she donated to those that seemed less fortunate than herself.

Only Amelia would think up such an event, Monique decided. The woman had a flair for raising money.

"Who's she donating the proceeds to this time?"

"The foster children and orphan program," Monique said.

Elaine had stopped reading and whistled. "These tickets are expensive."

"It's for a good cause," Monique replied.

Monique volunteered time at the orphanage at least once a month for an hour, doing whatever was needed. Many times the small children enjoyed being read to. And on all occasions the children loved hugs. In this case, she hoped Amelia Wakefield's bachelorette party was a success.

"The highest bidder gets a night out on the town, a restaurant of their choice and a Broadway show," Monique read, remembering the evening she and Nick had gone to see the famous Broadway show "Cats". She had enjoyed the show, but most of all she had enjoyed being with Nick. Looking back, she remembered how Nick had tantalized her with kisses afterwards, once he had driven her home. His kisses were similar to the kisses he had planted on her earlier this morning.

"What's the ticket price?" Elaine asked.

Monique told her.

"For those prices, I should get a weekend vacation," Elaine joked.

"If Mrs. Wakefield can do something valuable with her money, other than pamper herself, I have no complaints with her good deeds to humanity," Monique said.

"I agree, Monique, and we're happy that she spends her money freely in this salon, too."

"I'm not complaining."

"I think I'll check on things in the back," Monique said to Elaine. She planned to check the appointment books when she returned.

"Ladies," Monique spoke to the nail technicians as she entered the room. Then she realized that she'd forgotten to add "gentleman," recognizing Kenny, her only male nail technician. "Hi, Kenny."

"Hi," Kenny said, looking through his transparent shield and up from the nail he was sculpting.

Monique moved through the room, taking mental notes on sanitation and inhaling the spicy scent of nail polish. Clean, organized nail stations with shiny chrome lamp covers sat next to the wall, with well-groomed nail technicians busy at work. Monique smiled, doting on her sterling clean salon, with its wide-tiled floors that sparkled.

The mirrored walls were streak-free. Silk plants and pictures of smooth hands spread like a swan's wings were also free of dust.

The soft whine of the nail machines filled the room, along with chuckles, quiet conversations and the laugh track from a TV talk show.

Monique checked the bathroom. Green ivy plants hung from white plant hangers, and another picture of spread hands adorned the wall.

The room was as clean as it had been when she opened

Shagreen II. She moved out of the room and to the facial area, pleased that she had asked Nick for his assistance. Her businesses were her pride and joy.

Monique peeked into all three facial rooms. The two male employees were busy massaging effeuraging and stroking their clients' faces. It was as if their light strokes followed the soothing rhythm of the calming music.

Monique continued her stroll to the room where her one female facialist was busy preparing for her next patron. The young woman looked up briefly from her work, spoke and proceeded with her preparations.

Monique had purposely hired the male facialists. She figured they would build her business. Women loved men to service them.

Satisfied that her employees were happy, Monique made her way down to the dispensary. The room was locked. Remembering that she had left her key up front, Monique slid the window open and reached in and flipped the light switch. The cool dispensary smelled of strawberries and fresh apple aromatherapy facial masks. Pedicure slippers in new packages on the shelves sat next to containers filled with complexion brushes.

Hiring Elaine was the best choice she'd made in a long time. Grateful that she no longer had to worry about the salon's care, Monique made her way back to the front to check the books and the appointments.

Monique sat at the computer. Sales were up, clients were making and keeping appointments. With Nick's assistance, maybe Shagreen II would finally pull out of the red. She wondered if Nick had been successful at convincing Faceology Equipment Co. to lower her payments and cease to sue her for full payment.

"Monique," one of the facial technicians came to her. "I have an emergency. My son is sick and I need to pick him up from school."

"Sure, you can leave," Monique said to the young man.

"I have an appointment in the next ten minutes."

"Don't worry, just go. I'll take over," Monique said to the facialist.

"I'll call Elaine if I can't come in tomorrow," the facialist said to Monique. He hurried from the salon.

Monique went to the facial room and sterilized her hands. She took a clean white smock from the closet in the facial room, slipped into it, then checked the service book. The woman was getting a plain facial. Monique checked to make sure the infrared lamp was working properly, then she checked the steamer.

The facial table had been changed with clean sheets and pillow cases. Monique checked her watch. She expected her client to walk in at any minute.

"Monique, this is Felita," the receptionist said as she ushered the woman in.

"Hello," the woman entered the facial room, and spoke to Monique.

"Hi, come in," Monique said, giving the attractive woman a white terry robe before showing her the dressing room.

Minutes later Felita was back and allowed Monique to make her comfortable on the table.

Monique cleansed the woman's face with a rich creamy cleanser and removed the substance with a warm white towel, using upward strokes.

As she worked, her mind wavered back to Nick and their business breakfast. If only she was free to love him, her life would be complete.

Monique was certain that Nick had a choice of women. What if she . . . was just another name in his black book. Monique let the thought disappear while she wiped the client's face lightly with herbal astringent.

She turned on the steamer. "Are you comfortable?" Monique asked, making sure her client was snuggled under the sheet, cozy and warm.

The woman smiled and gestured with her hand, indicating that she was all right.

Monique turned the steam a notch higher now, letting it flow over the woman's face. The soothing music and the warm steam lulled the woman to sleep. She woke when Monique applied the mask.

While the mask hardened on the woman's face, Monique reminded herself that she couldn't allow herself to be distracted by Nick's romantic persuasions. After Nick completed the work for her, she planned to keep a distance between them.

She removed the client's mask and checked her watch. It was past her lunch break. She applied lotion to the woman's face and showed her to the makeup room.

From the phone in the facial room, Monique called Colleen.

"Are you free for lunch?" Monique asked.

"Of course I am," Colleen's voice came across the line.

"I'll see you in five minutes," Monique said, hanging up, hurrying to get out of the building.

Amelia Wakefield had an appointment. Monique didn't want to run into her. She seemed to be a nice person. But for strange reasons that Monique was unable to explain, Amelia's presence gave her a feeling of uneasiness. Monique decided that she didn't like the woman and left it at that.

Just as Monique was leaving the salon for lunch, Jacqueline walked in and up to the counter.

"I would like to make a paraffin manicure appointment," Jacqueline said.

Monique noticed the woman scanning the shelves that held the leather purses, while Elaine checked the appointment book for a vacancy.

"The earliest appointment I can give you will be Tuesday, at three-thirty," Monique heard Elaine say to the potential client.

Jacqueline turned her attention back to Elaine. "Perfect," she said. "I would like for you or this woman to perform my services." Jacqueline pointed to Monique.

Monique caught the surprised look in Elaine's eyes.

"I'm sorry, Miss . . ."

"Jacqueline," she said. Her eyes seemed rimmed with sudden anger.

"Jacqueline, Miss McRay or myself do not service the clients unless it's an emergency."

"This is an emergency." Jacqueline's voice sounded raw and tart.

Monique and Elaine exchanged glances. Perhaps it was her own uneasiness, but an urgent small voice warned Monique to dismiss the woman as gracefully as she could. She didn't know the woman, but Monique was sure they would never be able to satisfy her. She already had an attitude.

Quickly, Monique tapped the computer and pulled up the appointments for the next week. "Elaine, three-thirty is not open."

"But it is . . ." Eventually, Elaine seemed to understand Monique's meaning and suddenly followed Monique's lead.

"I'm sorry," Elaine said. "I made a mistake."

"I don't think so," Jacqueline's fury shot out at Elaine and Monique. "I heard that you little witches were choosy about who you served."

Monique raised her hand to quiet Jacqueline. "Please—" Monique said, but Jacqueline didn't let her finish.

"Clients are always right," Jacqueline spat the words at Monique. "And for some reason you"—she pointed a long blood-red nail at Monique—"you don't want me in your salon."

"Will you please lower your voice and calm down," Monique said, as several clients waiting for services looked up from reading their magazines.

Those that were engaged in conversations stopped talking and listened to Jacqueline, who had flown into a rage.

"You have refused to service me. Therefore, I can speak as loud as I please."

"Will you please leave," Monique said, straining to keep the volume on her voice low.

"Yes, I'll leave. But when I finish the smear campaign on this business, you won't have to tell clients to leave because you won't have any clients to service." With that said, Jacqueline stormed out.

Shocked at the woman who had just come in and threatened to close her business that she was struggling to keep open, Monique felt a tinge of anger mingled with fear.

"Who is that woman?" Monique asked Elaine.

Elaine seemed just as surprised as Monique.

"I don't have the slightest idea."

"She works at that newspaper over on Circle Drive," one of the clients who had heard the commotion said.

"Don't pay her any attention, the paper is a rag," another client stated.

Monique was grateful for the client's soothing remarks. However at this point, she could not afford a smear campaign.

"Monique darling," Amelia Wakefield had obviously gotten off her facial table when she heard the confusion. Dressed in a long white terry robe and wearing a collagen treatment on her face, she had run into the lobby.

"We're fine, Mrs. Wakefield," Monique said, ushering the woman back into the facial area.

The anguish Monique was experiencing brought on by Jacqueline's threat was almost too much to bear. It was beyond her why this person had chosen to attack her business. Monique went to the computer and checked the past appointments from the time she had opened Shagreen II. There were no indications referring to a person by the name Jacqueline registered in her computer. Learning that the woman worked at a newspaper made Monique shudder inside.

Destroying her salon's reputation would be as if her hard work and her struggles in life would have been in vain.

"Monique." Monique heard Elaine call out to her.

She rose from the computer and went over to where Elaine had just finished helping a client decide on a piece of jewelry in the case below the counter.

"Yes," Monique said, her voice edged with worry.

"I think we should call the paper and report her to her boss."

Monique sighed heavily. "Her boss is probably itching for some nasty piece of gossip. I'm sure he or she would let Miss Jacqueline print exactly what she wants."

"You're probably right." Elaine frowned.

"I checked the client list, and there is not one client that has the name Jacqueline." Desperate to find out who the woman was, Monique called Tamika.

"Shagreen, how may I help you?" Tamika's voice came across the line, clear and professional.

"Tamika, will you check the computer and see if we have ever had a client that goes by the name Jacqueline."

"How far back do you want me to check?" Tamika asked Monique.

"Check the appointments for the last year."

Monique waited while Tamika checked to see if they had ever serviced a client with the name Jacqueline. She would deal with the woman's last name later, since neither she nor Elaine had asked Jacqueline her last name.

"Monique, there was a woman in earlier this morning. Her name is Jacqueline."

"Do you have her last name?"

"Yes, her last name is Woods."

"Describe her," Monique said to Tamika.

"She was tall, thin, light brown and rude. She gave the technicians a hard time. And she asked for you."

An acute case of agonizing stress spread through Monique.

"Where does she work?" Monique wanted to make sure that the client who informed them of Jacqueline's employment was correct.

"She works for a newspaper." Tamika told Monique the name of the paper that had opened for business a few months ago.

The stress that had spread through Monique settled in her throat, bringing with it the acid taste from the coffee she drank at breakfast.

Monique's face grew hot. "Thank you, Tamika," her voice was barely a whisper.

Monique walked to the kitchenette and took an antacid from the cabinet. She dropped the small pill inside a glass and added water. The wretched pain she felt because some person with nothing better to do but pounce on her business was indescribable. Monique drank the distasteful medicine.

The phone in the kitchenette buzzed. Monique answered it.

"Colleen is on line two," Elaine's voice came across the extension line.

"Thanks," Monique said, punching the lighted button on the phone.

"I thought we were going to lunch," Colleen said to Monique.

"Colleen, I have not been having a good day," Monique said. "But as soon as I pull myself together, I'll pick you up."

"You sound upset. What happened?"

Monique proceeded to tell Colleen, leaving nothing out.

"This must be the day for crazies. One woman came in and asked for a French roll."

"That shouldn't have been a problem."

"Yes it was. My girl didn't have no hair."

Monique chuckled.

"And pitched a fit when I told her the price for a weave."

Monique laughed, almost forgetting her problems.

"I'll see you in a little while," Monique said to Colleen, who always made her feel better.

The suffocating tightness she had felt at her throat slowly dissolved. Physically, Monique felt better. However, her spirits seemed to sink further as she gathered strength to leave the salon.

Fear and anger seemed to have tied themselves together in one humiliating knot at the pit of her stomach. She had never received anything but compliments on the services that her clients received at both her salons.

Monique understood clearly that there was no one to blame but herself for refusing to grant Jacqueline Woods an appointment. She had, however, surrendered to the quiet voice inside her. As a result, she was responsible for the endangerment of Shagreen II.

Just thinking of the damage that Jacqueline Woods could perform with a few swift taps on her computer keys was shattering. The very thought twisted black fear around her heart. Monique struggled to cease the apprehension that coursed through her. What good had it been for her to go to great lengths to save a business that she would ultimately lose?

FIVE

Nick slid behind the wheel of his mini BMW and drove to Omar's. After checking out the cafeteria, he had changed his mind; if he was going to eat in a lively restaurant, Nick figured he might as well have lunch at Omar's. At least the people that made the noise would be people he knew.

By the time Nick reached Omar's the fall air had chilled a little more, the sun that had been shining brightly earlier had found a hiding place behind gray clouds. That thought brought to mind just how miserable he had been without Monique in his life.

Nick got out of his car. Taking long strides toward the restaurant, he soon entered the building.

Several women sat on the brown wooden benches, legs crossed, swinging their feet and clutching their purses. Nick stood at the entrance behind the gold and red stained glass and searched inside for an empty stool at the bar.

"Would you like a table for two?" the young waitress asked him.

"No," Nick said, when a woman stepped in front of him and addressed the waitress.

"Your advertisement states that if customers wait longer than ten minutes, lunch is free. We have been sitting here for twenty minutes and we want free lunches."

"That advertisement is not for this area," the waitress began to explain.

"Oh no, sister," Nick heard the woman raise her voice.

He moved past the woman when he spotted an empty space at the bar, allowing the music, laughter and everyone's simultaneous talking to drown out the potential customer's tantrum.

It had been a while since Nick had gone to Omar's. The familiarity of the room welcomed him. Photographs of famous baseball players and other famous people covered the walls, leaving spaces between for an autographed baseball bat or some other memory.

Nick pushed his hands in his jeans pockets and headed over to the bar where Stone and Brant were watching the highlights of the Bulls basketball game from the night before. Nick straddled a stool and sat, joining the guys.

"Come on, Brant, pay me," Stone said when the scores from last night's games were posted on the television screen.

"Man, you wouldn't have known the team won if you hadn't been here," Brant protested, taking his wallet out.

"Like I'd never found out?" Stone said, laughing.

"Shhee, you got lucky," Brant said, looking over at Nick. "What's up man?"

"You got it," Nick said to his younger brother, while half listening to Stone and Brant argue back and forth. Nick turned his attention to the midday news after Brant took out a bill and laid it in front of Stone.

While watching the news, Nick ordered lunch. He waited for his sandwich and scanned the dining area. Monique was engaged in a conversation with her friend Colleen.

Nick allowed himself the pleasure of watching Monique from a distance. When Monique turned in his direction, Nick shifted his gaze back to the midday news, and to his memories of the morning he had spent kissing Monique in the parking lot.

From time to time, he watched Monique out of the corner of his eye. If she thought he was going to give up and forget about their relationship, she had better think again. He had a long ways to go before he was over her.

The young waitress set his sandwich before him. Nick bit into the steak sandwich, determined not to allow Monique's presence to distract him.

Just as he took his third bite, Roger Cummings walked in and headed straight for Monique and Colleen's table. Roger sat down as if he was expected.

Jealousy ripped at Nick's heart. He knew Roger Cummings, a private detective who once worked for Jerry Mack. For reasons Nick couldn't explain, he had a feeling that Roger was a sneak.

Monique and her friend had Nick's undivided attention.

What was the connection between Roger and Monique? Nick considered the question, reflecting on how he had seen them together just before he and Monique broke up.

Another streak of jealousy crept from the pit of Nick's stomach and burned his face when Roger slipped his arm around Monique's shoulder and gave her what seemed like a light squeeze. Nick put the sandwich down and drained the bottle of soda he'd been served. *If Monique and Roger were lovers, why didn't she tell me?* The thought winged its way across Nick's mind. He set the bottle on the counter and made eye contact with a waitress so he could pay for his lunch.

"I'll see you back at the office," Nick said to Stone, who was engaged in a friendly debate with Brant over who was the best tennis player.

Instead of giving Nick a verbal answer, Stone nodded while continuing his debate with Brant.

Nick got up and walked over to Monique. His intentions were to tell her that he had called Faceology Equipment.

"Monique, as soon as the paperwork is completed, we'll talk," he said, holding her gaze.

"Sure." She smiled up at him.

Nick spoke to Colleen. He turned his attention to Roger, casting him an icy stare. "Roger."

"Hi, Nick," he heard Roger say.

Nick walked out of the restaurant. It was Monique's choice to date another man. She was single, fun, beautiful and despite all the troubles she had managed to get herself into with her creditors, she was an excellent business-woman. Still the fact remained, Nick considered whole-heartedly, Monique owed him and she was going to pay.

"Roger, how many times do I have to tell you that my business and personal life is none of your business?" Monique asked Roger, who was quizzing her on the amount of money that she owed Faceology Equipment and at the same time warning her to stay away from Nick Parker.

"Monique, since when did we stop being a team?"

"Since we grew up, Roger," Monique said, annoyed at Roger's need to help her solve every problem that she encountered. Visions of seeing Nick just minutes ago flashed before her. Monique placed her hand over her heart and forced herself not to think about him.

Colleen ate quietly while listening to the argument be-tween her best friends.

"So, who's the lawyer?" Roger asked.

"Parker and Stone." Monique took a sip from the warm tea she had ordered to calm her nerves after they had been racked earlier in the day.

"You can't leave that guy alone, can you?"

"Roger, who I choose to associate with is none of your business."

"Did you tell him?"

Monique set the cup down and squeezed a drop of lemon juice from the slice into her tea. "No, Roger," Monique answered with defiant curtness before taking another drink from the herb tea.

"Monique, you know if you tell him, he'll think less of you."

Monique forced herself to settle down before she spoke with quiet desperation. Forbidding herself to allow Roger to upset her further, she turned to him.

"First, I have no reason to discuss my past life with Nick Parker or anyone at this time."

"Good, keep it that way." Roger seemed satisfied that Monique was keeping a distance between her and the man he despised. "I wouldn't want to see you get hurt again," Roger said. "Guys like Nick Parker have images to protect."

Monique struggled to compose herself, while Roger plunged on with his unsolicited advice. She looked out the window at the oak tree shedding its red, gold and brown leaves. They floated against a light wind and finally settled on the ground beneath the oak tree.

Roger deliberately reminded her of the pain she'd suffered six years ago when her ex-fiance refused to marry her because she had been adopted.

The grim sob that had once caught in her throat at the embarrassment she'd felt and the hurt she'd suffered had dissolved over the years. With iron control, and the will to refrain from an outburst she was sure would turn heads in the restaurant despite the noise, Monique spoke to Roger with even determination. "And second Roger, did it ever occur to you that most times I am not interested in your advice?"

Colleen, who had been quiet and attentive through the discussion between her two best friends, laid her head against the booth's back and laughed out loud.

"And next, I would appreciate it if you would stop trying

to protect me." Monique's voice rose slightly over the noise. "Do I make myself clear?"

She met Roger's gaze without flinching.

"Don't make a scene, Monique. I was trying to help."

"What did I say?" Monique said, forcing herself to a quiet calmness.

"I'm sorry if I upset you Monique, but I don't want you to forget where you came from."

Monique knew that Roger's intentions were good. He had consoled her through many crises, and had taken time out of his busy schedule to escort her to charity benefits, and even to the movies when she didn't feel like spending a weekend night at home alone. Nonetheless, her intentions were to remain friends with Roger and nothing more.

Monique studied Roger's face closely, determined to make him understand. He was not her guardian angel, and he was not in charge of her life, social or otherwise. Another picture of Nick's handsome face flashed across her mind.

"How can I forget with you reminding me?" Monique noticed Roger's throat move as he swallowed hard.

"I have some free time." Roger's voice was husky. "Do you want me to pick up where we left off on the project?"

"First, I'll have to talk to Nick, then make a budget," Monique said. For the first time she felt a sense of confidence when she spoke regarding her finances.

"Okay . . . all right, I'm not going to comment." Roger held up both hands as if to ward off any response he had for Monique's decision to confide in Nick.

Colleen, who had been listening quietly except for the laughter she'd enjoyed when Monique proceeded to put Roger in his proper place, spoke up.

"Roger, I agree with Monique. What difference does it make who Monique dates or does business with?" Colleen's words trailed off, while she gave Roger a half-mask look, as if she had discovered some secret.

"That's it."

Roger grinned. "So Monique knows I care a lot for her. If she was my wife, she wouldn't have to worry about people like Nick Parker handling her business."

"Roger, don't talk about me as if I'm not here," Monique said. Then she added for the record, "And no, we're not husband and wife material." Monique gestured for him to get up so she could leave.

As much as she wanted to love Nick freely, if he proposed to her, she wasn't sure if she would accept.

Roger raised his long lean body from the booth's seat. He pulled the black cap that rested between him and Monique over his thick black hair and waited for Monique to stand.

When Monique stood, Roger walked the women out to Monique's car.

The chilled air reminded Monique how undecided her love life was. It was like the sun that had peeked earlier from behind the clouds, as if undecided whether to shine or not.

Monique unlocked her car door and got in. She wound the window down and allowed Roger to lean over and talk to her.

"Monique, if you married me, all of your problems would be solved."

Monique turned to Colleen. "Besides the fact that he is classless, he is also crazy." She faced Roger then. "No thanks."

As usual, Roger appeared amused. A rich chuckle came across his lips. "I'm leaving for Philadelphia in the morning," Roger said. "Can we have dinner tonight?"

"I'm working late," Monique replied, planning to work on the payroll at her original Shagreen, before the accountant picked it up.

"I'll stop by the salon."

Roger, as always, was persistent. Monique decided that

it would be best if she and Roger talked at her home. "I'll be home around nine tonight," Monique said.

Roger nodded, then smiled and walked to his car.

"Monique, that's not the first time Roger asked you to marry him," Colleen said.

"Colleen, you know as well as I do that Roger is not serious."

"Maybe." Colleen pulled the seat belt over her shoulders and clamped it across her waist. "But it never struck me until now that Roger could be serious," Colleen said.

Monique started the car's engine. She ignored her girlfriend's remarks. Roger Cummings never made her heart flutter. He was her friend. It was Nick Parker who was responsible for the sizzling passion that rose within her at the sight of him. The mere touch of Nick's hand made her heart flip-flop. It was Nick Parker that she wanted to love.

Monique drove out onto the street, considering Colleen's remarks about Roger's feelings for her. She, Colleen and Roger had lived together for the first ten years of her life. Monique had been the first to be adopted. Yvonne and John McRay adopted her. Later, Colleen was adopted. Roger remained at the orphan institution until he graduated high school.

Nonetheless, over the years, the three remained friends. Roger was protective of Monique and Colleen as if it was his duty. And he often teased that he and Monique would marry the day after their college graduations.

"Roger would make some woman a nice husband," Monique said. He was no longer the angry poor boy who was once a ward of the state.

"Maybe," Colleen replied. "If he doesn't chase her away."

"Why would he do that?"

"As overprotective as Roger is, he'll make a saint take flight."

"Monique pulled up to the curb in front of Colleen's "Clip and Bob" salon beside a hunter green sports car with a tan rag-top. At first she thought it was Nick, until she saw a man that she didn't recognize get in and drive off.

However, seeing Nick's car tempted her to recall the fire he had started in her that morning. Monique calmed herself.

SIX

Radiant golden light illuminated the upstairs Pella windows in the Parkers' home. Pitch pine needles lined the driveway. Thick green hedges nestled close to the house. The usual blossoms that lent cheerful hues to the neat, manicured green lawn were no longer perched atop the shrubs, a sure sign of an approaching winter.

"Is Sharmain really getting married, or is she just talking?" Nick spoke in quiet, withdrawn, worried tones.

"I understand that she's serious," Nick's father replied.

Nick walked a few paces and stopped. "I've wanted to open a camp for years," Nick said. He shook his head. It didn't seem that his dream was going to materialize if he didn't take action.

"Son, you know how your grandmother is," Mark reminded Nick.

"I understand."

"Sharmain gets married, the land is hers," Mark Parker warned Nick.

A frown creased Nick's forehead. He trusted his grandmother, but this time, Lucy Morgan was making a mistake.

Nick nudged the toe of his shoe into a patch of pine needles that hugged the curve of the driveway, giving them a swift impatient kick. Under no circumstances would Sharmain destroy his plans.

One of the golden lights that lit the upstairs in the house faded to black. The sheer white curtain fluttered.

"Let's go inside," Mark said, moving toward the house.

Nick pushed his gloved hands down into his overcoat pockets, clutching the tiny pink wrapped box that held the diamond brooch he had purchased for his grandmother's birthday.

It was time to play his trump card. Cousin or not, Sharmain was not going to walk away with the land that he needed to help the inner-city children. He would wage war on Sharmain, and make her life a bitter battle.

As Nick walked with his father, he summed up his life. He had been fortunate to have good parents who could provide for him and his brother. Unfortunately, there were children that had no homes, and barely enough of the daily necessities in their lives. Summer vacations and winter camps were dreams that many had not attempted to imagine, knowing that their dreams would be in vain. Nick intended to change that image.

Nick let the door close behind him with a soft thump as he and his father ambled through the foyer. He stopped and put his grandmother's birthday gift in the silver tray that was purposely placed on the table to hold Lucy Morgan's tiny expensive gifts. He pulled off his coat and hung it in the closet before he continued on to the dining room.

As he passed the closed double doors to the living room and study, Nick noticed Sharmain standing at the top of the stairs. Her smile was a smirk to say the least, Nick decided as he made his way to the dining room to join the family.

The family was already seated at the lengthy white table in the dining room.

Nick noticed that his mother hadn't wavered from tradition for their grandmother and her mother's birthday. Clara had set the table with her best bone china and silverware. A pink bouquet of roses from Florida centered the table.

Nick spoke to his brother Brant, to Brant's wife Daniella, to his mother, and to his grandmother before he took a wet-wipe from the box on the hutch, wiping his hands. He pulled back a white cushioned chair and sat next to his grandmother, giving her a kiss on her plump rosy cheek.

"Hi," he said, admiring his grandmother's pink ankle-length lounge outfit. Her glossy hair was the color of rich silver, complimenting her buttery complexion.

Nick settled in his chair, giving Sharmain a brief nod.

Mark took his place at the head of the table next to Clara. After Mark said the grace the family settled down to Clara's mother's birthday dinner.

Roasted cornish hens with sourdough oyster stuffing, homemade potato salad, candied yams and tender collard greens were all Nick's favorites. Two large pitchers of iced tea the color of black coffee sat on the serving table next to the kitchen door.

The polite dinner conversation made an about-face when dinner was over and the family sat at the table sipping iced tea.

Lucy Morgan pushed her wheelchair farther away from the table.

"Granny, do you need help?" Nick stood to assist his feisty eighty-nine-year-old grandmother, who was bound to a wheelchair because she had taken a nasty fall months earlier.

"Oh, I'm fine." Lucy Morgan spanked her grandson's hand playfully.

Sharmain, who was sitting on the other side of her grandmother, gave Nick a mean smirk. "The land is mine," she mouthed the words.

"Not yet," Nick mouthed back. Nick's calm demeanor always took flight when he and Sharmain were in the same room.

It angered him that Sharmain was shallow and only wanted to line her pockets, when there were so many children that needed attention and a healthy environment in which to grow into respectable, educated adults. Nick tried to dismiss his deliberations. It was clear to him that Sharmain only thought of herself and the next five-hundred dollar purse she planned to buy.

Brant, who had just witnessed the silent fight, gave Sharmain an icy gaze and began discussing his latest project at Parker's Art. "Daniella and I donated several acres of land to the Community Center."

"Brant, that's wonderful," Clara smiled with pride at her youngest son.

"I didn't know you owned any land," Sharmain said between sips of iced tea.

"We donated some of the land Granny gave us for our wedding present," Brant said, shooting Nick a swift smile.

"That's great," Nick agreed.

"If we can help a few people out of the projects, I think it'll be worth it," Daniella said, pressing her palms against her seven-month's pregnant stomach.

Nick watched Daniella, and wished that he and Monique were married and she was pregnant with his child. If only she would let him love her, Nick mused. Monique was determined to keep a distance between them. Nick cut his musing and turned his attention back to the conversation.

"Are you building the houses?" Mark asked Brant.

Brant grinned. "No, daddy."

"All right. Because you got that business to run." Mark Parker drained his tea glass and turned to his wife, who was looking at him. "What?"

"Parker's Art belong to Brant now, Mark, don't get started," Clara said.

"Clara, I don't mind giving, but you can give away too much," Mark said. "But it is an excellent idea." Mark smiled as if to please his wife.

The quiet conversation came to a halt when Lucy cleared her throat.

"Sharmain is thinking of marriage," she said, her voice strong. "I haven't signed any papers or made any definite decisions." She looked in Nick's direction. "But if Sharmain is the first to marry, I plan to give the land to her and her new husband." Lucy's gaze went to Sharmain, then back to Nick.

"Granny, thanks." Sharmain smiled.

"I didn't give it to you yet." Lucy Morgan rested her hands in her lap and seemed to have been studying her decision. "Sharmain, when do you plan to get engaged and set a wedding date?"

"As soon as my fiancé gets a job, which will be soon," Sharmain said.

Nick shot Brant an undereyed glance.

"I see," Granny said. "Well, sometimes finding proper employment takes time."

"I agree." Sharmain said, smiling.

"What kind of job is he looking for?" Lucy inquired.

"He sent out several resumes to real estate companies," Sharmain answered. "He hopes to manage one of the larger companies in Atlanta."

"Interesting," Nick said.

"Of course he's managed real estate companies before," Sharmain said, giving Nick another nasty smirk.

"So, what happened to make him leave the company?" Clara asked.

"There were complications and he didn't feel he had to deal with them."

"What sort of complications?" Nick wanted to know.

"Yeah, what happened?" Brant added.

Lucy cleared her throat, interrupting her grandsons. "We all wish your fiancé the best of luck in his job search." Granny looked around the room and smiled at her family.

"Granny, once the land is mine I can do whatever I want with it, right?" Sharmain asked.

"I would think so," Lucy said.

"I plan to sell the land once we're married," Sharmain said to her grandmother. "My fiancé knows two or three businessmen who would like to build a shopping center." She directed her next statement to Brant. "Which is not a bad idea. People need a place to shop, right?"

"If you say so," Brant replied.

"Homes will be built on your land." Sharmain reminded Brant.

"Land that I donated."

Nick gave Sharmain a dangerous look. "I didn't think the land was for sale."

"If I decide to give the land to Sharmain, I'm sure she and her husband will make the best decision," Granny said.

"Why are you concerned Nick?" Sharmain's tone seemed to hold a slight bitterness, as if she wanted Nick to shut up.

"Sharmain, the land has been in the family for years," Brant said when Sharmain interrupted him.

"Why're you worried. You have your share."

"That's what worries me," Brant replied. "You have no idea what those guys are going to build on the property."

"Whatever." Sharmain shook her head, forcing a smile that refused to reach her eyes.

"And you don't care," Nick said, a hint of anger edging his voice.

Nick finished his tea. His cousin was making plans to sell property that his grandmother hadn't signed over to her. He couldn't let that happen.

Besides, the conversation was turning into an argument.

"Sharmain, how do you think you sound? Your plans are to marry a man who's unemployed, and it looks like he can't keep a job." Brant poured himself another glass of tea.

Nick noticed Daniella nudging Brant with her elbow, as if she wanted Brant to settle down.

"What's it to you?" Sharmain shot back at Brant.

"I guess keeping the land in the family is not important to you, since your only concern is money."

"Oh no, Brant Parker, you did not go there." Sharmain turned on Nick. "I guess those are your thoughts, exactly."

"Exactly."

Granny, Mark, Clara and Daniella exchanged glances.

"I just bet the two of you can't sleep at night for hatching a plot to keep Granny from giving me that land." Sharmain directed her statement to the Parker brothers.

"Trust me Sharmain, you aren't worth the trouble," Nick said.

"I don't know," Brant said, ignoring Daniella's second elbow nudge. "Hatching a plot to keep that freeloading fiancé of yours off that property is not a bad idea."

"What's their asking price?" Nick asked. If his plans to own the land didn't work, he planned to buy the land from his cousin for a higher price. Plan B was bound to work.

Sharmain took a sip of tea, then set the glass down. "The asking price?"

"Yes," Nick said.

When Sharmain finally disclosed the figure the businessmen offered, the family let out a gasp.

A round of mumbles and groans came from the family members. Nick felt a wave of heat rise to his face. "That much, huh?" Nick tapped his foot against the carpeted floor. He was prepared to pay whatever the cost was, if he had to buy the land.

"I think it would be wise for you to hold off on making plans to sell the land, Sharmain," Clara commented on the discussion for the first time since the subject of giving land was discussed that evening.

"I agree," Mark nodded.

"I think it's fair," Sharmain said. "If Granny is planning on signing the land over to us, we should look for buyers."

'How can you make a deal on property you don't own?" Brant wanted to know.

"Easy," Sharmain shot back, turning her attention to her Aunt Clara.

"If your sister was my real mother, you wouldn't have a problem with me owning the land and selling it, would you, Aunt Clara?" Sharmain reminded her aunt, as usual, that she was not really related to Clara or the Parkers. Her real mother had died when she was a small child. She was six years old when her father married Clara's sister, Kate.

"Sharmain you know that I don't have a problem with you being my sister's stepdaughter. You are family. But I would have a problem with anyone in this family who has plans to sell that property," Clara replied.

"Greed has a special way of wiping out family values," Nick stated firmly.

Sharmain opened her mouth to speak, but was stopped by the wave of Lucy's hand.

"Nick and Sharmain, if you will excuse me," Lucy said, registering her gaze on her grandchildren. She rested her wrinkle-free hands in her lap, then moved her chair back an inch or two.

"Now, I wanted to have this discussion to hear how everyone felt." She turned her attention to Nick.

Nick had no intention of discussing his plans with the family. Saying too much would give Sharmain ammunition. He needed as much mental firing power as possible.

"I think the decision is up to you, Granny," Nick said. Lucy nodded.

"What do you think, Aunt Clara?" Sharmain asked.

"My thoughts are not important to you."

"Let me take a wild guess. You probably want your precious Nick to own the property."

"Don't you start with me . . . girl." Clara got up and went to the kitchen for the lemon cake and coffee.

"Unlike all of you, Granny wants me to have it." Sharmain smiled sweetly.

"I'm thinking about it," Granny said. "I've learned tonight that you would like to sell the land." Granny stopped talking and waited for Clara to set the candleless lemon birthday cake on the table.

"Sharmain honey, this land was given to me for a wedding gift. When Clara and Mark married, I gave them a portion of it." Lucy drew in a deep breath and exhaled slowly. "Brant has his portion. We all know why I didn't give Nick a portion of the land when he got married." She rolled back to the table, giving Nick a quick understanding nod, before she carefully cut herself a thin slice of lemon cake.

"Nick, I don't think you're getting married again anytime soon," Sharmain smiled at him.

Nick checked his watch. This conversation was getting sticky. "I might."

All eyes at the table fell on Nick. Clara smothered a smile. Mark nonchalantly cut a slice of cake.

Brant and Daniella exchanged questioning glances.

"Do you see what he's doing?" Sharmain asked. "I knew he would do this."

"It's not a problem," Lucy said. "If Nick gets married before you, he'll have to stay married for six months. And the same applies to you." Lucy cut a small piece of cake with the side of her fork, and slowly put the sweet-tart dessert into her mouth.

"Are you really thinking of marriage, Nick?" Clara asked, her pearl white smile widening. She seemed pleased to learn that her elder son was considering marriage again.

"I'm considering the possibilities," Nick said, realizing

that was what he'd done when he learned that his grandmother was thinking of giving her land to the next closest family member.

"Of course he considered marriage, about ten minutes ago," Sharmain said.

Nick ignored her. To him, she was exactly what he'd thought of her all his life, and earlier that evening. This time he didn't hesitate to add greedy, tacky, and having no manners to speak of. His intentions were to own the land one way or another, with as much grace and tact as he could.

His mind was made up. However, there were complications. Who was he going to marry on short notice?

Nick's beeper vibrated in his suit coat pocket. He took it out and checked the number. Jacqueline Wood's number flashed across the narrow lighted screen.

"If you'll excuse me, I have to go," Nick said, glad he had an excuse to leave.

He got up and leaned over, planting a kiss on his grandmother's cheek.

"Your gift is in the foyer with the others." He felt his grandmother's fingers clutch his lower arm, giving him a delicate squeeze. "I'll see you all later," Nick said. With long strides, he left his family in the dining room.

Monique walked into her house and turned on the light, filling the living room with a warm white welcoming glow, exposing the cream-colored wing-back sofa and the two lavender wing-back chairs. She closed the vertical blinds over the sliding glass door that led out to the terrace on the side of her house. She gave the puff of the balloon valance a light tug.

She and Colleen had lost the game. It didn't matter, though, the game was fun. However the conversation between some of the women had been about Nick and his new girlfriend, Jacqueline. The woman's name set off an alarm in Monique. It was clear to her now why Jacqueline had thought it necessary to humiliate her in front of her customers. However, it didn't make sense. She had never seen Jacqueline until she came into the salon. Did Jacqueline know that she and Nick had been lovers?

After careful consideration of the woman's actions, Monique conceded that she wasn't the least bit interested in Jacqueline and Nick's love affair. However, she was concerned that Jacqueline might follow through with her threat to demolish her salon's reputation.

Monique decided not to mention Nick's girlfriend's action to him. If Jacqueline was insecure, that was her problem.

Nonetheless, Monique's body didn't agree with her. Her heart fumed at the very idea that Nick was loving another woman. She calmed herself. Nick was single and free to love whomever he chose to love.

Monique went into the kitchen and took a bottle of water from the refrigerator. She drank half of the water before going to the living room and turning on the television to perish her loneliness.

The last segment of a comedy show was ending. Monique curled up on the sofa and, while she half-watched the show, she allowed her thoughts to waver back to the evening's conversation that had captured her attention at Colleen's card game.

When Monique had left the room to assist Colleen with the refreshments, she hadn't expected to hear the latest gossip. At least not the gossip concerning the man she wanted in her life. She had set the peppered cheese and crackers on the serving tray and listened to the grapevine news on who was loving whom.

Finally Nick's name was mentioned. Jacqueline's name followed shortly afterwards, connecting the two as the newest lovers in town.

Monique tried to dismiss her deliberations. *It didn't matter what Nick did with his life or who he dated. There was no room in her life for romance anyway. She had more pressing issues to attend to,* Monique reminded herself, tucking her sour grapes away in the back of her mind, only to have another thought make an easy slide into her reflections.

Nick was a special man. She could not compare him to any man she had ever dated. He was the type of person that took care of business. He was hard working and the best lawyer money could buy.

Monique closed her eyes, her long black lashes fanning out almost to her high cheekbones.

The laugh track rollicked from the television, filling her living room. Monique lowered the volume and waited for the evening news, struggling to keep her mind off of Nick. She got up and took a magazine from the rack. She tried to read. The magazine wasn't working. Especially when Monique considered how quickly Nick had gone on with his life, a slow rippling pain settled at the bottom of her heart.

The doorbell drew Monique away from her deliberations. It had to be Roger. He'd promised her that he would stop by before he left for Philadelphia.

Monique turned off the television and went to let him in.

Nick Parker stood in her doorway, his tall muscular frame towering over her. Surprised, Monique allowed her gaze to travel over him from head to toe. His wavy, jet black hair lay close to his head. The charcoal suit, shirt and matching tie made him look as if he had just stepped out of the co-ed fashion magazine that she had tried to read.

"Hi," he said.

Monique noticed the worried lines around Nick's eyes.

"Come in," she offered, feeling the flutter that swept through her and circled her heart whenever she was in his presence. Forcing her emotions to settle, she stepped away from the entrance and allowed him to enter her home.

Nick held out the folder to her, then took off his coat. "I hope this will solve your problem."

Monique took the folder and opened it, while Nick pulled off his coat and hung it on the coat tree near the door.

"I hope you approve of the actions I took on your behalf to set up a budget with Faceology Equipment." Nick said, explaining to Monique that he had called the company a second time and worked out a payment plan that he was certain she could stick to. "I can always talk the company into changing the plan, if it's a problem."

"No, thank you," Monique said, looking at the cover letter, then motioning Nick toward the sofa. "Please, sit." She walked over to join him while briefly scanning the contents in the folder.

Nick continued to stand once he reached the sofa, as if he preferred to notice Monique's reaction to his professional handiwork. Finally, he sat.

Still reading the information, Monique smiled. She opened her mouth to speak as she read the information, but the words caught in her throat.

"   ," she said when she could finally speak.
"   "

                                                    with the terms

the red lipstick that she'd worn to Colleen's card game. If Nick wanted to take her to dinner, she certainly wasn't going. "I can't go out tonight, Nick."

A frown creased Nick's forehead. He leaned further back onto the sofa and looked away. "I need . . . I want you to marry me."

Monique's mouth opened and closed. Once again, she found herself lost for words. When she was able to make a sound, she gasped. Then she shook her head.

"No," she finally said.

"It'll be for a short time."

"No."

"Let me explain my position." Nick waited for a second or two before continuing. "I need a wife. My grandmother is giving land to the next person in our family that gets married."

He waited for a moment before he continued. "I want to build a camp for the inner-city children and teens in this town."

Nick looked at Monique as if to see if she was following him. "Monique, this is just not any camp. The children would have a place to spend their summers—a place other than the streets," Nick stated.

Monique heard what sounded to her like Nick's voice. She also observed to her like pl cern to help young than him with another woman. Monique felt the green-eyed monster tugging at her heart.

"No, Nick, I can't marry you." She locked her gaze with his. It would be unfair to her to marry him. Nick had a way of bringing passion from deep within that she had forgotten existed.

"The children will have an opportunity to learn new ways to have fun and to socialize, Monique."

"I realize their needs." And she did. "I can't . . . marry you."

Nick's warm gaze swept over Monique. "Please."

Monique had listened to Nick's testimonial. He was sincere in his plea to make a better environment for the inner-city children. She too, was involved in the well-being of the children who spent their after-school hours at the Community Center.

"Nick, please don't ask me to do this." Monique looked away. It was almost impossible to refuse him anything, but being his wife was too much for him to ask. "I think if you explain your reasons to your grandmother, she would at least give you a parcel of the land," Monique said, hoping desperately that she could change Nick's mind.

"My grandmother is aware of my intentions," Nick said. He crossed one leg over his thigh and continued. "My desires to make a better place for the children in this town hasn't altered her demand for strict family values." Nick uncrossed his leg and planted his foot on the floor. He rested both hands on his thighs and lowered his head as if studying the pile in the carpet.

"I think you should speak to your grandmother," Monique said, wanting to end the discussion on marriage.

The concept of her living in the same house with Nick, knowing that he would be seeing his lover, was disturbing.

"Monique, if my cousin was going to use the land for a useful purpose, I wouldn't object to her owning the property. But, she intends to sell it to the highest bidder." Nick gave Monique a side glance. "To build a shopping strip."

"So, she can marry, and sell the land to you," Monique suggested.

"No. Anyway, she wants too much for it."

Monique shifted herself on the sofa. At least Nick was honest. He wanted to marry her not because he loved her, but because he wanted to own property. No matter how good the cause, she was nothing more to him than the means to own dirt. Monique tried to come to terms with Nick's reasons for wanting a marriage of convenience.

Pondering over Nick's reasons, she decided they were valid. But still she couldn't bring herself to be his wife.

"You mentioned that you might need me to do you a favor, but marriage is out of the question." Monique studied his handsome face. She'd never seen him worried, nor had she had the opportunity to see him angry. Annoyed, maybe.

Now Nick's expression was a mixture of both. One she'd never experienced. Nick's eyes narrowed as he straightened. The small scar on his face seemed to harden on his jaw line.

"Please."

"I'm sorry Nick." Monique avoided his pleading gaze. "I can't marry you."

Nick rose to his full height, all six feet three-inches. He pushed his hands in his trouser pockets and faced Monique, his eyes matching the hard line etching his jaw.

"You will marry me for six months, or I will send you a bill."

"But Nick . . ."

"You have a choice."

Marriage was out of the question. It didn't matter if she hadn't completed her project. Nick wasn't marrying her because he loved her. He wanted six months of her time. But business was business.

"Six months," Monique said, getting up mulling over her choices.

For the first time she regretted having asked Nick to help her. She should have known that the favor he would request from her would not be an easy one.

Paying for the services Nick had performed on her account, to save her business was more than she could afford to pay.

Monique assailed her regrets. Most of the times in her life she had lost. She couldn't lose her salon.

"It will take longer than six months to complete the camp," Nick said. "But we will have to stay married for that amount of time before the land is deeded to me."

"Nick, your grandmother is going to know that this marriage is not true." Monique hesitated. "Your cousin certainly is not going to believe it." Her voice trailed off, as she continued to worry. "Do you think we're going to fool all your family?"

"Monique, I'll worry about that."

"What do you mean, you'll worry about that?" Monique snapped. She considered another choice. She could ask her mother to lend her the money. But, no, if she could do that, she would've asked Yvonne McRay to lend her the money before she went to Nick.

"Okay. But I'm doing you this favor because I can't pay you."

"I understand."

"Are you sure we can masquerade as a happily married couple?" Monique was curious to hear Nick's response. After all, the whole town knew they'd been friends at one time. Still, she was certain that his cousin would see through their scheme. A scheme that she wanted no part of. How could Nick force her to marry him?

"We'll have to be seen in public. My parents usually invite everyone over for Sunday dinner. Especially during the holidays. We'll pretend to be in love."

Monique didn't like what she was hearing. She walked over to the fireplace and pushed the green plant that was setting perfectly on the mantel over an inch.

Monique's vow to stay uninvolved with the opposite sex, and with Nick Parker in particular, had been shattered. A knot tightened in her stomach and slowly crept near her breast. Monique sat on the edge of the sofa. Nick was working on her last nerve.

Monique didn't look at Nick. She wouldn't give him the pleasure of seeing her squirm. Pretending to be in love with him was like adding kindling to a smoldering fire.

"I think we should reconsider the romantic gestures." She finally turned and faced him.

Nick tilted his dark head. "If you're involved with someone, he'll have to understand."

"Involved?" Monique started and then stopped. She didn't have the slightest idea where Nick had conjured up a romantic relationship for her.

Monique stood, still remembering that Nick was involved with Jacqueline. "I don't think Jacqueline will think too highly of you and I tying the nuptial knot," Monique said, noticing what seemed to be a surprised expression on Nick's face.

"Jacqueline was a friend." Nick moved closer to her.

Monique stepped back and met Nick's gaze. She found the thought of sharing close contact with Nick for six months unsatisfying.

"Nick, your mother is a very good client. If she knew what we were planning, it could become a serious problem," Monique said, hoping she could convince Nick that it was immoral to marry for convenience, regardless of how good the cause.

"My mother doesn't interfere with my decisions."

"Will this be a justice of the peace wedding?" Monique dismissed his comment.

"If that's what you want," Nick said. "I prefer a real wedding."

"When do you want our wedding to take place?"

"We could get married in November, before Thanksgiving," Nick said.

It was September. Monique would have to throw together a quick wedding. With Colleen's help, she was sure the two of them could pull it together by November. "Is the first week in November okay with you?"

"Sounds good," Nick said.

"Nick, I don't know."

"About what, the wedding date?"

"No. I don't pretend well," Monique replied. However, she would have to fake her emotions. She had no intentions of becoming more emotionally involved with Nick.

"Neither do I," Nick said. "But I will take a chance on just about anything to build the camp."

Facing her dreadful future, Monique knew that it was easy to lose sight of reality. She had fought to release the memories of his warm, drugging kisses that had made her blood pound. She hadn't totally forgotten, but with time she knew that one day Nick would be a pleasant memory. Now there wasn't a chance of forgetting.

"Monique, if we don't show affection for each other, we might as well not bother."

Unable to deny Nick almost anything, she had arrived at the moment of reckoning. By her own action, she was opening the door to a place that was to stay closed until her project was completed. While conflicting emotion tore at her, Monique had no choice but to agree. "Okay," she said.

"I think we can pull this off," Nick said, as if he was aware of Monique's indecision.

"You mean act as if we're in love," Monique said, with clear visions of Nick's passionate kisses. At that moment, her memories crept out of the deep recesses of her mind where she had carefully buried them the night she had resolved their love.

Nick nodded. "Especially when my cousin Sharmain is in town."

"Where does she live?" Monique asked, wondering how often she would she have to demonstrate her false passion, and hoodwink Nick's cousin Sharmain.

"Atlanta. She visits the family for holidays, and our grandmother's birthday."

"Hmm, six months," Monique repeated the words almost to herself. *All I have to do is stay calm, cool and in charge of my senses.*

"I'll draw up a contract and bring it by for you to sign." Nick reached out and pulled her into his arms. His lips grazed hers, sending hungry sensations spiraling through her.

At first Monique struggled. Her defenses ceased. She sank against his hard chest, allowing Nick's kiss to deepen. He pulled away, lifting his head. His gaze burned deep into her soul. Monique felt hot blood inch through her veins. Nick kissed her again. Suddenly, he dropped his hands to his side. He walked to the coat tree, took his coat and put it on.

Nick walked to the door, opened it and stepped out onto the porch.

"Good night, Monique," he said. Taking swift steps, he went to his car. Monique closed the door. There was nothing separating them now but the upcoming weeks before she promised to be his wife. She had finally settled one disaster, only to find herself in another disaster worse than the first.

Finally, Monique went upstairs to her bedroom. One minute she had been bored almost to tears, making peace with her dull life. The next minute Nick Parker stood at her door, offering her an ultimatum. She would deal with the problem. But how was she going to allow herself the pleasure of Nick's closeness, then pretend that her emotions didn't matter?

Monique went to the closet for her nightgown. She took the lime green gown from the rack. She draped the nightgown over her shoulder and opened the vault on the closet wall. She lifted the box from the vault that held her past. Slowly Monique opened her memoirs.

For several minutes, Monique stood in her closet, touching pieces of her gloomy past. She traced the cracks in the tiny black shoes with a long, slender finger, before cupping the worn heel in her palm. She would never forget where she came from. She placed the shoes back in the box, set them inside the steel vault and locked it.

As soon as Monique finished her bath, she sat on her bed and dialed Colleen's number.

"Are you busy?"

"No, what's going on?"

"Colleen, I just did something that I need to talk about."

"You didn't hurt Roger."

Monique chuckled in spite of herself. Roger would probably be furious with her decision. But Roger didn't pay her bills.

"Am I keeping you and George from anything?"

"No, he's in the study working on a real estate deal," Colleen said. "I can come over if you want me to."

"It's not necessary," Monique said. But it was vital that she talk to her best friend.

Disturbing apprehensions and hope swept at Monique as she tried to dismiss her feelings for Nick. His kiss had held no pretense. And she, despite her restraint, had drunk the sweetness from his lips.

"Okay, so this is not a discussion that we'll want to have a strong drink over."

"No, Colleen, two cups of strong black coffee will do the trick."

"I'll be right over."

"Colleen, you don't have to come over. Let's talk tomorrow morning.

"Okay, but I think you need to talk tonight," Colleen said.

"Tomorrow, Colleen." Monique hung up.

SEVEN

On Saturday morning Monique went downstairs and put on a fresh pot of coffee. She took the mocha cream from the refrigerator and filled the creamer. It was going to take most of the day to plan her and Nick's wedding.

Monique had gotten herself into many disasters over the years, but this one was up for an award.

First, she had hired a young woman who was supposed to manage her salon and had not only left her business in disarray, but had left without giving her decent notice. Her salon had suffered and she had suffered, and to mend the financial threads that her salon hung by, she had promised a marriage contract to a man that she was attracted to.

Monique knew full well there was no place in her life for the relationship she was about to assume in payment for legal services. Now, as she stood in her kitchen, Monique hoped that she had completed the cycle for wreaking havoc in her life.

It was just after ten o'clock when Colleen rang the doorbell, interrupting Monique's thoughts.

"What happened?" Colleen asked, going straight to the kitchen and pouring herself a cup of coffee, with Monique joining her.

"Colleen, if nosy was an educational requirement, you would have a master's degree."

Colleen gave Monique an impish glance. "Watch it."

As they settled themselves at the kitchen table, Monique dropped one cube of sugar into her coffee and waited for it to dissolve before she cooled Colleen's curiosity.

"Nick and I are getting married," Monique stated while stirring her coffee slowly.

"Excuse me?" Colleen cocked her head to one side as if she was more shocked than surprised. "Why? . . . I mean, what?" Colleen couldn't complete her question. "I knew something happened at that meeting."

Monique circled the rim of her cup. The only thing that happened after her and Nick's meeting was that he had kissed her senseless.

"I'm doing him a favor." Monique struggled to maintain an even tone, while explaining to Colleen that her marriage to Nick would last for six months. The marriage was payment for his services in saving Shagreen II.

"Well, girl, let's plan this wedding. I know you're having one."

"Yes, but I'm not sure if I want a wedding."

"Anyway," Colleen said, testing her coffee to see if it was cool enough to drink. "You're getting married and that's all that matters."

"For six months."

"Right!"

"Colleen."

"Now let's get started." Colleen got up and grabbed a pad and pencil from the kitchen counter drawer. On her way back to the table, she began writing and talking at the same time. "Let's see. Gown. White, of course. Flowers."

"Will you stop. I would like to vent my frustrations."

"Go ahead, you're getting married."

"It's not real."

"Same thing."

"Colleen, this is a marriage of convenience for Nick. It's not like he and I are in love."

"Who's not in love . . . you or Nick?" Colleen looked from the pad she was writing on.

"That's not the point," Monique said, suddenly remembering that she and Nick were supposed to fool his family, especially his cousin Sharmain.

"Let's plan the wedding."

"Yes!" Colleen said, raising her fist in triumph.

Monique took the Yellow Pages from the closet in her kitchen. She and Colleen went to work, looking for bridal and floral shops. Monique wrote the numbers of the shops that sold wedding invitations.

"Monique," Colleen said to her girlfriend, "I think we should find a seamstress for the gown first."

"Colleen, if I didn't know any better, I would think it was you who was getting married."

"I know, it's so exciting," Colleen chuckled.

Monique shook her head. There was nothing that Colleen loved better than going to weddings.

Monique sat quietly, flipping through the Yellow Pages, taking notes on all the gown shops in town. She remembered the shop she had passed on her way to the hotel.

"I have a perfect wedding gown shop," Monique said, making Colleen remember the wedding gown shop and giving her the address.

"Yes." Colleen smiled. "That shop is perfect."

"Hum-um," Monique murmured, allowing her mind to waver to Nick. He seemed to know exactly what he wanted. Nonetheless, there were no excuses for him to give her only two choices. Marry him or pay him. She had chosen the former, and she hoped she wouldn't live to regret her choice.

Colleen looked up from a wedding invitation ad. "This company does excellent work," she said, taking her ballpoint pen and scribbling on the pad how she thought Monique and Nick's wedding invitations should appear.

Monique McRay
and
Nicholas Parker
Request the honor of your presence
at their marriage

Monique studied the wedding invitation scribbling that Colleen had written, imagining the writing in italic type on fine paper.

"What do you think?" Colleen asked, grinning.

"If our marriage were real, it would be nice."

"Monique, you worry too much. Do you know how many women would say yes to Nick's invitation to marriage, real or not?"

Monique imagined that a couple of women would've jumped at the chance. "Maybe," Monique said, not wanting to give Nick Parker the credit of being hunted and wanted by women. "I'm not other women."

"Let me enlighten you. If Nick just wanted to marry in order to own a piece of land," Colleen said, waving her hand to match her nodding head, "he would've married Jacqueline."

"Colleen, you don't understand." Monique dismissed Colleen's evaluation.

"Yes I do, he wants to marry you."

The phone rang before Monique could argue with Colleen.

"Hello," Monique answered, hearing Nick's voice on the line.

"Have lunch with me," Nick requested.

"Nick, I'm busy. Can we have lunch another day?" Monique waited for his response while she fought the unwanted affection that began rising in her.

"I need to talk to you." Nick's voice came across the line, as if he was coaxing her to share a meal and conversation with him.

"I hadn't planned on going out today."

"We have to be seen together, remember?" he reminded her.

"What time?"

"I'll pick you up at one o'clock."

Monique hung the receiver back on its cradle. Looking back, she knew it would have been better to borrow the money that she owed Nick.

"Colleen, I'm having lunch with Nick. We can continue tomorrow night."

Colleen smiled. "I'll be here," she said, getting up. "Have fun."

Monique slipped into a rust knit dress, matching brown heels and matching purse. While she went downstairs to wait for Nick, she hadn't thought to ask him where he was taking her for lunch. The sound of his car pulling up into her driveway cut her thoughts.

She watched from her living room window as Nick uncoiled his long body from his tiny car. A warmth that she hadn't expected swept through her as she observed how handsome he looked in his dark tan suit.

A second later, he rang her doorbell. Monique opened the door, determined not to let him inside. She didn't trust herself to be alone with him.

Nick circled his arm around her waist, pulling her to him, and he touched her full red lips with his. "I hope you don't mind having lunch with me at the lake house."

"No," was all Monique McRay could say. She had gone to the trouble of keeping him out of her home, only to be alone with him anyway. Her heart fluttered from the touch of his lips.

Nick drove, not saying much to her, and she in return didn't force a conversation. Monique sat quietly, enjoying the country scenery. Crimson-and-yellow leafed trees stood at the edge of the curved, black road. A white church was set back in the distance.

Finally, Nick turned his car into the lake house community and soon parked in front of his varnished wood home.

"We won't be living here," Nick said, getting out and going around to open the door for her.

"Where will we live?" Monique asked when she was out of the car and climbing the short steps with Nick.

"I have a home in town," he said, unlocking the door. He stepped inside and waited for Monique to enter.

The living room was masculine, with a black leather sofa and chairs, and glass cocktail and end tables trimmed with silver chrome. Black lamps covered with gray shades sat on the end tables. One huge green silk tree sat near a side window.

Monique dropped her purse on the sofa while Nick removed his suit jacket and laid it over the arm of a leather chair.

"I hope you like my cooking," Nick said, gesturing her to the kitchen.

"I don't know. What did you cook?" Monique said, wrinkling her nose.

"Lobster with wine sauce."

"I love seafood," Monique replied, surprised that Nick could cook. On second thought, she realized that he may have ordered the food from a restaurant.

"Did you make lunch yourself?"

"Sure I did." Nick grinned, leading Monique to the table he had set in the small dining room that had a perfect view of the lake.

Nick returned, setting a garden salad in front of her and one at his place setting. He left the room and quickly returned with the lobster and a tray with a bottle of wine.

While they ate and drank wine, Nick talked about his work. Then the conversation changed.

"Monique, while we're married, I don't want you to see anyone else," Nick said after he had drained his wine glass.

"I had no intentions of seeing anyone." Monique eyed Nick closely.

"Is Roger a friend?" Nick pushed his chair away from the table, crossed and rested one leg on his thigh.

"Roger and I are friends, and have been friends for years."

"All right."

Monique got up and walked out on the deck. She looked out at the lake that resembled clear blue silk. She didn't believe Nick. He had a lover, and was concerned that she remain faithful. Had he forgotten that their marriage was business? Regardless, she would never have an affair. Monique rested her hands against the deck railing.

"I didn't mean to upset you." Nick was behind her now. She could feel his breath on her neck.

Monique turned around and found herself closer to him than she wanted to be. The outline of her breast almost touched his chest. "Yes," she said, looking up at him, unable to stop him from lowering his head and delivering to her lips a drugging kiss.

Monique felt her emotions skid out of control as she clung to him, returning Nick's sweet kisses that promised more than she was willing to give. Without warning, he lifted her in his arms and carried her to his bedroom.

A small voice screamed to Monique to find control. She closed her mind to the warning and allowed herself to bask in Nick's love. His mouth covered hers, and with one stroke, he unzipped her dress.

The phone rang, swirling Monique back to her sound judgment. She pushed against Nick's chest, struggling to move from underneath him. In her struggle, she heard him curse.

Nick reached for the phone. "Yeah?"

While he spoke to whoever had called him, Monique

got dressed and, without saying good-bye, she walked outside and took the first bus home. Monique settled in her
seat, thanking the heavens for telephones.

EIGHT

Two American flags were set on each side of the wall behind the judge's brown podium.

The courtroom was almost empty, except for a few clerks, Nick, his client, Mrs. Amelia Wakefield, her stepson, his lawyer, and the bailiff.

Nick and Mrs. Wakefield sat at the mahogany table, facing the judge. Across from them, Amelia's stepson sat with his head down. "His mother is forcing him to do this, you know?" Amelia said to Nick, who was busy studying Amelia's late husband's medical files.

"Maybe," Nick said, not taking his eyes off his work.

"She'll do anything for money. That's the way some people are."

Nick stopped reading the medical records. He couldn't agree more. He was forcing Monique to marry him. He turned his attention back to the file in hand. *It's for a good cause,* he reminded himself, remembering how he had forced Monique to make a choice.

"Come to order. All rise," the bailiff instructed.

When the judge was seated, Amelia's stepson's lawyer stood.

"Your honor, Mr. Wakefield is declaring that his father was not of sound mind when he willed his holdings and other businesses to his wife, Amelia Wakefield." The lawyer went on discussing his case and defending his client in deep detail. "It is even believed that Mrs. Wakefield may have forced her husband to sign these documents, your honor."

"Objection, your honor," Nick cut in, interrupting the lawyer.

"Mr. Livingston, can you show proof that the defendant forced her late husband to sign the will?"

"No, your honor."

"Sustained. Stick to the facts, Mr. Livingston."

"Yes, sir."

Finally, Nick stood to defend his client. As he did so, he wondered what the judge would do to him if he learned he was forcing Monique to marry him.

"Your honor, my client is the sole heir of her late husband's estate and all his holdings." Nick passed a copy of the medical records to the judge. "He was of sound mind when he signed all documents stating these facts."

The judge read the medical information. After making a note, he passed the papers to the bailiff to give to Nick.

"I object, your honor. They were alone when Mr. Wakefield signed the will."

"Can you prove otherwise, Mr. Parker?"

"Yes sir, your honor."

Nick retrieved a video from his briefcase and passed it to the bailiff to be played. Mr. Wakefield's voice came across the speakers.

"I bequeath my property and all my holdings to my wife, Amelia Wakefield . . ." The court listened to the remainder of the tape.

"You are a darling." Amelia Wakefield hugged Nick while they were leaving the courtroom. "Where did you get that tape from?"

Nick smiled. "It's all in a day's work."

After court, Nick sat in his office and drew up a contract on his computer pertaining to his and Monique's marriage. This type of information was off limits to his secretary. The less anyone knew, the safer his chances were for getting the property, and building the camp. *And the woman you wan,* his subconscious reminded him. Nick ignored the small voice and proceeded to complete the contract. Nick completed the marriage contract and read it before making a copy for Monique to sign. Suddenly a strange sensation settled in his stomach. He wanted the property, but not at the expense of his law career. If someone found the contract, he would be disbarred.

An even more scary thought clicked across his mind. *What if Monique reports me to the bar association?* He wasn't sure if Monique would destroy his career, but he was sure about one thing, she didn't love him and she wasn't happy about their arranged marriage.

Nick deleted the contract, deciding that a verbal agreement would be safer. If Monique wouldn't except the verbal agreement, he'd have to go back to his plan to buy the property from Sharmain.

Nick knew Monique didn't want him. That was the understatement of the year. She had run the day they had lunch, and refused to answer any of his phone calls. But who else could he marry? Another woman may not have gone along with his decision.

When Monique resolved their relationship, he had been lonely. He'd met Jacqueline at a party Stone had given to cheer him up. Stone had also invited every available woman from his little black book, Nick was sure of that.

Jacqueline was among them. Through loneliness and the desire to forget Monique, he had turned to Jacqueline for companionship. After seeing her several times, Nick knew she wasn't the woman for him. Jacqueline wanted more than he was willing to give. Lately, she had called him. Nick hadn't returned her calls. He had simply refused to have anything to do with the woman.

Nick paced over to the window and looked out over

the city. He would spend six months of his life with Monique, under the same roof. He suspected it would be the hardest months of his life. He would control himself. He would stay out of her way. He didn't have the slightest idea how he was going to stick to his promise. Nick walked back to his desk. He was strong. He would stay away from Monique. *Liar,* a small voice spoke up in the back of Nick's mind.

Nick walked out his of his office on his way to Shagreen. He stopped by his secretary's office. "Doris, I'm out."

Fifteen minutes later, Nick walked into Shagreen, inhaling the light scent of subtle sweet cologne. "I need to speak to Monique," he said to the receptionist.

"Sure, may I tell who wants to see her?"

"Nick," he said, scanning the room. He had never seen so much makeup in one place at one time. Expensive black, brown and tan leather purses set on shelves that protruded from a mirrored wall. But, like Monique, the room was tastefully done.

"You can go in," Tamika said, directing Nick down the hall to the left to Monique's office.

Nick knocked on the door.

"Come in," Monique said, looking from the budget she was working on.

Nick walked into Monique's office, observing the plaques, certificates and awards decorating the wall. Monique seemed comfortable seated behind her L-shaped desk.

"Hi." Nick pulled back the chair in front of her desk and sat. He crossed one leg, resting it on his thigh.

While Monique was on the phone, Nick noticed the picture in a gold frame sitting on a case that matched her desk. He assumed this was Monique's mother. The woman was attractive. The same lemon complexion. The same black hair, only shorter. Her eyes were narrow and her lips much thinner than Monique's full lips. He wondered if

Monique's mother would give her blessing to her daughter if she knew what was taking place between them.

At that moment, Nick really didn't care about the deal he was about to make with Monique. He had plans. He wasn't stopping until his plans materialized. If he was lucky . . .

Monique hung up the phone and gave Nick her attention.

"I'll read the contract," she said, as if waiting for Nick to present her with a list of rules for their marriage.

"I think a verbal agreement will be better." Nick studied her facial expression.

"Verbal?" Monique frowned.

"Yes," Nick said not taking his gaze off her.

"As long as there are no changes after we're married, it's fine with me," Monique replied.

"I would like for us to spend as much time together as possible," he said. "We need to continue to show our affection for each other while we're in the presence of my family . . . and your family."

Monique nodded, agreeing with Nick.

"We need to share a bedroom," Nick continued.

"We will not sleep together and we will not sleep in the same room," Monique raised her voice.

"Monique, husbands and wives sleep together."

"Of course they do. But our marriage is not really a marriage and I want my own room."

Nick looked away for a moment.

"All right. We'll also need to be seen in public places," he added to his verbal list.

"As long as it's not an evening I'm working late." Monique pushed away from the desk. "I have a card game every Friday night."

"You'll have to give that up," Nick ordered.

Monique rolled herself closer to her desk, and tilted her head to the side. "I think you misunderstood me."

"I understood you, but for the next six months we're going out on Friday nights."

"Excuse me." Monique's tone was argumentative now.

Nick uncrossed his leg and leaned closer to Monique's desk, still looking at her.

"I didn't come her to fight with you."

"Who's fighting?" Monique held his gaze. "Just because we're getting married, does not mean that I'm changing my life style for you."

Nick leaned back in his chair. "Do you want to do this or not?"

"Yes, but I can't stop working and go out with you, just because we have a verbal contract."

"We'll compromise," Nick said, hoping that he and Monique could come to a mutual agreement on their sleeping arrangement.

"Speaking of compromising, you didn't mention how we were going to pay for this wedding."

"It doesn't matter." Nick raised up, reached into his back pocket and took out his wallet. He slipped a credit card from between the folds and laid it on the desk.

Monique pick up the thin card and held it. "Owning that property means that much to you?"

"It's what the property can do." Nick stated flatly, determined to stay in control of his emotions. There were too many children in town with nothing to do but get themselves sent to juvenile hall. He saw it every day in the court system. "They're good kids, Monique. They don't deserve what they're getting out of life."

"I know," Monique said, wishing she had not gotten herself tangled into Nick's goodwill web.

"My staff and associates are having dinner tonight. I would like for you to come with me."

Monique pulled out the desk drawer and stuck the credit card in her purse.

"I'm really busy. Can we go out another night?"

"I would like to introduce you to everyone."

"Nick, is it necessary?"

"All right, we can go out once a week." Nick rested his arms on the arms of the chair.

Monique got up and walked to the door. "Nick, do you really want me to have dinner with you and meet your staff, or do you want us to have dinner?"

"We can do that," Nick said, smiling.

Monique stood near the door, holding it open for Nick. "I'll pick you up around seven."

He reached out and drew her to him, lowering his head to kiss her.

"There are no relatives here, so we don't have to pretend," Monique said, reminding Nick of his promise.

"It doesn't hurt to practice." Nick leaned over and brushed his lips against Monique's. "We'll talk."

NINE

Monique closed her door and sat on the edge of her desk. No solution came to mind as to how she was going to get out of this predicament. This was her own fault. Going dancing and having dinner with Nick's associates were not in the contract.

Monique touched her lips where Nick had feather-kissed her. She wouldn't think about him. She had too many things to do. She went around and took her wedding checklist from the drawer.

Tonight, Monique and Colleen were leaving work early to put the final touches on the wedding arrangements. She also had a meeting with the caterer.

There had been a problem with the menu. The catering company that she hired called Monique and explained that fresh shrimp for the hors d'oeuvres would increase the price of their service.

Monique never imagined a wedding was rated ten on the stress scale. At any rate, Monique was convinced that she and Colleen had put together the fastest wedding in the Northeast, considering that it was the first of November.

Then there was the seminar in Florida to prepare for.

Monique pushed in the numbers to Shagreen II. Elaine answered on the first ring.

"Shagreen II."

"Did you call the travel agent and purchase your ticket for the seminar?"

"Yes, I did. I wouldn't miss that seminar for nothing."

"I wanted to make sure you were attending," Monique said, hanging up and calling Colleen.

Colleen's phone rang three times before the receptionist answered.

Monique was about to hang up when the young woman finally took her call.

"Is Colleen around?"

"One moment."

"Colleen, are you going with us to the seminar or what?"

"I'm not going. I'll keep an eye on your salons and check on the final touches for the wedding, if that's okay with you."

"Thanks, Colleen, I don't know what I'd do without you."

Monique was closing the salon early tonight. She went to check with the technicians and facialists to see if they needed help with anything. Everyone had served their clients and were closing down their stations.

Monique went out front and prepared the deposit slip for the bank.

An hour later, she headed home. As soon as she walked inside the house, she went upstairs and started packing for her trip to Florida. Just as she was packing her shoes, her doorbell rang.

"Yes, Roger." Monique moved aside so that Roger could enter. Roger walked in, rubbing his leathered gloved hands together. "Wow, it's cold out," he commented on the weather before acknowledging Monique.

"It certainly is, Roger," Monique moved toward the thermostat to raise the temperature.

"I need to talk to you." Roger moved as if to get a better look at Monique. His gaze seemed to hold a hint of suspicion.

"Did you bring the information that you found about my birth parent or parents?" Monique gestured him to follow her to the kitchen. Shimmers of light from the back streetlight flitted into Monique's backyard and streamed through the half opened blinds into her dining room.

"No," Roger answered.

Monique went over and closed the blinds. She turned around to find Roger slipping out of his coat. He draped it over the back of a chair, then reached for a cup from the cabinet.

"Roger, I would like to know the information in the report."

"Monique, I'm sorry. I thought I had it with me, but I left it in my office."

"You can tell me."

"It would be better if you read it for yourself."

"Is it good or bad?"

"When I give you the report, you'll know." Roger replaced the cup on the shelf and retrieved a tall wineglass from the wine rack.

"I had my hopes up," Monique said, sounding disappointed.

"Other than building your hopes up, how was your day?"

"Busy as usual, but good." She answered Roger's question, wondering what the conversation was leading to.

Roger opened the refrigerator and chose between the two bottles of wine. Chablis or blush. He chose the chablis, uncorked it and filled his glass.

"I finally got a chance to read the newspaper about an hour ago. I read your wedding announcement," he said before turning the wine up to his lips and taking a long swig.

"So?" Monique said, her voice filled with authority and challenge.

"I thought you were through with that guy?"

Monique took the plant that was sitting in the windowsill and placed it on the table. She didn't intend to discuss with Roger the arrangement she had with Nick.

"I changed my mind," she said, taking a glass off the shelf to join Roger with a drink.

"Why don't I believe you?"

"Why should you not believe me?" she answered, filling her glass with wine.

"You're making a mistake." Roger took another drink of wine and set the glass down on the counter.

Monique set the bottle down. "Roger, you know as well as I do that lovers break up and make up all the time."

"First of all, when we were in Omar's, Nick acted as if he was all business, except for the look he gave me."

"We made up." Monique decided that keeping her answers short was best, keeping in mind that Roger was a private detective.

"Did you tell him?"

"No, I didn't tell him that I was adopted."

"Do you plan to?"

Monique took another sip of wine before she answered him. She planned to tell Nick eventually. It wasn't important that he knew. "I intend to tell him."

Roger drained his glass. "You're setting yourself up to get hurt."

"Roger, I wish that you would stop saying that. Nothing is going to happen to me." She was calm as she spoke, as if she believed the words she'd just spoken.

"If you think for one moment that he'll want you after he learns that you're adopted and have no family background, he'll dump you the same—"

"Don't you say it," Monique's voice rose. "I will not stand here and listen to you rehash my broken engagement."

"Because you know it's true," Roger said, pouring himself another glass of wine.

"That's why I hired you—to find at least one of my parents."

"I have most of the information. But you won't let me complete the job."

"When I can afford you," Monique wailed. Their argument was getting out of control. Monique felt her eyes brimming with tears. Roger was a constant reminder of her past. Monique snatched a paper towel from the roll and headed for the door. She thought she heard the bell ring while she and Roger indulged themselves in a yelling match.

"Nick," Monique whispered his name.

"Are you all right?" Nick brushed past her and headed to the kitchen, with Monique trailing close behind him.

"I'm fine," she said, shifting her gaze from Nick to Roger.

"Nick, this is Roger Cummings," Monique started to introduce them, then remembered she had heard Nick speak to Roger while they were at Omar's, calling him by name.

"I know," Nick cut her off. "He worked for Jerry Mack's P.I. firm. "What's going on?" Nick asked.

"We were having a discussion," Roger said, finishing the wine.

"Yes we were, and Roger was about to leave," Monique said, taking his coat off the chair and handing it to him.

The two men stood glaring at each other for a while before Roger finally made his way out of Monique's house.

When they were alone Nick took off his coat and hung it on the coat tree near the kitchen door. He stood before Monique, his tall muscular frame towering over her. "What was that all about?"

Monique decided that telling Nick part of her life story wouldn't be that bad. It was right that she told him. It wasn't as if her engagement or marriage to him would suffer because of her past. Her reasons for not wanting a serious relationship and a real marriage were simple. She needed to know if there were any serious diseases in her biological family tree.

Monique led Nick into the living room and sat. She folded her legs underneath her and got comfortable. After what seemed like the longest pause ever, she spoke with quiet firmness.

"Nick, I'm adopted." With an iron will, she composed herself, swallowing back tears that threatened to surface.

Monique noticed Nick's lips part to speak. He didn't seem surprised at her revelation, nor did he appear disturbed.

"How long have you known?" Nick's voice broke with a husky whisper.

"For years," Monique said, leaving out significant information.

The flicker of apprehension that threatened to race through her at Nick's response to her news faded and was replaced with memories the evening she told her ex-fiancé's mother she was adopted. Mike's mother acted as if Monique had committed a crime.

"Roger is looking for your parents." Nick leaned in closer to Monique.

"Yes," Monique said.

Nick didn't say anything. He looked as if he was in deep thought.

"I hope you find them," Nick finally replied, covering her hand with his. "It must be hard for you, wanting to know who they are."

Monique felt tears brimming and burning her eyes as her heart swelled. Nick was understanding and kind. Still she couldn't bring herself to love him completely, until she learned her background.

One tear rolled from each eye as the warmth of Nick's husky voice floated out over her.

He moved closer and drew her into his arms.

"Monique," Nick tilted her head back so he could look into her face. "Is this the project that you've been working on?"

"Yes," she said, fighting to control the next tear.

"Don't cry." Nick touched his thumb to her cheek, wiping the tear and kissing the salty spot. "Shhhh."

Unable to speak through her tears, Monique nodded. Nick's pleading with her to stop crying only made her fight harder to control the tears that were falling.

"That's the reason you broke off our relationship?"

Monique nodded and untangled herself from Nick's comforting embrace. She went to the powder room in the hall underneath the stairs for a tissue to wipe her tears. She hadn't meant to cry. But the thought of her life hanging on the outcome of Roger's findings broke her heart.

When she returned, Nick was standing. He held out a small black velvet box.

"I came over to give you this," Nick said, flipping the top and exposing a 4-karat diamond ring.

Monique could hardly believe Nick had gone to so much trouble for their engagement. She was almost speechless as she held the ring, admiring the diamond set in the center of green petals.

"Don't you think you went a bit overboard?" She smiled, beginning to feel like herself again.

"We have to make it look good." Nick took the ring and slipped it on her finger. He leaned down and brushed his lips against her cheek. "If you feel like you need to talk tonight, give me a call."

Later that night, Monique took a long, hot bath. She cracked her bedroom window so the chill of the night would mix with the heat in her home. Finally, she slipped between her warm blankets and slept.

Her ex-fiancé stood at the altar, watching while Monique and her adopted father John McRay walked down the aisle to the rhythm, 'Here Comes The Bride.' She smiled, taking slow, steady steps to her soon-to-be husband. When she reached him, it was Nick facing her instead of the man she was supposed to marry. She smiled up at him. The minister spoke, reading the vows.

"Will you take this woman to be your lawful wedded wife?"

"No," Nick said, walking out of the chapel, leaving her in tears.

Monique tossed in her sleep, small whines slipped from her throat. She ran. Not after Nick, but away from the church, her adopted parents and from herself. "She's not real, she doesn't know who she is, get her away from me," she heard Nick say.

Monique sprang up in bed. "Oh my God, oh, oh." Her heart pumped hard in her chest. Monique lay awake for a long time, staring at the ceiling, assessing her life. For once in her life she was glad her marriage to Nick would last for only a short time. *Maybe Roger is right.*

In the wee hours of the morning, she dozed off, allowing her subconscious to attack her once more.

Nick's fingers were warm and gentle against her taut breast as he peeled the black lace away, exposing her smooth lemon skin. His lips moved to hers. They both drank each other's sweet kisses, like sipping heady goblets of rich wine. In the meantime, his strong hands caressed delicate parts of her body that had never sampled such intimacy. He drew her closer. She could feel the heat of his breath against her neck and her cheek as he made a heated trail back to her lips. Again he kissed her long and deep. Suddenly, he vanished.

Monique woke from the sound of her moans. She rubbed her eyes and rolled over, tired from her dreams. *Woman get a grip,* Monique told herself, getting out of bed.

TEN

Clara Parker filled in the dollar amount on her mono-grammed check. "You have a wonderful business, Monique," Clara complemented her on the services she had just received.

"I'm glad you enjoyed yourself," Monique said, smiling and taking the check that paid for Clara's beauty package: manicure, pedicure, clay pack facial and brow wax.

"I'm certainly looking forward to you becoming a part of our family."

Monique forced a smile. It wasn't easy to be the fraud she apparently was. If Nick's mother learned of their mis-guided trick to bamboozle the family and half the town, she was certain that Clara Parker would be paying for beauty packs at the next aesthetician salon in Teaneck, New Jersey.

Monique never had reasons to think that Mrs. Clara Parker was a spiteful woman. However, she was sure Clara would announce to the town their false plans, and forbid her friends from patronizing Monique's businesses. Monique simply couldn't afford to put her salons in danger. She had struggled to keep them. If Nick's scheme didn't work, she wouldn't be responsible for the pain she intended to inflict upon him.

"Thank you." Monique managed to say as politely as she could.

Nick had already informed her that his cousin would be visiting his parents.

"I'm looking forward to the family meeting you," Clara said before leaving Monique.

"Thank you," Monique said, smiling as Clara left the lobby, holding the door while Tamika walked inside from lunch.

"Monique, you didn't tell me you were getting married."

"Is this on your need-to-know list?" Monique asked the receptionist.

"No, but I would love to go to the wedding."

"Your invitation is in the mail," Monique said, smiling at her flirty receptionist.

"Yes!" Tamika said, excited.

"Tamika, control yourself," Monique said, noticing Amelia Wakefield moving to the counter to pay her bill.

"Darling, I'm absolutely thrilled over your engagement to Nick," Amelia beamed. "He is my lawyer, you know, and a good one, if I must say so myself."

"Thanks, Mrs. Wakefield," Monique said. Not only did Monique dislike Amelia Wakefield, she despised her comments. In spite of her feelings for Amelia, Monique had mailed the woman an invitation. After all, her marriage to Nick was business. Her business teetered on the fact that if she lost one client because of her dislike for them, it would mean Shagreen II was in danger of failing.

"I must say, you do know how to pick them." Amelia waved a heavily jeweled wrist.

Monique responded with a nod as she watched the elegant woman's expression. Amelia Wakefield was the icon of glamor, and was acting as though Monique had just chosen the prize roses from the garden.

"Listen, since you're engaged, you're no longer in the running for the bachelorette auction." Her smile widened.

"So I have decided that as a client of your establishment, I am inviting you and your friends to lunch."

"How nice," Monique said, forcing another smile.

"I'm telling you this because I can imagine your schedule is tight. So try to keep your calendar open the week before your wedding."

That evening Monique sat amongst Nick's colleagues at their dinner in the restaurant, while he introduced her as the future Mrs. Parker.

While they ate dinner, Nick's colleagues congratulated her and Nick and wished them the best that married life had to offer.

When the dinner was over and the dinner party was sipping wine and listening to the live band, Nick stood and took Monique's hand, leading her out on the dance floor, joining several other couples.

Monique allowed Nick to gather her in his arms. With slow dance steps, Nick guided her.

"You know, you never did tell me why you left me the day we had lunch." Nick looked down at her.

"You wouldn't want an explanation now."

"I wouldn't mind," Nick said, drawing her even closer. Monique could feel his heart beat against her and the tautness that coiled in his body.

"I'll tell you one day," she said, wanting to drown out the affection she was beginning to experience.

Nick leaned over and kissed her softly on her lips.

Please don't do that. Monique stopped dancing. "I'm ready to go home," she said. She needed an excuse to get away from Nick. It seemed that he used every opportunity to make her swirl with passion. Monique had begun to recognize feelings that she thought were dead.

* * *

Sunday, the day Monique would officially meet and have dinner with Nick's family, had finally arrived. She chose a royal blue calf-length dress, blue heels and gold accessories. She sprayed a small amount of oil sheen on her soft permanent wave hair and brushed the wavy tresses until they seemed to glow. Monique took careful measures to apply small touches of makeup and just a dab of her favorite red lipstick. The idea of marrying Nick because she was in his debt was discouraging. If his family knew . . . Monique pushed the thought to the farthest recesses of her mind, where she stored all of her secrets and humiliations.

In time she would know her past. Whether the information Roger found was favorable or not was yet to be determined. She would save her worries for other important matters, like holding on to Shagreen II.

While Monique and Nick drove to his parents' house for dinner, Monique took the liberty of asking a few questions. Families always interested her. "What's your grandmother like?" she asked Nick.

"She's eighty-nine, but feisty," Nick said with a soft low chuckle. "Even after she fell a few months ago."

"The fall must have caused her serious injury," Monique said.

"Granny fractured her hip," Nick said. "But she didn't injure her sharp wits."

"I think it's wonderful that you still have your grandmother," Monique said, smiling. Her smiled faded. If Nick's grandmother was as sharp-witted as he said she was, she doubted that Nick was fooling his grandmother at all, with their make-believe marriage.

"Yeah, I'm glad she's still around."

Monique turned in her seat, facing Nick. She wanted to see his expression. "I'm sure we're not fooling your grandmother."

Nick chuckled. "I don't know." Nick slowed at the street

that led to his parents' home and made the turn. "I have a chance to fulfill a promise I made to myself. I intend to go through with it."

Monique didn't miss the seriousness in his last statement.

"I wish we could do this another way," Monique said.

"And deprive me of the privilege of having you for my wife?"

"Is that supposed to be a joke?"

Nick laughed. "No, it's not a joke. Think of it this way. You're getting what you want. I'm getting what makes me happy."

"If your grandmother figures out this transparent engagement, we won't be getting married." Monique leaned back against the soft leather seat.

"You'd like that, wouldn't you?"

Monique shivered from the memories of Nick's kisses. "Our marriage would be wonderful, if it wasn't for our agreement."

"Are you saying that you would rather we didn't have a contract?"

Again Monique reflected on the smoldering passion that Nick was responsible for igniting in her. "I didn't say that."

"What are you saying?"

"I would like to have a real marriage."

"To me?"

Monique didn't answer his question. Instead, she looked at him for a few seconds.

Nick chuckled, as if he could feel her eyes on him. "You worry too much," Nick said, stopping the car in his parents' driveway behind Brant and Daniella's pickup and cutting the engine. "But, I hope your answer is to me."

Monique was not comfortable attempting to fool an old woman. "Why does it have to be about you?"

Nick got out and walked around and opened the car

door for Monique. He slipped his arm around her waist and they walked like old lovers to his parents' home.

"Why can't it be about you?"

"Are you flirting with me?" Monique said, intending to change the subject.

"Yes, and all you have to do is pretend to flirt with me," Nick said, ringing the doorbell.

Sharmain opened the door. "Look who's here, the fake love birds." She tossed her head and walked to the dining room were the family was waiting for Nick and Monique.

After dinner, everyone went to the great room. Nick and Monique stood at the sliding doors that led out **onto** the patio. While Brant and their father watched the football game, the women talked. Clara, her mother and Daniella discussed everything from recipes to the latest styles in winter and fall clothes, while Sharmain sat on the other side of the room staring at the television.

Nick slipped his arms around Monique's waist. "They like you," Nick said, nuzzling the side of Monique's face with his lips.

"Were you worried that they would dislike me?"

"No, I thought maybe you were concerned."

Monique turned and looked up at him. "I like them too."

"You just don't like me."

"Nick, please," Monique said, smiling.

Nick touched his lips to hers. Monique felt her blood rush through her. "Don't do that," she said when Nick released her.

Monique walked over to the sofa and sat beside Daniella, while Nick joined Mark and Brant.

As Monique made herself comfortable on the sofa, she noticed Lucy Morgan wheeling herself over to the bookshelf, taking a family photo album from a low shelf. She rolled back to Monique and handed the book to her.

"I always say, if you're going to marry a man, you must

see his childhood pictures," Lucy said, smiling. "Gives you an idea what your children are going to look like."

Monique laughed in spite of herself. She'd never thought of it that way. However, unlike Daniella who was expected to deliver her and Brant's baby any day now, there would be no children for her and Nick.

Monique spread the book out, sharing the album with Daniella. She turned the pages in the photo album, stopping when she came to one of Nick's pictures.

"I think he was about six years old in this one," Lucy said, a pleasant smile curving her tinted red lips.

Even at six years old, Nick was tall, dressed in blue short pants, yellow and blue polo shirt and blue sneakers. His eyes squinted against the sun and the flash of the camera as he embraced a tan collie.

"Ooh, he loved that dog," Granny said, leaning over in her wheelchair as if she were seeing the picture of her grandson for the first time.

Monique smiled at the obvious admiration Nick's grandmother had for him, as she read the printing written at the bottom of the photo. "Nick and Caesar."

"He was a beautiful dog," Monique said, turning the page.

Lucy's smile faded into a more serious demeanor. "Caesar wandered out of the gate one day, and Nick never saw the dog again." Her age-old eyes sparkled. "He hates losing anything." Lucy folded her hands across her waist and waited, as if she was anticipating a response from Monique.

"How awful," Monique replied, looking up from the photo album.

With yours and Nick's crafty act of passion, you're not fooling Lucy Morgan. Monique banished the clever thought.

"I think that dog was the only living thing Nick loved at that time, except for his family," Lucy Morgan said, still eyeing Monique with a careful gaze.

"Nick must've been hurt," Monique responded, not exactly liking the way the woman was directing her conversation.

"I thought his heart would break." Lucy unfolded her arms and rested them on the chair's handle. "I hate it when my grandchildren hurt."

Monique forced a smile as she attempted to grasp the meaning of Mrs. Lucy Morgan's words. If Lucy Morgan had an inkling that her intentions were to bring emotional pain to her grandson . . . Monique didn't want to know what would happen to her. It was as if she didn't have to keep a watchful eye on her heart. If she read Lucy Morgan right, anything that went wrong in her and Nick's marriage was going to be her fault. Monique's heart fluttered this time, but not because of Nick's passion. She had cast herself in a dangerous mold. The only way she could win was to trust that she had made the right decision to marry Nick.

"I'm sure Mr. and Mrs. Parker found him another pet," Monique said over the men's loud cheers as their team made a touchdown.

"No, Nick never did own another pet," Lucy replied. A cheerful smile replaced her somber expression, and it was as if their conversation had never taken place.

Nick's grandmother quietly turned her attention to Sharmain, who was making her way across the room to sit beside Monique.

"If you ladies will excuse me, I think I'll take a nap." Nick's grandmother wheeled herself out of the room.

"So, you're supposed to be the woman that's marrying Nick?" Sharmain asked Monique, crossing one long slender leg over the other, letting one shoe dangle from her foot. Her short black hair was styled into two-inch curls away from her oval-shaped face. Her dark eyes seemed to flash a hint of mischief.

"Yes, we're engaged," Monique said, giving the album

to Daniella, who had been sitting quietly through the previous conversation.

"I'm sure Nick has his reasons." Sharmain's smirk matched the icy tone in her voice.

Monique shifted in her seat, uncomfortable with Sharmain's insinuations. Breaking the news to Sharmain that she was marrying Nick for nontraditional reasons would be like refusing to assist a drowning man with a rope for a new chance on life. Her business depended on her marriage to Nick. Besides the fact that Nick's affection for her was a lie, she hated being insulted.

"Excuse me?" Monique said to Sharmain.

"I think you heard me. But I'll make myself clear." Sharmain allowed her dangling shoe to drop from her foot as she uncrossed her legs. "How much is he paying you to marry him?"

A twinge of irritation bordering on anger raked at Monique's insides. She had no one to blame but herself for allowing herself to be coaxed into a marriage to save her business, and at the same time allowing Nick the pleasure of accomplishing his dream. However, she would not dignify Sharmain's remark with an answer.

"I said we're engaged," Monique said with frosty, determined control.

"Nick may have you and Granny fooled with the pretense that he loves you, but I know his reasons for marrying you, and love don't have nothing to do with it."

"And you're sure about that?" Monique asked, feeling her irritation turning more to anger.

"When my cousin Nick marries you because of love, that will be day hell freezes over."

Monique rose from the sofa with one fluid move. She was a guest in the Parker's home. It was her first visit, as a matter of fact. It wasn't polite to make a scene in the presence of the family.

"Could we go to another room and discuss this matter properly?" Monique asked Sharmain.

"I don't see why we can't. There's no one stopping us," Sharmain said, getting up off the sofa.

"Excuse me," Monique said to Daniella.

"Sure." Daniella turned her attention back to the game.

Monique walked out of the room and waited near the door for Sharmain to lead the way to a private place where they could discuss the matters of her and Nick's pretense of affection for each other.

Sharmain opened the door to the living room, and walked inside. Monique closed the door and quickened her pace, hot on Sharmain's heels. She slowed her pace as she moved past the cocktail table, glancing at the painting hanging over the powder blue sofa. At the moment Monique felt as strong as the mountain that was painted on the canvas.

"What is it that you want to say to me?" Sharmain asked.

"Let me explain something about me, to you." Monique pointed a finger at the woman and placed one hand on her slender narrow waist, her fingers spread out over her hip. "Nick and I are engaged and we are going to get married." Monique swallowed hard. If it was fight or flight, she chose battle.

"Not if I have anything to do with it," Sharmain shot back.

"Believe me, Sharmain, there's nothing you can do to stop this wedding."

"Yes, I will. After I convince my grandmother that Nick has betrayed her, there won't be a wedding."

"Tck," Monique made a clicking sound with her lips and placed a long, manicured finger to her full red lips. "I must remember to inform your grandmother of the time you wrote those bad checks . . ." her voice trailed off, as if she was allowing the information to soak in. "And I think you went to jail for . . . let me see if I can remember." Monique paused for a second as if she was thinking. "Yes, I think you spent a week in that disgusting place."

"That's a lie," Sharmain snapped.

"Really?" Monique asked nonchalantly. "Then I suppose that your boyfriend didn't lose his job and his real estate license because he spent his client's escrow money."

"Who told you that?" Sharmain's voice trembled as if she were close to tears.

Monique smiled, grateful that Roger Cummings was her friend. "That's not your business. But your grandmother may be interested in this information."

"That's blackmail."

"I know." Monique stepped out of the room and into Nick's arms.

"Are you all right?" Nick asked, releasing his grip on Monique.

"I'm fine," she said, inhaling his heady cologne.

Sharmain squeezed past Nick and Monique. "The two of you deserve each other. But Nick, I will get you for this, if it's the last thing I do."

"What happened in there?" Nick asked, pulling Monique to him, nuzzling his lips against her cheeks.

Monique was sure the embrace and kiss were for Sharmain's eyes only. "Sharmain and I had a woman-to-woman discussion."

Nick chuckled under his breath. Then without warning, he covered her lips with his, parting them with the tip of his tongue.

Monique felt the electricity coil inside her, making her emotions skid and sway, losing control while Nick's kiss deepened.

"Lord, Lord, and Lord, the two of you make me sick!" Sharmain shouted.

Monique and Nick unraveled themselves from their kiss,

and watched Sharmain head back into the room with the others.

"Mission accomplished," Nick said.

"Maybe," Monique said. Her warning to Sharmain was sincere. She had worked too hard to lose Shagreen II. She wasn't going to lose her business because Sharmain and Nick were engaged in a personal war.

Holding hands affectionately, Monique and Nick joined the family.

Monique and Nick said good night, and went home. Halfway to Monique's house, Nick stopped at the traffic light and turned to Monique.

"What did you say to Sharmain?"

"I blackmailed her," Monique said, telling Nick what she had found out about his cousin.

Nick leaned his head back and laughed.

Monique smiled and gave Nick a wink. She settled back against the seat, turning her attention to the beautiful homes lit with soft white lights and well-manicured lawns, while Nick's soft chuckles floated out to her.

Soon Nick drove into Monique's driveway. While Monique unfastened her seat belt and gathered her purse, Nick got out of the car, walked around and opened the door for her. He held her hand, assisting her. When they reached her front door, he took her key and turned the lock.

Once inside her living room under the soft glow of lamp lights, Nick pressed her to him, and kissed her.

Monique pushed against his chest and out of his embrace. She walked to the kitchen "We're alone. There's no need to pretend." She went over and closed the blinds.

"It may have been a show for you, but I wasn't pretending."

"We have an agreement. That's all. The engagement,

the marriage," she reminded him. Monique felt the tears sweep up through her and threaten to fall. "It's all a lie."

"It wouldn't be a lie if you weren't so uptight about being adopted and what the world thinks about you!" Nick's voice rose.

"Well it means everything to me."

"Why? Give me a reason." Nick's voice seemed clouded with annoyance. "One that makes sense."

Monique gave Nick a short laugh. But the laughter didn't reach her eyes, or her angry facial expression. "You don't understand," she said, her voice rising with each word. "I would like to know if my parents' were healthy, sound-minded people."

"You don't seem to have a problem." Nick moved closer to Monique.

"That doesn't mean that I'm satisfied."

"The people that raised you don't seem to have done a bad job."

"You're right, Nick." Monique heard her voice quiver as she spoke.

"Then I don't understand the problem," Nick said.

"Of course you wouldn't understand. You never lived—" Monique stopped. She wasn't ready to tell Nick that she had lived in an orphanage before she was adopted.

"I never lived where, Monique?"

Monique wiped a tear that slid down her face. "Go."

"I'm not leaving until we have finished this discussion."

Monique took a towel from the rack and wiped her eyes before Nick reached out and gathered her in his arms.

"I've told you how I feel about you."

Liar, a small voice in Monique said. Again, she pulled away from him, not wanting him to console her.

"What's wrong now?"

Determined to stay in control, Monique closed her eyes for a moment and swallowed her tears.

"You don't feel anything for me."

"How did you come to that conclusion?"

"Nick, please. The whole town knows about your lover." Despite not wanting to sound like a jealous woman, Monique shouted the words out to him.

"Lover?" Nick asked her.

"Give me a break. Everyone knows about Jacqueline. I had the pleasure of meeting her myself."

"Monique, Jacqueline was a friend and that was all."

"Was a friend?"

"I don't see her anymore."

"I'm supposed to believe that, when the woman came into my salon and threatened to write bad publicity."

"When did she do that?"

Monique waved her hands. "Don't worry about it. I wouldn't want you breaking up with her because of me."

Monique noticed the anger that seemed to settle in Nick's eyes.

"I wouldn't lie to you."

"Really?"

"Monique, I love you."

Monique reached out and took Nick by his arm. She began walking toward the kitchen door. She stopped at the coat tree. "Get your coat and go."

Nick pulled on his coat. "Throwing me out is not going to make me change the way I feel about you."

"Just go."

"I don't want to leave you like this."

"Out!" Monique pointed her finger to the living room door.

She watched Nick leave through teary eyes. When he was out of her house, Monique took brisk steps up the stairs, went to her room, threw herself across the bed and cried.

The more she faced the dreadful truth, the harder she cried. She loved Nick and wanted to be his wife for more than six months. But the reality of it all was that her dream was doomed, never to come true.

Nick sat in his car in front of Monique's house for a long time before he headed for home. He had promised himself that he wouldn't show any affection toward her. He would follow their agreement and show their love in the presence of his family only. He hadn't kept his promise, unlike Monique who had kept to the rules.

Nick gazed at Monique's upstairs window. If they hadn't gotten into a fight, he would never have known that Jacqueline was spewing gossip and making threats.

Nick started his car and headed home. As he reached the street that led to his lake house, he made a U-turn and drove back toward town.

Two miles later, Nick walked into the apartment lobby and took the elevator up to the tenth floor. He rang the doorbell and waited for what seemed like a half-hour.

Jacqueline opened the door, dressed in a short pink lounge outfit that stopped just above her knee.

"If you came to tell me that you're engaged, don't bother. I read it in the paper," she said to Nick, pulling him inside her apartment.

Nick pulled away from her and pushed his hands into his trouser pockets.

"We have to get a few things straightened out," Nick said, moving farther into the room and away from Jacqueline.

"Don't tell me. You broke off your engagement to that . . . person, who owns those little pedicure shops." She waved her hands as if the very thought of Nick being engaged to another woman beside herself was distasteful. Jacqueline smiled up at Nick. "Her services are disgusting to say the least. You can't be serious about marrying her." Jacqueline stopped talking, as if she was waiting for a response from Nick. When he was still silent, she continued. "She is—"

"Shut up." Nick said, grinding out the words through clenched teeth.

"You can't be serious. When I read that announcement, I thought it was a mistake."

"If you write one negative word about Shagreen or Shagreen II, you will have to deal with me."

"You're kidding."

"I'm very serious."

"Nick, you and I had a small disagreement. We can still be friends."

"No, we cannot be friends." Nick turned and headed for the door.

"But Nick."

He opened the door, stepped out into the hallway, and took the elevator to the lobby.

ELEVEN

The next morning, Monique stopped by Shagreen to meet with her staff before taking a flight to Florida to attend the aesthetician seminar. She was tired and listless from the small amount of sleep she'd gotten the night before.

All night she had drifted in and out of sleep, dreaming and remembering the touch of Nick's strong hands caressing her body, his demanding kisses.

After the meeting, Monique went to the salon kitchenette and poured herself a cup of coffee. While she sipped the steaming liquid, her mind reeled with memories of Nick and the fight they'd had—the tears that she had let spill freely because of her jealousy. How she had gotten herself in a predicament that she had to save her salon was beyond her. There had to be another solution to her and Nick's madness.

Her ponderings were interrupted by Tamika, who walked in carrying a long green box.

"These are for you, Miss McRay," the receptionist said, setting the box on the counter.

"Thank you," Monique said as she went over and lifted the cover off the box.

One red rose lay atop a small envelope. Monique slipped the envelope from underneath the rose and removed the small card. She read the message from Nick.

Monique,

Please reconsider changing our contract. We can make our marriage last a lifetime.

Love,
Nick.

Monique slipped the card back into the envelope and into her suit coat pocket. Did Nick actually think she wanted to change their marriage contract?

She couldn't deny her feelings for him any longer. But there was simply no space in her life to love him without fearing the information from her past. She had resolved their relationship once. As soon as their six-month marriage expired, he would be out of her life completely.

The aesthetician seminar would be just what Monique needed to get away from the hustle and bustle of her life in New Jersey. Her whirlwind engagement to Nick and the quickie wedding she was planning, took away energy that she had planned to use.

Storing her memories of Nick in a safe space in her mind, Monique checked her watch, as she headed out to her car to pick up Elaine.

As soon as she got into her car, Monique turned the key in the ignition, starting her car. Instead of pushing the gear into reverse and backing out of the parking space, Monique sat for a minute studying the front of the salon and the sign SHAGREEN engraved in large thin letters across the salon's window, as if the sign held a solution to her problem.

She could tell Nick that she had changed her mind and the marriage would be off. It was as simple as that. It wasn't as if she would never pay him for the arrangement he'd made for her with the company to pay for the equipment. The problem was that she couldn't pay him for his service and Faceology at the same time.

She pushed her worries to the back of her mind, and

drove out of the parking space, turning the radio to the contemporary jazz station. The music usually kept her mind free from thinking about her problems.

Ten minutes and several traffic lights later, Monique drove up to Shagreen II. Before she could get out of the car, she noticed Elaine walking out the salon to her car. Monique reached down and pulled the release button that open the car's trunk, then leaned over and unlocked the passenger's door.

"Hi," Elaine spoke getting into the car, settling down and securing herself with the seat belt, after she had loaded her luggage in the trunk of the car.

"Good morning," Monique returned Elaine's greeting, driving out onto the street. "Is everything all right at the salon?" Monique asked. She learned from experience, that inquiring about her business was important.

"We have no problems," Elaine smiled, reaching into her purse taking out her phone. She dialed the number, waited for a moment, then spoke into the receiver.

From the one-sided conversation, Monique could tell that Elaine was talking to her man-friend. Monique turned her attention away from Elaine's phone conversation, and recalled the invitation she had offered to Elaine to stay at her mother's condo while they were in Miami. Elaine had been grateful for the invitation, but confessed that her man-friend was joining her.

The beep of the phone indicating that Elaine had turned her phone off, drew Monique out of her musing.

"I think you might enjoy this night club," Elaine said, after she had slipped her phone back in her purse and took a business card from her wallet.

Monique stopped at the red traffic light, took the card from Elaine, and read the address of the hot Miami club. "Elaine, you know I need to enjoy myself." Monique laughed, easing up off the brakes as the traffic light

"I'm happy to see you too," Monique said, giving her mother a hug.

"Listen," Yvonne said, after she and Monique had released each other from their embrace. "I'm sorry I can't spend anytime with you today." She smiled, showing beautiful white teeth, accenting the hint of strawberry lipstick she was wearing. "I have a lunch date."

"That's fine, maybe we can talk tonight," Monique said, not sure if her mother would be free that evening either. A few years after her mother became a widow, she had started dating again. With all the excitement in her life, it was hard for Monique to keep up with her mother's schedule.

Yvonne's smile widened. "I'm gong on a dinner cruise tonight, but we can have breakfast tomorrow morning."

"Whew!" Monique chuckled. "You have more excitement in you life than I do."

When Yvonne finished laughing, she clasped her hands. "I don't. intend to become a wrinkled up old lady yet."

Peals of laughter floated from Monique. She checked her watch. "There's a special session before the seminar . . . and it's starting in about an hour. So I'll see you in the morning."

It was too bad that she and Nick didn't have a relationship that allowed them to walk on a sandy beach while ocean waves rolled to shore, sweeping up around their ankles and legs. It was too bad that she and Nick would never enjoy the last late rays of the afternoon sun, snaking into the horizon.

They each had their needs, their wants and their thirsty desires to fulfill. The rules they'd set for themselves didn't include private romantic moments. They had allowed themselves the pleasure of tasting the sweetness of each other's kisses, in the presence of friends and family, and in controlled moments.

The morning of the seminar, Monique and her mother,

Yvonne, had breakfast at a local restaurant down the street near Yvonne's condo. The bright morning sun perched in a clear blue sky and glinted warm rays over them. "How's business?" Yvonne asked Monique.

"Business is great," Monique replied, not mentioning that she had had financial difficulties.

"I'm proud of you, you know."

"Mother, it's hard work."

"Good, hard work never killed anybody," Yvonne McRay said, her laughter ringing out over the sound of sea gulls, singing and flapping their huge wings, that seemed to add a sense of serenity to the morning.

"That's true," Monique said, enjoying the wisps of wind that blew off the ocean, cooling the balmy morning's air.

"Monique, I am just as happy as you are about your wedding," Yvonne said, looking at her daughter.

Monique sipped the ice water, then cut a small piece of the cheese Danish. It was best if she didn't discuss her and Nick's wedding.

"I'm happy," Monique said, wanting to change the subject, concerning her fake holy matrimony.

"Monique, is anything wrong? Did you and Nick call off the wedding?"

"No," Monique said, enjoying the cool wind that lifted her hair, exposing her bare shoulders.

"Are you sure you're ready for marriage?" Yvonne asked Monique between sips of purified ice water. Yvonne McRay's smooth, wrinkle-free, lemon complexion seemed to glow against the morning sun, denying any indication of her sixty-three years.

"Yes, I'm ready." Monique made sure she answered the question, saying exactly what she imagined her mother wanted to hear.

"You don't sound excited," Yvonne said, seeming to pay closer attention to her daughter. "I hope you're not getting married because you're thinking about your biological clock.''

"No, Mother," she said. Without warning a truthful thought winged across her mind. *I have no choice.*

"Marriage is a serious matter, Monique." Yvonne seemed to have been studying Monique's eyes for an answer, the way she did when Monique was a young girl.

Monique turned away, giving her attention to roller-blading couples. She had learned years ago that she couldn't fool her. Any slight change in her attitude at this point would give Yvonne the message that she wasn't being totally honest with her.

"I think I'm making the right decision to marry Nick," Monique said, making sure that she kept her eyes from meeting her mother's soft black eyes.

"Well, if you're happy, I'm happy for you. It's just that so many people get married thinking they're making the right decision, and two years later, they're on their way to divorce court."

"I understand," Monique said, feeling a tight squeeze grip her stomach. She was aware of the ramifications, and what to expect from her marriage to Nick. But she couldn't disclose this to her mother. Yvonne would never understand. The woman would rush to her rescue, writing a check to pay Nick what Monique owed him, and Faceology Equipment too.

It was getting close to the time for Monique to leave for the seminar. She pushed away from the table, sort of relieved that she had a seminar to go to, although it was always a pleasure to spend time with Yvonne. At any rate, this visit was making Monique uncomfortable. She wished that she and Nick were already married and divorced. Monique took her purse from the tabletop and offered to pay for breakfast.

"Breakfast is on me," Monique said, reaching into her purse and taking out money.

"If you insist," Yvonne smiled. "Will you be going out tonight?"

"I think I'm going to that club Elaine told me about," Monique said, getting up from the table. "Unless you want me to do something with you tonight."

"Oh, no," Yvonne laughed softly. "It's just that my friend and I have tickets to a play and dinner tonight." Yvonne seemed to smile at the mention of her man-friend. "As usual, he surprised me with tickets."

Monique wasn't surprised that her mother was dating again, after her husband John died a few years ago. Nonetheless, Monique had no intention of attending a play with her mother and her male friend.

Monique laughed. "Have fun. I'll see you in the morning."

As usual, the seminar was packed with information, products, equipment, salespeople and people Monique hadn't seen in a couple of years. While she checked the price of an infrared warming lamp, her cellular phone rang.

"Can we meet in a few minutes?" Nick's voice came across the wireless line.

It dawned on Monique that she hadn't told Nick she would be out of the state. "No, we can't meet," Monique said. Before she could tell Nick where she was, he interrupted her.

"Why can't I see you?"

"Because I'm in Miami at a seminar."

"I think you should've told me that you were leaving town."

Monique couldn't think of any reason for Nick to know every move she made. They hadn't planned one of their dinner dates that was for the sole purpose of showing the townspeople and his family that they were the loving couple Nick insisted that they pretend to be. Besides that, she was glad that she wouldn't have to deal with his loving embraces and long hot kisses.

"I don't think it's your business to know every move I make." Monique was determined to stay in control.

"I think so."

"It's not in the contract."

"It goes without saying."

Nick didn't sound pleased to Monique. "I don't agree."

"We'll see about that," Nick said. "Did you receive the rose?"

"Yes." Monique felt her heart swell with passionate feelings that she had buried before taking her flight to Miami.

"Will you reconsider?" Nick's voice came across the wireless phone, edged with a warmth that melted away a tiny portion of the promise she'd made earlier to herself.

Monique's memories surfaced, reminding her that she and Nick had verbally fought the night before.

"No, Nick, it's not a good idea."

"Other than the reason that you're adopted and searching for at least one of your parents, what other reasons are there?"

"Nick, I think we should talk about this later."

She could hear Nick's soft breathing crossing the airwaves. When he didn't answer her, Monique said good-bye and hung up.

Monique moved away from a crowd that walked over to the massage table she'd been observing. She planed to purchase the table sometime in the near future for her first salon.

Monique moved to a table were the newest facial packs were being sold. As she studied the masks, she allowed herself to remember the evening she'd had dinner with her ex-fiancé's parents.

The purpose of the dinner had been to announce their engagement. Her ex-fiancé's mother hadn't concealed her feelings for Monique once she learned that Monique had been in an orphanage until the age of ten. The woman had set her glass down hard on the table, splashing driplets of red wine onto the white lace cloth. She hadn't minced words when she reminded Monique that she had once been a ward of the state and had no family to speak of. Suppose Monique and her son had children. The pitiful things would lack a family tree, other than the one her son would provide. Suppose Monique's family was riddled with disease and a life of crime.

Monique's cellular phone rang, hurling her out of her deliberations. "Hello," she answered.

"Don't hang up on me, woman," Nick's voice seemed lined with a cool edge.

Monique imagined Nick with one hand on his narrow hip, the phone laid against his ear and standing ramrod straight.

"Monique, are you there?" The sound of Nick's voice disengaged her musing.

"Yes," she said, pushing her visions to the deepest corner of her mind. She walked out of the crowded room and stopped in the corridor.

"I need an answer."

"I'm not going to discuss this with you, neither am I going to fight with you." Monique walked back into the room. "I am in a room filled with people," Monique whispered into the phone, keeping her voice low. The woman standing next to her, surveying the infrared lamp, cocked her head as if to hear Monique's side of the conversation.

"Fine, but we will discuss it." The phone went dead.

Monique punched the off button on her phone. It seemed to her that Nick was finding more reasons to add information to the verbal contract. She walked to another part of the room. She had the right to privacy. It would be different if their engagement and marriage were real.

By the end of the seminar, Monique still had lots of energy. She took a cab to her mother's apartment, undressed and took a long, hot shower. She made sure she kept all thoughts of Nick locked in the deep crevasses of her mind.

Reminding herself that she was going to the club Elaine told her about, Monique showered and dressed. She decided that the short white sleeveless dress and gold heels would be perfect for her evening out on the town. She carefully applied her makeup and brushed her hair until it hung down over her shoulders. A pair of gold earrings completed her outfit.

Monique took her purse and went downstairs. She took a cab to the club and walked in. The first person she saw was the dermatologist from the seminar.

He was a tall dark man with skin the color of black coffee and beautiful white teeth. He was wearing a pair of black dress pants and black shirt and loafers, instead of the expensive suit and wing tips he wore during his lecture earlier that day.

"Hi," Jeremy spoke to Monique.

Monique returned his greetings cheerfully, glad that she had run into a familiar face.

Jeremy found them a table and they ordered drinks and enjoyed each other's conversation, which was mostly centered around their work. Jeremy told Monique he was engaged, and she in return told him about her engagement to Nick, regardless of how phony it was.

As the evening drew close to midnight, Monique had found Jeremy boring socially, but interesting professionally. It was as if she was getting a personal lesson in her profession.

The band played a slow song and Jeremy asked Monique to dance. Just as they walked out on the dance floor and Jeremy circled his arms around her waist, Monique felt a touch on her shoulder. She turned her head slightly and looked into Nick's angry eyes.

"Excuse us," Nick said to Jeremy. Nick's focus went back to Monique.

"Let's go outside."

Monique smiled at Jeremy and allowed Nick to slip his arms around her waist and walk with her out to the patio section of the club.

Once they were seated at a table and Nick ordered drinks for them, he turned his attention to Monique. "Is he your reason for not telling me that you were coming to Miami?"

"No, he's not. And how did you know that I was at this club?" Monique asked as she watched Nick's eyes narrow.

"I ran into a woman outside that recognized me. She said that she worked for you."

"Elaine." Monique looked around. "She must be inside."

"I don't know," Nick said, getting back to the subject. "Who is he?"

"Nick, Jeremy is a dermatologist. He lectured at the seminar."

"Oh, yeah," Nick said.

Nick sounded angry to Monique. "Why're you upset?"

"You flew to Miami without telling me." Nick's voice sound civil, yet traced with anger. "And what do I find when I get here? You locked in some man's arms."

"Jeremy is engaged. Not that it's any of your business." Monique sipped her drink.

"And so are you." Nick drank a small amount of his scotch.

Monique looked out at the palm trees that towered at the edge of the ocean. "Our engagement is different."

"Besides the small verbal contract, I don't think so," Nick shot back.

"Nick, I'm not going to fight with you."

Nick leaned back in his chair.

It seemed to Monique that Nick's anger was not ceasing. Monique checked her watch. "Are you ready to go?"

"I just got here," Nick said. "Let's go inside."

Once inside, Nick took Monique in his arms and they danced. The touch of his soft thick mustache against her cheek sent shivering waves over her. The familiar fluttering around her heart returned, and Monique knew that a marriage to Nick would be the hardest thing she had ever done in her life.

Nick bent his dark head and kissed her lips.

Not willing to resist, Monique enjoyed their intimate moments.

"I'm going back to Jersey in the morning. I think I should get home," Monique said. Her evening with Nick was leading down a primrose path, a trail that she wanted to get off.

"Stay with me tonight," Nick said, tightening his grip on her waist.

"I can't."

"Monique."

When she didn't speak, she felt Nick release her.

Monique and Nick walked out of the club. Nick got them a cab. He rode with Monique to her mother's apartment and walked her inside.

"I'll be home tomorrow night," Nick said while they stood in Yvonne's opened front door. Nick leaned over and kissed her.

Monique couldn't speak. She just watched him as he walked to the elevator, pushed the button and waited for the elevator's arrival. She closed the door and leaned against it. *Big, big mistake. Don't marry him.* Monique ignored the annoying thought. She was going to marry Nick Parker.

* * *

Wisps of cold autumn air blew against Monique's face as she hurried to her car outside the airport. The sky was gray, a warning that rain was threatening to fall. She leaned her head against the back of the seat and closed her eyes, deciding whether or not to call Nick and let him know she was back home. She didn't want to deal with him tonight. Suddenly, she found herself wishing she was back in Miami. In Miami, she had no problems. Maybe she had had two problems, she countered. Nick had arrived unexpectedly, and he had sparked flames around her heart.

Not to mention that she hadn't told her mother the truth or the real reason she was marrying Nick. Monique felt guilty. Yvonne had taken her in when no one wanted her. She had given her everything she ever dreamed of or wanted, and she was repaying the only mother she'd ever known with half-truths, thanks to her involvement with Nick Parker.

However, this was not Nick's fault, and she couldn't blame him. The whole matter was her own doing. She could have given up on Shagreen II. It wasn't as if she didn't have another business. Regarding those issues, Monique realized she had made the biggest mistake in her life.

Nick Parker was not a man to tangle with. He had used her situation to get what he wanted, and now she was stuck. Monique slowed for a yellow light, then sped off. Her thoughts trailed back to her problem. She had solved one problem. In return, she had accumulated another.

She said a silent prayer. *With your help, I will get through this. I promise you, I will never make another mistake like this again.* Because her true problems had yet to begin.

Living in the same house with Nick would pose a challenge, one that promised to test her heart, mind, body and soul. She was stuck between passion, desire and a need to be loved.

TWELVE

Nick took his computer, several law books, a set of luggage with his clothes along with his suit bags and laid the items in the back of his BMW while Stone tied Nick's easy chair down on the back of his truck.

"I think it will hold," Stone said to Nick, tightening the loop into a knot around the recliner.

"Yeah," Nick said, not in the mood for conversation. The moving company he'd hired, canceled at the last minute. There were problems with the moving van. The company promised to reschedule Nick's move for the next week. Nick declined the company's offer, asking Stone to help him move.

"Are you all right?" Stone asked his best friend.

"I'm fine."

"I'll see you at the house," Stone said, climbing into his truck.

Nick gave Stone a thumbs-up sign and made a second trip back to his lake house, checking to make sure he had locked the door. He was moving back into his house at the Carriage Place in town. He hadn't lived there since his divorce. Not that it had anything to do with his feelings for his ex-wife, she'd never lived in the house. Weeks before the house was completed, Debra asked him for a divorce. Nick agreed to give it to her. Their marriage had been hanging by threads as it was. What they both thought they did not exist. Debra was lonely and starving for his attention, while he worked late building a clientele for his law firm. Their times together were limited. At first, she had spent time visiting her family in New York. In a way he had been pleased with her choice. When he had been home, he had been busy, preparing a case or watching sports.

Nonetheless, Nick had still been hurt when he realized that his wife had found pleasure in the arms of another man. He had tried to make sense of how lonely she must have been. He couldn't. After he learned of her affair, their marriage was broken beyond repair. As much as he had loved Debra, he had hated her after the affair.

Out of desperation, he and Debra had tried to make the marriage work. They had gone to a marriage counselor, but their careers clashed, and many of their appointments had been canceled.

The canceled appointments continued until they both decided it was better that they go their separate ways. Debra had her buyer's career and his law practice was too much of a strain for their marriage to stand. Under the pressure of it all, their frayed marriage had unraveled, fallen apart and scattered like worn threads from old fabric.

Not once while they attempted to mend the pieces of their marriage, did Nick have any desire to make love to her.

When the verbal fights had begun, he couldn't resist reminding her that she had allowed another man to make love to her.

Their battles became more heated with each passing day. Nick had moved out of their townhouse and to his house on the lake. Debra moved to New York with her family.

Their brand-new, four-bedroom house that had been designed and built by Parker's Art stood fully furnished and empty of their presence.

Once, Nick made an attempt to live in the house. The house was too big for one person, so he moved back to his house on the lake.

Now, he was ready to marry again. This time, he didn't have to worry about the marriage working. Monique wasn't in love with him.

Nick started the engine and drove away from his house. His vision of Monique seeing another man was enough to make him burn with anger. Nick's car swung around the curve faster than he intended. He slowed the car down, remembering his last accident, when he had swung the same curve too fast not long ago. The result put him in the hospital, leaving a gash on his jaw.

Ten minutes later, Nick drove into his driveway in front of the house he had had built years ago. He took his luggage out of the car.

Once inside, he went upstairs to his bedroom, a few doors down from the bedroom where Monique would be sleeping. Nick set the suitcase on the floor against the bedroom wall, and made a second trip back to the car for his shoes. Just as he returned to his room and set the shoes in the closet, he heard Stone's truck horn.

Nick went out to the garage and took a knife from the shelf. He rolled the dolly out of the corner and out to Stone's truck.

"You took your time getting here," Nick said sharply to Stone as he climbed on the back of the truck and cut the rope that secured his chair.

"I had to make a stop," Stone said, helping Nick strap the recliner onto the dolly. They guided the furniture off the truck. "Why don't you just tell Monique that you want to marry her forever, instead of six months, man?"

"I suggested it. Why?" Nick said as he reached around the chair and opened the front door. He gave the door a swift push, opening it wider and rolling the chair inside his house.

"That way you won't have to take your anger out on me."

Nick stopped, setting the dolly flat against the floor. "Do I look like I'm angry?"

"No, you're pissed off." Stone jerked the dolly and rolled it into Nick's study.

Nick gave Stone a quick glance. Stone was right.

"Let's go to the garage," Stone said, positioning the chair against the wall.

Determined to ease the tension that had tightened the muscles in his body, Nick nodded, agreeing to go with Stone. Working on the car would take his mind off of Monique and the harsh reality of having to live with her and not being able to touch her.

Nick grabbed his jacket and he and Stone headed out to Stone's truck.

"It's not too late to change your mind about marrying her," Stone said.

"It doesn't matter, it'll be over in a few months," Nick said, hoping Monique would change her mind and stay with him forever.

"Right, convince yourself," Stone said, turning the key in the ignition.

When Stone parked in front of the garage, Nick was the first to get out. He walked inside the warm building and took his tan coveralls from the locker he shared with Stone. He pulled the jumper on and popped the hood on the red and white 1957 Ford. Stone got in the car and sat behind the shiny red steering wheel.

"Don't start the engine until I check the oil," Nick said, twisting the cap and slowly pulling out the oil stick. He held the stick up to the light.

"Is the oil okay?" Stone rolled down the window and yelled out to Nick from behind the wheel of the Ford.

"Looks good," Nick said, lowering the stick back into the slot. Did you mend the radiator?"

"No, it's still leaking," Stone said, "but I can start the engine."

Nick's mind was unoccupied now from any thoughts of Monique and how he was going to live with her. Helping Stone repair his car was something he and Stone often did when they were in college. For Nick it was a way to keep his mind free from thinking about all the weekend parties he missed while he studied for his law degree. Now his hobby was serving to keep his mind clear from thinking about Monique McRay.

"Start the engine," Nick yelled out over the sound of welding blowtorches that some other men who had recently joined them in the garage had turned on.

Stone turned the key in the ignition. The car's engine turned over and stopped.

Nick checked the battery. "Stone this battery is shot," he said, rubbing the brown rust that coated the battery.

Stone got out of the car. "I have a jumper cable."

While Nick leaned against the car and waited for Stone to return, his mind wavered. He wished he could jump-start Monique and change her feelings for him.

THIRTEEN

Monique checked in with the vendors for her wedding as soon as she returned from her trip. The flowers were ordered, the small wedding chapel was ready, and the invitations were sent to the guests. The food, the reception hall and her gown were ready.

It suddenly came to Monique that Nick hadn't called her. His actions were those of a man who was seriously engaged or a man that was already married and was upset because his wife had left town without informing him.

Monique opened the window in her bedroom and let in a gush of fresh air. The evening air held a chill. She closed the window and went to her small study where she had a list of suitable renters for her house for six months.

One young woman was interested, but she thought the rent was too expensive. Monique crossed her name off the list. Her house was worth every dollar she was charging. The house had three bedrooms, an eat-in island kitchen, lots of closet space, a garage, two and a half baths. Not to mention the magic Daniella had worked to decorate the house. Monique looked at another application. Three men in their late thirties wanted to rent the house. Their application stated they were in the construction business. Monique laid the application aside. She shuddered to think what three burly men would do to her almost perfect home.

Her next application was from a young lawyer at Nick's law firm. Monique read the information and added him to the pile that she was considering, imagining that Nick had told him about her house. She dismissed her thought and headed upstairs to the bedroom closet where she kept her most personal memories in the vault. She took out the box that held the blue ribbon, a pair of white socks and black patent leather shoes. Monique concluded that one day soon, she would discard the items from the past. The items had once held happy memories of the day Yvonne and John McRay adopted her. That part of her life was over.

The sound of a car pulling into her driveway brought her back to the present moment. From her bedroom window, she noticed Nick's car. She put the box back into the vault and went downstairs to let him in.

"Hi," Nick said, pulling off his coat and laying it over the wing-backed chair. He pushed his hands inside his pockets.

Monique watched Nick move closer to her. So close, she could smell the scent of his cologne.

"Did you take your blood test?" Nick asked, his eyes seeming to burn into her.

"I'll have to set aside time to do that," Monique said. Going to her small study, she checked her appointment book. "I'll see if I can get an appointment this week."

"We also need to decide where we're going on our honeymoon." Nick spoke the words in the same cool, businesslike tone as before.

"We won't be going on a honeymoon."

"Don't you think it'll look suspicious if we don't go away together?" Nick asked.

"I've made plans to take a trip."

"Where're you going?"

"I don't think it would be wise to tell you," Monique replied, noticing how Nick watched her through narrow, slanted eyes before taking another step toward her. Monique pressed herself against the desk, refusing to make close contact with his hard body.

He stood before her now. His warm dark eyes seemed to smolder with a special warmth. But when he spoke, Monique realized that Nick's voice and eyes were not in agreement.

"I would like to know where you're going."

"I prefer that you didn't know."

"What if something happened . . . to you?" Nick sounded worried.

"Nick, don't worry."

Without another word, Nick walked out of the study, took his coat off the chair, and put it on. He opened the door and walked out into the chilly evening without looking back at Monique.

Monique closed and locked the door. She leaned against the wall. *Don't even think about thinking,* she told herself.

Amelia Wakefield browsed through the catalog of one of her favorite stores to shop. It was a tough decision to shop for Monique's wedding gift. For some time she had been trying to decide what would be best for the beautiful young woman. The silverware, or china. *No,* she thought. Maybe she shouldn't give her anything. Amelia threw the book aside. How could she have been so foolish? Monique barely knew her. If it weren't for the salons, Monique wouldn't know her at all. But somehow it mattered that Monique was aware of her presence.

FOURTEEN

Monique sat at the table with Amelia Wakefield, sipping hot blackberry herb tea while she waited for Colleen to join them.

Amelia was dressed in a hunter green suit, and white pearls circled her neck. Her hair was pulled back into a tight bun, exposing small matching pearl earrings. Soft fluffy bangs stopped a quarter of an inch above her arched brows.

Amelia smiled while she struck up a conversation about her bachelorette party.

"I was hoping that you would've been able to attend." She smiled. "At the time I planned this party, you weren't engaged to Nick Parker."

"No, I wasn't." Monique smiled as politely as she could.

"However, I must say that men with Nick Parker's status and power are the only right choices to make when one is choosing a marital partner."

"Maybe. I haven't given it much thought," Monique said, imposing iron control to refrain from telling Amelia Wakefield that she didn't want to talk about Nick Parker.

"Well, there are certainly more important things to give your thought to." Amelia paused and took another sip of tea. "I mean, have the two of you discussed children?" She held her cup in midair as she appeared to study Monique.

Monique took a deep breath. "We aren't having children," Monique replied, drumming her fingers lightly against the pink tablecloth. Not only was Amelia annoying, she was also nosy.

"But dear, why not?"

Because lovemaking is not allowed in this marriage, Monique wanted to say. She didn't divulge that information. "We've decided that it would be best if we didn't have children."

"Oh, I see." For once, the elegant Mrs. Wakefield seemed lost for words. "Are there any special reasons?" Mrs. Wakefield finally asked.

"Yes, but they are private," Monique assured her.

Colleen joined Monique and Amelia just in time. Monique felt her tension stretching like a rubber band on the verge of snapping.

"Ladies," Colleen said, sitting daintily in a chair and setting her elite designer purse on the edge of the table. Colleen's winter white wide-tail dress spread down over her ankles, barely touching the tops of green suede heels.

Monique smiled. She also knew that Colleen was aware of her uneasiness in Amelia's presence. It didn't matter. Monique was a businesswoman. If one of her clients wanted to treat her to lunch, she was polite enough to accept.

They talked about everything, from the wedding plans, to how happy Amelia was that Monique was marrying the right man.

Monique stayed quiet as Amelia went on about how lucky Monique was. Amelia acted as though Monique had gone fishing and caught the largest trout in the sea. Before lunch was finished, Monique proceeded to tell Amelia just that.

"Dear, it's true. He has everything a woman wants in a man," Amelia told Monique.

Monique looked at her watch. "I'm late for an appointment. Thanks for lunch, Mrs. Wakefield," she said, getting up from the table.

Amelia Wakefield had managed to pluck her last nerve. She was getting out of that woman's sight as fast as she could before she said something that would damage her owner-client relationship.

That same day, just as Monique was about to leave work and go home, Colleen called her and asked Monique to stop by her house. Monique hesitated, almost refusing Colleen's offer. She wanted to pack her clothes and have them ready to move into Nick's house before she went on her trip after the wedding.

But with determination, Colleen convinced Monique that the information she had for her was too important to speak about over the phone.

"I'll be right over. But Colleen, I can't stay long," Monique said, knowing how, when she and Colleen got together, they talked for hours.

Shortly after Monique's phone conversation with Colleen, she drove home and, instead of going inside, Monique crossed the lawn and walked to Colleen's house.

Monique took brisk steps up the concrete walkway that was lined with short green bushes. Her tight brown dress pulled against her hips as she tripped on the toe of her high heels while walking up the steps. Monique rang the doorbell and waited for her friend to open the door.

Colleen opened the door and flipped the light switch. A rainbow of colorful balloons and streamers hung from the ceiling and swayed out from the corners of Colleen's living room. The house smelled of delicious catered food.

"Surprise!!" Fifteen or more women rose from hiding spots behind the sofa and chairs and appeared from the kitchen and dining room to greet Monique at her bachelorette party.

"Gotcha," Colleen said, laughing.

Someone turned on the music with a fast rhythm. A tall, good-looking man dressed in green doctor's scrubs slid out on the floor and held Monique's hand, swinging her in a circle.

In spite of herself, Monique laughed at the stunt Colleen had pulled as she allowed the dancer to swing her around, following his rhythm.

While Monique and the guy danced, the women formed a circle. Clapping their hands to the beat and moving their feet and swaying to the music, they chanted, "Go ahead, dance baby dance!"

Suddenly, the man released Monique's hands and, with one rip, he peeled off the green scrub top and flung it out into the crowd of women.

It sounded as if all the women screamed, except for Monique. All she could visualize was Nick's bare broad chest instead of the dancer's muscular physique. Just thinking about Nick in ways she knew she shouldn't made her flutter.

With another rippling sound the dancer had stripped down to his jockstrap.

Just as the dancer did that, one of Colleen's technicians pretended to faint. Laughter filled Colleen's living room.

It had been a long time since Monique had so much fun and laughed so much.

After the male stripper left the party, the women presented Monique with gifts.

"Wait a minute, this one is mine," Elaine said, passing her gift to Monique.

Smiling, Monique carefully unwrapped the gold and white package. She lifted the top and pulled out a pink lace teddy with a matching garter belt. The women broke into peals of laughter.

"I think I can top that one," one of Colleen's technicians said, passing her gift to Monique.

Monique removed the long white sheer laced nylon lounge outfit and held it up for the others to see.

Tamika leaned over to get another look at Colleen's technician. "Miss thing, where are the panties?"

"She don't need no underwear, girlfriend." The women joined Colleen in her laughter.

In spite of it all, Monique was grateful for the gifts and the party, even though she knew she would never use any of sexy the lingerie in Nick's presence.

The food was served and enjoyed while the women listened to music and drank grasshoppers with more than the normal amount of liqueur.

The evening grew into midnight as the women sipped drinks and told stories of their lost lovers and whom they wished they had married until they spotted one of their ex-lovers on the streets.

"Monique, you remember Frank Lamont?" one of the women asked.

"Yes," Monique said, remembering the last time she had seen him. Frank Lamont's muscular physique was similar to Nick's.

"I loved Frank. When he got married, girl, I thought my world would stop spinning."

"Is he still a hunk?" Colleen asked.

"His wife has dressed him in husband clothes and he don't look like I remembered."

"Did you speak to him?" Monique asked the woman.

"I spoke and kept going."

As the women shared their stories, Colleen got up and went to the phone, motioning for Monique. "I'm calling a cab to get these tipsy women out of my house."

Monique agreed with Colleen. Elaine looked as if she was in no position to stand, let alone drive.

It wasn't long before several cabs were parked along the curb near Colleen's house.

After the women were gone, Monique thanked Colleen for the party.

"Monique, every woman should have a wedding shower, and a bachelorette party." Colleen stacked the last of Monique's gifts on the sofa.

"You're right," Monique said, taking her purse and looking at the gifts.

"Can I take these gifts home tomorrow?" Monique asked, turning and walking toward the door.

"Sure you can," Colleen replied, following her girlfriend to the door.

Monique opened the door and stepped outside. She turned to Colleen.

"Thanks again," she said, quietly.

"You're welcome."

As Monique walked home, she allowed herself to think . . . *Everything is perfect, except my reasons for marrying Nick Parker.*

It wouldn't have made a difference to Monique if she didn't care. But she cared, even if Nick didn't.

Over the weeks that led up to her wedding, she had given the situation quite a bit of thought. If she was marrying a man who was adopted, she too would want to know his background. Maybe she was making too big an issue of the entire matter.

Monique quieted her thinking. Her and Nick's wedding day was approaching quickly. Soon, she would be Mrs. Nicholas Parker.

FIFTEEN

The day of the wedding, tall young handsome ushers dressed in cream tailcoat tuxedos with matching trousers and bronze cummerbunds seated the wedding guests in their proper pews in the church.

White bouquets gracefully decorated the edges of the church pews. Organ music piped preludes, "Wind beneath my wings," setting the mood for Monique and Nick's wedding. Monique chose the classical-inspirational music for forty-five minutes for the guests' enjoyment. Besides, the music seemed to fit the occasion. Nick was the wind beneath her wing.

Six bridesmaids waited in the church wing dressing room, careful not to wrinkle their long pink slender gowns.

Colleen darted around Monique's dressing room, assisting Monique with the final touches, checking her makeup and wedding gown.

"Monique, are you all right?" Colleen asked as she hooked the diamond necklace around Monique's long slender neck.

Monique looked at her girlfriend through the vanity mirror. "Colleen, I'm fine." She was, except for the butterflies in her stomach.

"Good," Colleen said, taking the veil from its cover and positioning it on Monique's head.

"Will you calm down." Monique gave Colleen's hand a light tap, as she clamped her veil in position.

"I don't understand you at all." Colleen lifted Monique's bouquet from the vanity table and held it in her hands. "You act as if you are going to the park."

Monique stood, lifting her long white gown, showing her white satin shoes. "If you want me to be excited about marrying Nick . . . I'm not."

"Keep your voice down, before Mrs. Parker hears you."

"She is outside," Monique said, thinking about the kiss she would have to share with Nick at the end of the wedding services. After today, she planned to keep her distance. This was her last kiss with Nick Parker. A warmth settled around her heart, reminding her how much she enjoyed being in Nick's arms.

"Colleen, you're a nervous wreck." Monique took the pink and white bouquet from Colleen. She had to do something to stop thinking about Nick.

"Someone has to be a nervous wreck, since you aren't."

"Colleen—" Monique was interrupted when her mother came into the room.

"Monique, you look beautiful." Yvonne beamed at her daughter.

"Thanks, Mother."

Yvonne McRay hugged Monique. "I wish you all the happiness with your new husband."

Monique blinked back tears. If only . . . she stopped the musing that had swept through her mind so many times since she had agreed to marry Nick.

Monique reached for a tissue to wipe the tear that was about to run down her cheek.

"That's the spirit," Colleen said, as if she was pleased to see Monique cry.

"Colleen, will you stop it."

Yvonne looked from Colleen to Monique. "Is something going on that I need to know about?"

"No, Mother."

A knock on the door sent Colleen to see who was on the other side.

"I want Mrs. McRay," Monique heard the young male voice.

"Mrs. McRay, the usher wants to seat you." Colleen waited for Monique's mother to give Monique a final hug before she joined the young handsome usher.

"Colleen, I think I'm getting cold feet."

"Keep your mind on Shagreen II," Colleen whispered. She went to lock the door, as if someone would walk in without knocking first.

"Right." Monique forced a smile. "I will get through this day in one piece," Monique said, walking with Colleen out of the dressing room, where she found Harry, her mother's male friend. She hooked her arm around his.

Six bridesmaids and six ushers marched down the aisle to the sounds of "When We Get Married."

Monique couldn't help but observe the picture-perfect moment. The bridesmaids and ushers marched up the aisle, followed by Colleen. The tiny ring bearer clutched the satin pillow, while the flower girl gathered pink rose petals from her basket and sprinkled the blossoms, allowing them to fall freely from her small fingers.

Monique and Harry stepped closer to the entrance. She could see Nick with his back to her, standing beside his best man, Stone.

Harry smiled down at Monique. "Well young lady, I hope that you'll experience more happiness than you ever dreamed."

"Thanks." Monique's voice was barely audible. Tears burned her eyes.

The organ player lowered the music she was playing for the bridal party, and with a loud touch of the organ keys, she began to play "Here Come the Bride." The music piped out of the organ filled the church with a hearty sound.

The guests rose from their seats and turned in her direction.

Monique noticed Nick turn to face her along with the wedding party. She couldn't help noticing how handsome Nick looked in his tuxedo. She moved slowly to stand beside him.

Monique stood next to Nick and faced the minister while he said a prayer.

She could hear teary sniffles coming from the front row. She was sure some of the crying was from her mother.

"Repeat after me," the minister said, directing his gaze to Nick.

"I, Nicholas Parker, do take Monique McRay to be my lawful wedded bride . . ." Nick repeated the words.

"To have and to hold, until death do us part." Monique repeated her vows. She fought back the tears. How could she stand in church and tell that lie. *God please don't let anything bad happen to me.*

"What God has put together, let no man put asunder." Monique heard the humdrum speech the minister was saying as she drifted in and out of silent prayer.

"If there is anyone here who has knowledge that this marriage should not take place, speak now or forever hold your peace."

Monique heard someone clear a throat. She didn't dare look at Nick. She was almost sure it wasn't Sharmain. She imagined it was Roger who made the loud throaty sound.

When no one in the audience rose to oppose Monique and Nick's marriage, the minister continued the ceremony, asking for the rings.

Monique and Nick exchanged rings.

"With the power of God, vested in me, I now pronounce you man and wife," the minister said. "You may kiss the bride."

Monique's heart swelled as Nick lifted her veil. His hands lingered for a moment before he pushed the sheer material away from her face, letting it fall backward.

Lowering his dark wavy head, Nick kissed Monique.

While enjoying the touch of his lips against hers, the undeniable, dreadful truth floated across her mind. She loved Nick. She couldn't deny her feelings any longer.

After a long moment, Nick stopped kissing Monique.

"Ladies and gentlemen, I present to you Mr. and Mrs. Nicholas Parker."

The organ played the recessional music, and the guests stood. Monique placed her arms in the folds of Nick's elbow and with swift steps they walked to the church entrance, forming the receiving line with the bridal party and their parents.

The newly married couple greeted and thanked their last guest. Amidst a circle of bubbles, they went to the limousine that waited outside the church to drive them to the reception.

The wedding was lovely, Monique reflected as she and Nick settled into the back of the limousine.

Nick moved over to Monique, and she didn't resist the kiss he planted on her lips.

At the reception, just before the main meal was served, Stone stood up and asked the guests to please stand with him.

Monique and Nick remained seated while Stone toasted the newlyweds.

"It is often said that a man with no bride has no pride." Stone held up his champagne glass. "Here's to my best friend, his pride and his lovely bride, the happiest couple ever. We wish them well."

The music began to play while clinking sounds from the champagne glasses filled the dining room. The guests toasted Monique and Nick's marriage.

"Colleen, did you bring my luggage?" Monique inquired once everyone was seated. She and Nick had planned to change into their traveling clothes right after dinner and their wedding dance.

"Yes," Colleen whispered back to her, while the waiters carried hors d'oeuvre trays, with escargot stuffed in large mushrooms, and shrimp toast.

Monique lifted the rectangular shaped toasted bread with the golden brown fantail shrimp and bit into the tasty seafood.

She looked over at Nick. He seemed to have been enjoying the food, while at the same time engaging himself in a serious conversation with Stone.

Monique turned her attention back to the guests. They seemed to have been enjoying themselves, drinking, eating and talking. She was pleased at the outcome. If she never had another wedding in her life, it wouldn't matter.

After the main course had been served and Monique had finished as much of the thick prime rib as she could, along with the tiny new potatoes, she pushed her plate forward.

"I'm riding to the airport with you," Nick said, cutting into the last piece of meat on his plate.

"That was not the plan." Monique smiled just in case one of the guests saw her and Nick talking.

"My flight leaves the same time as yours."

"It doesn't matter," Monique said between clenched teeth with a plastic smile. She didn't want Nick knowing her destination. Not that she thought Nick would want to come with her now, after she had made it clear to him weeks before the wedding that she was traveling alone. It was just that the pretense was over. They were going to live separate lives, in the same house. For Monique that was more than what she wanted.

"We are going to the airport together." Nick's tone sounded final.

Monique lowered her gaze to avoid Nick's eyes. If she

didn't know any better, she could have believed that Nick thought their marriage was real.

She stole a glance at Nick. He was talking to Stone again. Monique looked out at their guests. She was certain they thought she and Nick were the perfect couple.

Just as the band began to play, Monique noticed Amelia Wakefield smiling over at her and Nick. Monique smiled back.

The vocalists took their position in front of the microphone.

Nick took Monique by her hand and led her off the platform and out onto the center of the dance floor.

She allowed Nick to hold her tenderly while they danced to the song, "I Will Truly Love You Always."

As the male and female vocalists hummed the interlude, Monique rested her cheek against Nick's chest, unable to cease the uncontrolled passion that swept through her.

When the dance was over, Nick and Monique cut the wedding cake. The traditional procedures of the cake feeding were performed between them while their guests applauded.

The festivities continued as Nick removed Monique's garter and threw it in the direction of the men, who seemed not to care if they caught the garter or not. Stone caught it. The crowd cheered.

Finally, it was time for Monique and Nick to leave for their honeymoon. Monique turned her back to the women who had lined up to catch the forthcoming bouquet. She threw it over her head. She heard high heels snapping and scraping against the hardwood floor, as if a small stampede had joined the reception. Monique heard Nick and Stone laugh.

When she turned around, Colleen was clutching the bouquet.

"All right George, you know what that means," a man

from the back of the room yelled out, followed by roars of laughter.

Nick covered Monique's hand with his. They bowed to their guests, turned and walked together, going to pose for the photographs and finally to their individual dressing rooms.

Finally they returned to say good-bye to their guests. Monique was wearing a winter white pants suit, a winter white wide-brim hat, bronze heels and gold accessories.

"Nick, you and Stone can drop me off at Colleen's house. She's taking me to the airport," Monique said while Nick held the car door open for her.

"If Colleen wants to come along, fine. But we're going to the airport together."

"But, Nick . . ." Monique started and glanced inside the car at Stone who was sitting behind the wheel, appearing to wear an impatient look.

"Would you like for me to put you in the car?"

Not in front of all these people, Monique pondered, noticing the onlookers that were bidding them a safe trip and a happy honeymoon. Monique slid into the back seat and waited for Nick to sit beside her.

It wasn't long before Monique and Nick arrived at Newark International and boarded their separate flights.

She left Nick standing outside the airport entrance, talking to Stone, while she hurried to pick up her boarding pass to Paris.

Monique settled herself on the powder blue sofa in her living room suite at the Hotel Verneuil in Paris. As she tucked herself away in one of the vest pocket rooms, she took out her planner and checked her schedule, while listening and enjoying the contemporary jazz that filled her room. Tonight she planned to relax. She had one busy day ahead of her, attending another aesthetician seminar.

Without warning, Monique wondered where Nick had gone, and what was he doing, and with whom. Monique brushed the disturbing thought from her mind no sooner than it appeared, only to be followed by another thought.

What if she didn't want to leave Nick after six months? She deleted that thought and continued to listen to the music that floated out from the speakers.

The evening after the first day of the seminar, Monique planned to meet with her friends Germain Fleury, her brother and his wife Marie, who also owned an aesthetician salon in the city. The family had invited her to dine with them at the Alcazar.

Monique got up and stood near the window. The black knee-length flare satin lounge outfit swung loosely over her body like a tent. The outfit had been a wedding present from Colleen, and it included black satin two-inch heel, open-toed bedroom slippers. Monique gazed out at the trees, glinting with what appeared to be thousands of crystal-clear lights.

Paris is a city for romance, Monique mused as she looked out over the city. She was a married woman. No one in their right mind would believe that she was spending her honeymoon alone. It was business for her and Nick, nothing more, she reminded herself. It was true, they'd had passionate moments, but their agreement still remained, a promise for each other to accomplish their most-wanted desires. Business.

A light tap on the door drew her out of her musing. Monique walked to the door. She hadn't ordered room service. Germain Fleury made no mention that she would visit her, and no one except her staff, Colleen and her mother knew that she had taken a flight to Paris.

"Yes?" Monique peered through the tiny glass opening that reflected her visitors. She could only see the upper part of his gray suit coat, gray shirt and gray tie.

"Monique," she heard the familiar voice from the other side of the door.

It can't be, she thought, as she dismissed the familiar sound of the male voice on the other side of the door.

"Nick." The man on the other side of the door took a few steps back. Monique realized that it was Nick. Her gaze swept over his handsome face. Monique moved away from the entrance and allowed him into her room.

He walked into the room and pulled off his coat. "I wanted to spend time with you," he said, hanging his coat on the coat tree near the door.

Monique stood before Nick. Her efforts to avoid him were defeated. She had traveled to Paris to dissolve the pain that gnawed at her, reminding her that she would never have the man she had married. She had traveled to Paris to remind herself that she was a woman facing harsh lonely nights.

"Who told you that I was here?" Monique asked Nick.

Nick looked as if he was unsure if he should answer Monique's question. When he spoke, his voice was a husky calm whisper. "Colleen told me a few weeks ago that you were attending a seminar." Pushing his hands into his pockets, he walked over to the window.

"If you knew that I was taking this trip, why didn't you tell me?" Monique was more annoyed at Colleen for finding a way to put her and Nick together. First it was the sexy lingerie, now this.

"Since we're here, we can at least enjoy the city together," Nick said, not turning to face her.

Nick was right, Monique mused, studying his strong muscular body. She made a mental note to cancel her dinner date with Germain Fleury and her family.

"Are you staying in this hotel?" she asked.

"I'm next door," Nick said, turning slightly to answer her.

"As long as we are civilized, I see no reason why we can't

live in the same hotel." Monique spoke the words almost as if she was thinking out loud.

"Civilized?" Nick turned and faced Monique. "You mean as long as we don't make love." He vocalized her fears.

"That too," she said, braver than she felt.

"I think we should make a truce. We will have fun while we're here."

"I agree," Monique said.

Nick leaned over and kissed Monique's cheek. "If it's okay with you, can we have breakfast in the morning?"

"I have an early morning," Monique said, referring to the seminar. "Maybe tomorrow afternoon, we can go out."

"Good, I'll see you then." Nick touched his hand to her waist and kissed her lips.

Surprised that Nick had deepened his kiss, Monique touched her lips with her finger. She smiled to herself. She and Nick were going to enjoy each other's company.

At noon, after the seminar, Monique went to her hotel room and changed from her navy suit to a pair of stretch jeans, a black pullover and a black waist-length jacket and ankle boots. By the time Nick stopped by her suite, she was dressed and ready to spend time with him.

"Hi," Nick spoke while he waited for Monique to get her purse.

"Where do you want to go first?" Monique asked Nick.

"Anywhere you want to go." Nick grinned.

"I like this." Monique clapped her hands together and laughed.

They shopped on Avenue Montaigne, buying small gifts for friends and family.

Monique bought a pair of bushy-tasseled pearl earrings (one black, one white) for her mother.

On their stroll back to the hotel, Nick slipped his arm around Monique's waist and led her into a cafe, where they dined on oysters and drank pink champagne.

The evening ended too soon for Monique, as she and Nick walked back to their hotel.

"Nick, I had a great time," Monique said, feeling relaxed from the champagne she had drank earlier.

"You're welcome, Mrs. Parker," Nick grinned. He took her key and unlocked her suite door.

"Listen, I'll be back shortly," Nick said, giving Monique a squeeze.

Humm, maybe Nick and I will be able to live together after all, Monique played with the thought. He hadn't smothered her with his sizzling kisses, scorching her with unabashed passion. She could live with that.

Monique let the thought flounce across her mind while she showered. She took out the floor-length black gown with thin red straps. The gown had been among the lingerie that Colleen had given her the night of her bachelorette party. Monique massaged lotion over her body, then splashed on cologne with the same aroma. She slipped into the floor-length black gown.

Just as she was about to slip into the matching house coat, she heard a knock on her door. Monique hurried from her bedroom, looking through her peephole, she saw Nick standing outside her suite.

She opened the door. "Come in."

Nick had changed into black pants and a black shirt. He smelled like fresh soap mingled with the scent of his cologne. He held a bottle of red wine, covered with a thin sheet of frost.

"Have you taken up chilling wine in your room?" Monique half joked.

"The chef downstairs did me a favor."

"Made friends with the chef, already?"

Nick moved into the room. His laughter floated out to her. "When I'm in Paris, I usually stay at this hotel. And the chef knows what I like."

Nick went to the bar that set against the wall in the living room. He found the corkscrew and uncorked the wine.

Monique watched him from a distance in her living room.

"Are you sure you know the chef?"

Nick's thick black mustache tipped into a smile. "We don't know each other personally, but he knows what I like." Nick took two wineglasses from the shelf inside the bar and filled the glasses with the chilled wine.

He held out the wine to Monique, and seemed to wait for her to join him.

"Thanks," Monique said, going to him and taking the wine he held out to her.

First, Monique inhaled the fruity flavor before she joined Nick, sipping the vintage and savoring its smoothness. She settled on the sofa, and noticed Nick's approving glance.

"Will you turn on the stereo?" she asked when Nick passed the entertainment center to sit beside her.

Nick pushed the button, and the room was filled with contemporary jazz.

Nick sat beside her, his eyes seeming to feast on her cleavage. Suddenly, Monique realized that she hadn't put on the sheer house coat that would shield her bare cleavage. Monique sipped the wine, not worrying about her cleavage. She had more important things to occupy her mind, if she wanted to worry.

Monique moved close to Nick, resting her head on his chest. She only raised it when she sipped the wine.

"Monique," Nick called her name.

"Humm." She watched Nick set his half-empty glass of wine on the cocktail table before them.

"Do you know what you're doing?" Nick took the wine from her hand and set it next to his glass.

"Of course I do. I was drinking wine, and snuggling up to you."

"I thought you didn't like snuggling up to me?" Nick chuckled softly, circling his arm around her waist, at the same time keeping a safe distance.

Monique inched closer to him. For once she would throw her cares to the wind. Who cared if their marriage was for six months only? She was exhausted from denying herself pure passion. And she was tired of starving herself of all the affection she needed. She nuzzled his jaw with her lips.

"Do you know what you're doing?"

"Yes."

Without warning, Nick gathered her into his arms. Like a magnet, Monique was unable to tear herself away from him. Her senses reeled and skidded from Nick's touch. He lowered his head and kissed her. At first, his kiss was a light touch, brushing across her lips, leaving sensations that seemed as if a thousand feathers had stroked her lips until they tingled with hot pleasure.

Nevertheless, Nick's feathery touches sent heat waves shilly-shallying through her body.

Nick kissed her deeper then.

Monique unbuttoned his shirt, exposing Nick's hairy, hard-iron chest. She ran her fingers through the curly mask, stroking his chest with her fingers.

Nick leaned into her, his lips making a trail up her neck and to her lips.

"Monique, are you sure?"

"Yes."

"I'm not stopping."

"Don't stop." She pulled away from Nick, enough to work the lower buttons on his shirt.

Nick pulled his shirt from the inside of his pants. He unsnapped his trousers and discarded them on a nearby chair.

Monique watched Nick standing over her wearing nothing but a black bikini jock. Her good sense almost recovered her. Monique brushed her common sense back to where it had come from. She allowed herself to feast her eyes on Nick's physique, before he lifted her in his arms and carried her to the bedroom.

Nick sat her down and propped one foot on the bed beside her.

"If you think you'll be sorry later, I can stop now."

Without answering, Monique reached out to pull him to her.

Nick shook his head. "I like this," he said, sliding the silk up around her hips.

Nick stopped, taking his foot off the bed. He lowered himself. "I like this." He sank down on one knee.

Monique reeled from scalding passion she didn't know existed.

"Do you want to stop?" Nick's voice was a low husky whisper.

"No." Monique heard her own trembling whisper.

Nick set one foot on the bed again. He lifted her hips, pulling her to him, allowing steel to touch soft marsh.

Temperature-rising heat like raw currents raced through Monique, making her ignore the small warning voice that nagged at her to stop. Instead, Monique caressed Nick's broad shoulders, making a trail with her fingers to the back of his neck and finally through his wavy hair, and slowly she allowed her fingers to inch down his back, making Nick crush her against his iron-steel chest.

For once in a long time, Monique had no urgent desire to disentangle herself out of his embrace. She simply enjoyed the touch of Nick's tongue teasing her lips, parting them, promising deep sinking kisses.

No words were spoken as Nick eased and slipped the red straps of her gown off her shoulder and down her arms. He feasted his eyes on firm round mounds that peaked with each touch of his warm lips.

Arousal grew as his hands captured her hips and slid

downward, planting kisses on her center, making her float in and out of her good, once-strong, stable senses.

From somewhere in the distance, Monique heard smothered lamenting sounds. As she floated in and out of her rightful mind, she realized the sounds had slipped from her own lips.

With the strength she had left, she pressed her hands against his chest as he covered her and sank into flames of soft passion that sent her skidding and soaring into a private world where only she and Nick lived.

Her blood seemed to have turned to liquid fire as he sank, ebbing his way along a primrose trail, laced with fire, flames and unabashed desire.

Like powerful waves, rising and rolling out of the sea, crashing against rocks that rested on an empty beach, they explored. Again, as if from afar, the sounds of murmurs and low growls reached out and floated over her. As she clung to Nick, she realized that it was his own voice.

Lost in a world of satisfaction, Monique savored the moment.

The next morning, Nick sat up in bed and watched Monique sleep. His eyes lingered on her cleavage and her slightly parted lips as she slept. Nick lifted her in his arms and kissed her parted lips. He held her, wanting to ravish her with his love. Monique was the woman that had unleashed a fury of desire in him, making him realize that he could love again. He leaned down and planted another kiss on her lips.

How was he going to convince Monique to stay married to him? As the thought trailed its way through his mind, he realized a shocking truth. He could never give her up completely.

He watched her long lashes flutter, and a small frown

creased her forehead. It was as if she had had a terrible dream.

"Monique," Nick called out to her in a hoarse whisper.

"Humm," she let out a soft moan.

Nick lay back with Monique still cradled in his arms.

He had been honest with her when he asked her to marry him and truthful with his reasons. It wasn't that he hadn't cared for her. He did. Now his caring had taken a turn and love was the ultimate reason for wanting to spend the rest of his life with Monique McRay Parker.

Nick dozed, the feel of Monique's firm body still haunting him.

Drifting off into a fitful dream, *Nick stood before the judge's glossy mahogany bench. Two bailiffs stood on each side of him.* "Mr. Parker, you have lied to this court about your feelings for Mrs. Parker. I find you in contempt. Bailiff, take Mr. Parker to his jail cell!"

"Your honor, I didn't lie."

"Mr. Parker, are you saying to the court that you're willing to release Mrs. Parker from her six-month contract?"

"Yes . . . no, your honor. I love her."

The sound of the judge's gavel slamming against the desk brought Nick out of his dream. He sprang up in his bed, squinting against the bright winter sun's rays that streamed through Monique's Paris hotel bedroom window.

That evening, over dinner, Nick noticed that Monique was quieter than usual. After they'd finished their meals of chicken breast stuffed with truffles, Nick filled his wineglass and offered the wine to Monique.

"No, thanks," Monique said. Nick noticed that Monique had made little or no eye contact with him all evening.

"Why?" Nick wanted to know. They had spent what he thought were special moments together in Paris.

Monique captured and held Nick's gaze for the first time

that evening. She had known the strength of her passion for Nick when she agreed to marry him. She couldn't blame him for their lovemaking. She had been a willing partner in the process of their romantic moment, not to mention her enjoyment. Inasmuch as she wanted to blame their passion on the wine she had drunk, she couldn't bring herself to lay blame there either. She had only drank a couple of sips. The lovemaking had been her fault. She should have kept her guard up and not allowed herself to relax and throw her promises to the wind. Maybe it was the wine, and Paris, Monique concluded, defending her romantic actions.

"I think it's better for us if I keep a clear head."

"I'm not sorry for what happened last night, and I don't believe you are either," Nick said.

"I didn't say that I was sorry for our lovemaking."

"What are you saying?"

"That it won't happen again."

"Is that a promise?" Nick chuckled.

"Of course it's a promise. Do you think I would joke about a thing like that?"

Nick chuckled again. "We'll see."

"I don't see the humor," Monique said, facing the desirable truth. She and Nick had consummated their marriage. It wasn't supposed to happen. But it had. They had sealed a bond. But was it love? Monique was unable to answer her own question. She was aware that whatever they had together would last for a short time.

"Are you ready to go?" Nick asked her when he saw the waiter coming to their table carrying the leather pad that held their bill.

Nick and Monique's evening ended early. Their separate flights left the next day. They wanted to get to the States, rest from jet lag and be ready for work in a couple of days.

After dinner that evening, Nick walked Monique to her hotel room.

When they reached her suite, Nick took her key and opened the door, following her inside.

"Thanks for a wonderful evening, Nick," Monique said. She was genuinely grateful for the time they had spent together.

"You're always welcome, Mrs. Parker." Nick leaned down and brushed his lips against hers. Monique felt the familiar fluttering around her heart.

"Good night," he said, backing away from her, as if he was afraid their passion from last night would resume.

Once inside her hotel suite, Monique packed and reminisced about her and Nick's lovemaking. She discarded her thoughts and promised to be careful when in close contact with Nick Parker. He was more than a match for her, packing a powerful punch in the lovemaking arena.

SIXTEEN

The taxi dropped Monique in front of Nick's house on her return from the airport after her Paris vacation. Nick's home was surrounded with tall oak trees. Green hedges nestled close to the outside walls of the house, complementing the flowers that only bloomed in the spring and summer. Even with the chill in the air and the first signs of serious cold weather, the grass was green and plush.

As Monique entered her new surroundings, she was glad that she had a friend like Colleen. She and Nick had given Colleen the keys to the house the day of the wedding.

Colleen had volunteered to move Monique's things into Nick's house while she was away. That way, the young lawyer who had rented Monique's furnished house could move in.

Monique walked inside the house and waited for the cab driver to set her several pieces of luggage in the great room.

She tipped the driver and moved toward the kitchen, noticing two other smaller rooms scattered near the large island kitchen.

A long counter with a cutting board top sat in the middle of the floor. Two stools with multicolored cushions stood near the counter. In one of the kitchen windows were several pots of yellow flowers. Monique figured whoever cared for the house took care of the flowers. Nick once told her he wasn't good with plants.

She surveyed her new surroundings, paying attention to the cozy patio outside the kitchen window. The patio seemed to have been designed especially for parties. She noticed two umbrella tables and the covered pool. Monique took a paper cup from the rack on the purified water machine and pumped the blue nozzle, filling the cone-shaped cup with cold water.

As she left the kitchen, making her way to the stairs, she noticed the door to Nick's study standing open. Nick was sprawled out on the leather sofa, sound asleep. Papers that he'd obviously been working on were scattered on the floor near the sofa. The screen saver on the computer moved in circles flashing big red, blue and green dots.

Monique went into the study and stood next to the sofa where Nick lay sleeping. "Nick," she called out to him softly.

"Hum." He groaned, reaching out his hand, as if he was trying to touch her.

Monique moved away from him and turned off the computer. She went upstairs to her room, leaving the luggage in the foyer for Nick.

Monique climbed the stairs, still not satisfied that she or Nick would follow the rules stated in their six-month marital contract.

It was late when Nick woke and left the study. He didn't remember turning off the computer. On his way to his room, he noticed Monique's luggage near the door in the great room. He lifted the two heavy suitcases and carried them up to her room. He set one suitcase down and tapped on the door. When Monique didn't answer, he opened the door and walked in.

The yellow comforter on her empty bed was turned

down. Nick noticed the light in the closet was on. He carried her luggage to the open closet door.

For a second, he watched Monique standing on the short stepladder, reaching for a pillow. The long white nylon gown she was wearing was similar to the lounge she had worn the night in Paris when he made love to her. He watched her round hips silhouetted against the soft material of her gown and he swallowed hard.

"Hi," Nick spoke. Monique turned and almost lost her footing on the ladder. Nick reached out and steadied her, helping her down.

"Oh Nick, you scared the daylights out of me," Monique said, clutching his shoulders.

Nick held her in his arms for a while, inhaling her sweet subtle perfume and feeling her soft, but firm body against his.

"I'll get the pillow," Nick told Monique, not wanting to let her go. Reluctantly, he released her and reached for the pillow she wanted.

"Thanks," she said when he gave her the pillow. She smiled up at him, and Nick felt his body harden.

"Can I get anything else for you?" he asked, trying to ignore the rising effect Monique had on him.

"No, I think I have everything I need," she said.

"Are you sure?"

Monique tilted her head to one side. "Yes."

Visions of their lovemaking in Paris played with his mind. He turned away from Monique.

Promising to stay in control, Nick walked out of the closet. He didn't look back. If he did, there was no telling what he would do to her.

Nick went to his room, discarded his clothes in his bathroom, turned the shower to a chilled temperature and stepped inside the stall. He realized that this was one night he wasn't going to sleep. When his shower was finished, he went downstairs, poured himself a stiff brandy and headed back to his room.

"Colleen just for the sake of curiosity. Why did you tell Nick that I was going to Paris?" Monique asked her girl-friend the next day when she stopped in at Colleen's beauty salon to get a soft wave perm.

"Now you know I had to tell him," Colleen said, squeez-ing the plastic bottle filled with perm solution over the hair that was wound on the rods. "Did you guys have fun?"

Monique looked at Colleen's reflection through the styl-ing mirror.

"Yes, we had a nice time."

"So, the marriage got off to a good start."

"We have an understanding." Monique omitted discuss-ing her and Nick's intimate night together.

Colleen held the perm solution in midair. "I knew I was doing the right thing when I told him where you were going." Colleen gave Monique a knowing look.

"Colleen, I know that you have these wonderful fairy tale dreams, wishing that Nick and I will have an everlast-ing marriage. But the truth is, it's not going to happen," Monique said, remembering her first night living with Nick. They had kept their promises. She knew then that the marriage wasn't going to last any longer than they'd agreed to.

"Can I help it if I'm a true romantic?"

"The marriage is for six months, end of discussion."

While Monique sat under the dryer reading the latest magazine and waiting for her hair to complete the twenty-minute process, she was suddenly interrupted by a woman that sat beside her. The woman was thin, but looked as if she worked out a lot. Her hair was cut short, feathering around her heart-shaped face. The clear lip gloss she wore glinted against her copper skin.

"I'm sorry to disturb you," the woman said. She looked to be in her early thirties, Monique assumed.

"Can I help you?" Monique looked up from the article she had been reading, thinking the woman was interested in services from one of her salons, since she and Colleen recommended their clients to each other.

"I'm Debra, Nick's ex-wife."

Monique folded the corner of the page she'd been reading, closed the magazine and gave the woman her undivided attention.

"I understand that you and Nick were recently married."

"Yes, we were," Monique replied.

"Nick . . . I'm just surprised that he remarried," Debra said as she pressed her hands over her short dress.

"And why is that?"

"From the conversations that we've had over the years, I didn't think he would be interested."

"Oh?" Monique continued to listen to Debra. Nick had never told her why he and his wife had divorced. However, she had heard rumors in her salon that Debra and her lover were the reason she and Nick had divorced.

"You see, Nick is horrible with relationships. Besides, he loves his work."

Monique looked away from Debra and saw Sharmain waiting for her appointment. It took every ounce of Monique's strength to control herself. She was aware that Nick's cousin was interested in knowing if their marriage was legitimate and not just on paper. *Had Sharmain sent Debra to grill her?*

Monique shot Sharmain another icy glance. She had obviously never left town since she'd attended her and Nick's wedding, and now she was provoking trouble.

Monique decided to play along. "And your point is?"

"I don't know, maybe he's settled now, and has time for a wife."

Monique just looked at the woman. Did she actually think she would discuss her and Nick's marriage?

"Anyway, I hope that your marriage lasts," she said, shifting herself as if to get a better view of Monique.

Monique felt her blood rush to her face. "Don't worry, I am going to keep him," Monique said, knowing she had no intention of doing that.

Debra rose from the dryer's seat. She placed one hand on her hips. "My friend Sharmain believes that Nick married you for the land that belongs to their grandmother." She looked down at Monique.

Monique lifted the dryer lid and rose from her seat.

"Why would you believe anything Sharmain has to say?" Monique gestured toward Nick's cousin. "She went to jail for—" Monique said, loud enough for Colleen's gossipy clients who were in hearing distance.

"Debra, will you come here, please?" Monique heard Sharmain call to Nick's ex-wife and her best friend.

Clients in pink styling chairs swirled in the direction of the three women. Soft giggles and chuckles floated up over the hum of twenty-four-watt blow dryers.

"Um-hum," Monique said to herself as she took her seat underneath the dryer.

Monique took out her cellular phone and called Nick's office, warning him that Sharmain was determined to find out if they were seriously married.

"So, Sharmain has finally gotten her girlfriend to do her dirty work," Nick said.

"Not at my expense," Monique said.

"Sharmain is grasping at the wind. She can't hurt us," Nick said. "Have lunch with me."

"I have about another forty-five minutes before Colleen will be finished with my hair," Monique said, wishing that she had asked Colleen to do her hair earlier, before the clients arrived.

"Call me when you're finished," Nick's husky voice circulated out to her. The very sound of his voice made her want to stop the search for her parents and rip up their marriage contract.

"I'll call you," she said. She shut her phone off.

Exactly fifty minutes later, Monique called Nick.

"Stay there, I'm on my way," he said.

Monique hung up and went over to one of Colleen's technician's stations.

"Can I use this?" Monique asked the young woman, picking up a rubber ponytail twist.

"Sure, take one," the beautician offered.

Monique pulled her long waves up into a ponytail and wound the band around her hair. Instead of waiting for Nick in the lobby, Monique sat back in Colleen's styling chair and finished reading the magazine article, ignoring the latest gossip.

"My, my, my." Monique heard a woman from the front of the lobby, speaking in a loud voice.

"You can stop moaning over him, girlfriend, he's wearing a wedding band," Monique heard another woman say.

"And baby, I got a private number."

The women giggled. Monique looked up from her reading and noticed that Nick was walking toward her. His hand pushed down into his trouser pocket, moving his suit coat back, exposing his gray shirt that seemed to strain against his muscular chest.

"Come on," Nick said to her, as if he hadn't heard the comments the woman had made. He waved to Colleen, who was walking toward the front of the salon.

Monique sat across from Nick spearing her fork into bite-size lettuce, while one lawyer after another stopped at their table to speak to Nick. Each one who hadn't attended their wedding congratulated them, while Nick introduced her.

"I'm going to a meeting for a couple of days. Would you like to come with me?" Nick asked.

"You know I can't come with you. I have to work."
Monique cut a tomato slice into thirds and speared it with
her fork. "Anyway, we don't have that kind of relationship."

Before Nick could respond, another man from the dis-
trict attorney's office stopped and spoke to him.

When the man left their table, Monique checked her
watch. "I have to get to the salon. I've been gone all morning."

"I have to get out of here too," Nick said. After paying
the check, they hurried to his car. Nick sped through the
street. Neither of them talked to the other until he reached
Shagreen.

"I'll see you later tonight," Nick said, reaching out and
touching Monique's hand.

Monique smiled at him and nodded while she got out
of the car.

Monique sat on the sofa in the great room, reading her
mail. She put the bills on one side of her and the junk
mail on the other. She laid the Christmas cards in her lap.

Just as she opened the GQ magazine that had arrived
for Nick, the doorbell rang. Monique went to open the
door, only to find Roger standing outside.

"Monique, I know that I shouldn't be here, but I wanted
to know how you were doing," he said, not waiting for
Monique to let him in. He walked past her and into the
great room.

"Hello, Roger."

"Monique, this marriage can't be real."

"What makes you think it's not real?"

"I don't know. I guess I thought you'd wait until I had
completed the work I'm doing for you."

"Did you bring the information you promised me?"

"I'm almost finished," Roger said. He reached out and
covered Monique's hand in his. "He's not right for you."

"Roger, I am not in the mood." She moved her hand from his.

"Monique, I know you think he loves you, but if you ever tell him the truth . . ."

"I told him I was adopted and he knows that you're looking for one of my parents."

"He didn't say anything?"

Monique shook her head. "Not a word."

"I wonder why." Roger paced a few feet and back to Monique.

"Because the only person that's concerned about my past is you."

"So, the project is not an issue anymore."

"Of course it is. I would like to know the medical history and other important information that might affect my life."

"Do you love him?" Roger reached out and covered her hand again.

Before Monique could reply, Nick walked in.

"What're you doing here?" Nick set his attache case on the chair.

"I stopped by to visit with my friend . . . do you mind?" Roger placed his hands on his hips.

Nick's glance seemed to burn into Roger. "I'm going to my study for a few minutes. When I get back, I want you gone."

"Nick, Roger is here to visit with me." She cast Nick a penetrating look, annoyed at his attitude toward Roger.

"I want him gone . . . now."

"You're gonna stand there and let him talk to you like that?" Roger questioned Monique.

"Nick, you know that Roger and I are friends. He will leave when we finish our visit." Monique was aggravated with Nick's dislike for Roger. It was as if he despised the sight of him.

Nick looked away from Monique and turned to Roger.

"You got about two minutes to get out of my house," Nick said, glaring at Roger.

"So, what is this? Monique loses her rights to have her friends over?" Roger shot back. He reached out and touched Monique's hand.

Nick seemed to have ignored Roger's comment. He took a step toward his study, then turned, directing his comments to Roger. "And I don't ever want to see you touching my wife again." With that said, Nick went to his study.

"What did you do, Nick, blackmail her into marrying you? Because you don't love her."

Nick wheeled around and moved with ease toward Roger. Then, as if he had second thoughts, he turned and headed back to the study.

Roger shook his head. "You better pray that my findings are perfect. Because if there's one flaw, he'll kick you out the same way he's kicking me out."

"Roger, please go." Monique fought to control herself. She was determined to straighten the havoc she'd wreaked in her life. But not for the reasons Roger thought. Her salon was important to her.

Nick was back in the room now. "I thought I told you to leave."

"I'm leaving," Roger shrugged. Turning on his heels, he headed toward the door.

Monique waited until Roger was out of the house and she could see the headlights from his car.

"Don't ever talk to Roger like that again."

"I don't like him and I don't want him near you."

"Why, what has he ever done to you?"

"Monique, I believe Roger is a sneak."

"He's not." Monique's voice trembled.

"I don't want him in our house." Nick's voice raised.

Monique placed both hands on her hips. "Don't you raise your voice to me." It was crystal clear that Nick was angry. But she was not going to stop speaking to Roger because Nick disliked him.

Nick didn't defend himself. He walked away from Monique and went to the study.

Monique went upstairs to her room.

As she soaked in a hot tub of bubbles, calming her nerves, she let her anger dissolve. Whatever reasons Nick had for disliking Roger, they were between Nick and Roger. Roger was her friend and she had no intention of dissolving their friendship. Monique stepped out of the tub and prepared for bed.

A light tap on her door interrupted her from reading her and Nick's early Christmas cards.

"It's open," Monique said, knowing it was Nick, since they were the only people in the house. She didn't want to discuss her friendship with Roger and she didn't want to hear Nick accuse Roger of being a sneak anymore.

She went back to reading the card she was reading before she had been disturbed by his knock on her bedroom door.

"I'm sorry," Nick said.

Monique looked up from her reading. Nick stood in her room, wearing nothing but his black pj's and his bare muscular chest.

"What do you want?"

Nick moved over and sat beside her. "I said, I'm sorry."

"Are you sorry for being rude to Roger or being rude to me?"

"I'm sorry if I was rude to you, but I don't like Roger."

"Nick, has he ever done anything to you?"

Nick crossed one leg over his thigh. "No, but he wants you."

Monique gave him the card that she had finished reading. "Roger is like a brother to me."

"If that's what you think." Nick flipped the card open and began reading the holiday greeting.

Monique reached for another card from Lucy Morgan and began reading, when the phone rang.

Nick picked up the cordless phone from the coffee table and answered the call.

"Parker's residence," Nick said, turning to Monique. "Hold on." He held the cordless receiver out to her.

"Who is it?" Monique asked in a quiet voice.

"It's Jeremy," Nick said. His voice sounded as if it was edged with cold iron.

Monique took the phone from Nick. "Yes, Jeremy." She listened to the dermatologist. "You broke your engagement." She listened. "I'm sorry to hear that." Monique glanced at Nick. "Yes, that was my husband." Nick's gaze seemed to lock with hers as she spoke, and she looked at him. "No, I won't be attending the seminar." Monique pulled her gaze away from Nick. "Thanks for calling." She pushed the button to shut off the phone and set it on the cradle.

Monique finished reading the card from Nick's grandmother, then passed it to Nick. "This Christmas card is from your grandmother," she said, reaching for the bill from Faceology Equipment.

Nick took the card and read it. He laid the card on the table. "So Jeremy broke off his engagement."

"Yes," Monique said, ripping the bill open to study the contents.

"So, why is he calling you?"

Monique shrugged her slender shoulders. "He invited me to a seminar."

"You gave him our phone number?"

Monique stopped studying her bill. She drew in a breath and let it out as if relieving herself of the tension that she felt between her and Nick.

"Nick, our phone number is listed, or have you forgotten?"

"We'll have to get a private number," Nick said. He smiled at her.

Monique felt her heart swell from the touch of Nick's finger.

The harder she tried to ignore red warning flags that swayed across her mind, the more she knew she had to be careful. Nick Parker wasn't a man to be toyed with.

Without warning, Nick pulled her to him, crushing her against his hard body. Covering her lips with his, his lips were hot and hungry against hers, and out of control. Nick stood, pulling her up along with him. He clamped his broad hands around her waist and half carried, half walked her to her bed. He put her down and towered over her. Slowly he lay down beside her, pulling her down on him.

Monique felt her need to resist weaken as she allowed Nick to plant one heated kiss after another on her neck, face and finally back to her lips.

It felt to Monique as if her blood temperature had risen and her blood was inching through her veins like scalding hot liquid. She felt Nick's hand moving her gown up around her hips. She dragged herself from out of the world she wanted to sink into and not return until she had explored Nick completely.

"No," Monique heard herself say. It sounded as if the voice came from a stranger. Loving Nick was not what she wanted to do. The price was too high. Their short months together would be over. And she would be left with the memories of a one-sided love affair.

From somewhere deep within, she found her strength. She pushed against his strong, hard chest until Nick released her.

Nick sat on the edge of the bed for several minutes before he left her room.

SEVENTEEN

Turkey, ham, potato salad, vegetables, pies, and almost every cake filled Clara Parker's house with the holiday aroma. Monique decided that the Parkers didn't cut corners when it came to family holidays. Monique had decided after a few Sunday dinners at Nick's family's home that she was going on a diet before Thanksgiving. If she lost a few pounds before the holiday, it wouldn't matter if she ate a little too much and gained the pounds she'd lost before the Parkers' feast.

Clara, Mark and Granny were their gracious selves. Clara seemed to be trying to make Monique feel especially welcome, Monique noticed. She wondered if her mother-in-law was aware of her and Nick's pretend marriage. Although, Clara didn't say anything about her and Nick's relationship, she did mention that she was waiting for Monique and Nick to announce that they were expecting a child soon.

"Brant and Daniella are taking care of that department," Nick said when Clara asked Monique if she and Nick had been thinking of starting a family.

"No," Monique said. "It's too soon."

"It would be nice to have the grandchildren around the same age," Clara continued.

"It would be nice," Monique said, hoping the conversation would stray and she wouldn't have to continue discussing the impossible with her mother-in-law.

"Uh," Sharmain grunted. "I doubt if there'll be any children from this holy matrimony." She shot Nick a bold stare.

Nick pulled Monique closer to him. "If you say so, Sharmain."

He brushed his lips against Monique's cheek, sending a delightful chill through her that threatened to warm any minute.

"I wish you wouldn't do that," Monique whispered.

"It's part of the contract. Remember?"

"Sharmain, why are you so angry at Nick?" Lucy asked her granddaughter.

"Granny, you know as well as I do that these two are faking."

"How do you know?" Brant came to Nick's defense.

"You can't talk, Brant. That's probably the reason you married this woman." Sharmain pointed a finger at Daniella.

With that remark from Sharmain, everyone began talking at once.

"Stop, right now." Mark held up one hand. The room became quiet.

"Sharmain, there's not a peaceful moment when you're around," Clara said. "If you don't stop this foolishness, I'm not inviting you for another holiday."

"You see what I mean, Granny?" Sharmain said, refueling the argument.

While everyone was arguing, Nick took Monique's hand and pulled her from the sofa with him. Monique allowed Nick to gather her in his arms and give her a smoldering kiss. She felt her body tingle with delight as he kissed her. Suddenly, the argument stopped.

"They make me sick!" Sharmain said.

The family ignored Sharmain, and the conversation was pleasant again.

"We're going," Nick said to his family.

"So soon?" Clara raised up to walk them to the door.

"We'll see you soon." Monique smiled at her mother-in-law.

"I will see you next week," Clara said, smiling her pearl smile.

"Nick, is Sharmain disturbed?" Monique asked.

Nick laughed. "I don't know. But she seems to have a behavior problem."

Monique settled back in the car seat and enjoyed the scenery. The ponds and lakes in the countryside were slightly frozen. Monique figured Nick was driving out to the camp he was building. She hadn't seen the place and was somewhat happy he was going there.

Monique reached over and turned on the radio. Music filled the silence.

As they drove though the countryside, passing the tall pitch pines and cold bare fields and yellow pastures, Monique wondered what was on Nick's mind. She knew he wasn't sorry he had married her. He wanted the camp for the inner-city children. Monique wanted it all to be over. She didn't know how much more of her and Nick's madly-in-love charade she could stand.

EIGHTEEN

Monique placed the last green, gold and crimson bulbs on the Christmas tree that stood near the fireplace in the lobby at her original Shagreen. She rolled the tiny switch on the electric cord connected to the colorful bulbs, lighting the tree and creating a festive mood in the lobby.

All Monique had to do now was finish her Christmas shopping. She hadn't selected and purchased a gift for Nick.

Monique wasn't certain that Nick wanted a gift from her. He had stayed within the terms of their contract. He came home late at night. If she was lucky, she would see him the next morning before they left for work.

Monique admired the tree.

"All we need now are gifts to go under that baby," Tamika giggled.

"I think so," Monique said, taking a string of garland out of the box and laying it on the edge of the mantelpiece. The phone rang. Tamika answered the phone.

"It's your husband, Mrs. Parker."

Monique went to answer the phone.

"Yes," Monique said to Nick.

"We have a problem," Nick said. His voice sounded strained.

Monique held her breath and waited for him to explain. When he didn't speak, Monique nudged him on.

"What happened?"

"Sharmain is back in town, and she's staying with us."

"I thought she was spending the holidays with your parents." Monique was worried. Sharmain's living with her and Nick meant she and Nick would spend more time together. She knew Nick would do everything in his power to convince Sharmain that they were in love.

"Sharmain waited too long. Now there're no bedrooms. They're not going to send her to a hotel." Nick thought Sharmain would be staying at his parents' too, until she learned that his aunt and uncle had been invited.

"Yes, we do have a problem," Monique said, prepared to deal with Nick's intimacy. And she had no plans to put up with Sharmain's foolishness and useless tantrums.

"What're we going to do, Nick?" Monique asked, hoping that there was a remedy to get around having Sharmain as a guest in their home.

"I'll sleep on the sofa in your room." Nick finally replied.

"Fine," Monique said. So long as Nick slept on the sofa and not in the bed with her, she knew she would be fine.

"What about your clothes? Sharmain is going to know that we sleep in separate rooms if she sees your clothes in your bedroom closet." Monique kept her voice low, just in case Tamika was listening to her and Nick's conversation.

"I had the maid move my clothes to your room."

Nick had taken care of everything, except for the part where he was going to raise unabashed passion in her. This consideration brought to mind the passion he had raised in her while they were in Paris.

It was almost impossible for Monique to banish her musing over Nick, when she had planned to shop for his gift.

Monique decided to take the afternoon off and go Christmas shopping. She tallied the day's receipts and placed the checks and cash in her bank deposit bag.

"Tamika, I'll see you tomorrow," Monique said, taking her purse from her desk drawer and her coat from the closet in her office.

"Okay," Tamika called back to her from behind the counter.

Monique drove to the mall, still unsure of what gift to buy Nick. He had several expensive suits, and all the accessories. He didn't need a watch. Monique considered buying him a gold chain. She decided a gold chain was not a good idea. She had never seen Nick wearing jewelry around his neck.

Finally, as she pulled into the mall's parking lot, she had the perfect gift idea for Nick. He never wore a house coat. He seemed comfortable walking around in his pj's and his bare chest. It was pleasing to feast her eyes on his six-pack stomach and hard chest. However the sight of her husband's muscular physique managed to raise fiery passion in her.

Monique went to the bank and made her deposits. She didn't know exactly what to give her employees for a Christmas present. Last year, she had been generous. Finally, she decided to give them each a small amount of money. She decided to purchase Nick's gift, before going to the card shop to buy money holders for the cash she intended to give her employees.

The men's boutique was across from the bank. Monique walked into the exclusive shop and went to the sleepwear department. She chose a black silk robe, and had the salesperson wrap the box that held Nick's gift in gold paper, decorated with a red bow.

With that done, she shopped for her mother, Colleen, Roger and her in-laws. Her in-laws were the hardest to shop for since they seemed to have everything.

Loaded down with packages, Monique headed to her car. Her next stop was the supermarket. She could imagine Sharmain thinking it strange that she and Nick only had water, orange juice, and a couple of bottles of wine in their refrigerator.

At the supermarket, Monique purchased enough food to last for a week, and headed home.

Small lights lit the hedges that nestled against her and Nick's home. Two gold bells hung on the door. From the great room window, the Christmas tree was in clear view, flashing an array of colorful lights.

Monique drove into the garage and popped her car's trunk.

Seconds later, the maid came out to help her bring the packages inside.

"I hope you don't mind that I'm here," Sharmain said coming down the back stairway.

"Hello, Sharmain," Monique said as she took her gifts to the great room to place them under the Christmas tree. As she set her gifts down near the tree, she noticed two gifts. Monique picked the smallest gift up and read the tag. *From: Nick, to my darling wife.* Monique decided that Nick may have written the card for Sharmain's eyes only, and reached for the second gift that was for the maid, from her and Nick.

By the time Monique finished placing the gifts under the tree, Nick walked in.

He pulled off his coat and hung it in the closet near the door. He walked over and slipped his arms around Monique's waist, gathering her to him, planting a tender kiss on her lips, threatening to ignite a thrilling sizzle.

Monique circled her arms around his neck and returned his kiss before removing herself from his embrace and going to prepare dinner.

"Would you like for me to stay and help you with dinner?" the maid asked.

It seemed to Monique that the woman thought she needed her help, since she had never seen Monique prepare a meal before.

"No, you can leave now," Monique said as she washed her hands in the washroom near the kitchen door leading to the garage.

Sharmain was back in the kitchen now, sitting at the edge of the kitchen counter, drinking a bottle of water.

"Well, if you don't need me, I'm going to find Nick."

Monique nodded. She could imagine that Nick was prepared for his cousin.

Monique washed and cut the vegetables for the salad, along with three potatoes. She placed the potatoes in the oven to bake for an hour.

While she prepared the steak for broiling, Nick came in and stood beside her.

"Can I help you with anything?" Nick asked, standing close to Monique.

"Let me see." Monique wiped her hand with a dry dishcloth and placed one hand on her hip. It seemed apparent that Sharmain had plucked Nick's nerves. His facial expression was strained, as if he was agitated.

"You can set the table." Monique smiled up at Nick, then gave him a playful push toward the dining room.

"Honey, do you know how to set the table?" The "honey" was for Sharmain, just in case she was eavesdropping.

"I'm not sure. I think I can," Nick said, making his way to the dining room.

"I can ask Sharmain to help you," Monique teased him.

"No, I'll figure it out."

Monique went to Nick's study for a bottle of brandy. She stood in the study's entrance, watching Sharmain go through Nick's desk drawer.

"You can check his attache case. You might find what you're looking for," Monique said, going to the cabinet and taking a bottle of brandy.

"I was looking for a ballpoint pen," Sharmain said, as if she was surprised to see Monique in the study.

Monique gestured to the desk where a container held four gold cross pens.

"I didn't see them," Sharmain said.

"Right." Monique turned and left the room. She was certain that Sharmain was looking for information to prove that her and Nick's marriage was in name only.

Monique set the brandy on the counter and went to find Nick, who was in the dining room arranging the silverware in the correct order next to the china.

"I found Sharmain in the study, going through your desk," Monique said, helping Nick with the silverware setting.

"She won't find anything." Nick took the water glasses from the china cabinet and set them on the table in the proper order.

"You're sure," Monique said as she and Nick left the dining room.

"Yeah," Nick answered, glad he'd deleted the marriage contract he had typed for Monique to sign.

The oven's timer buzzed. "Will you take the potatoes out and set them over there?" Monique asked Nick, gesturing to the small counter next to the stove.

Nick Parker seemed to be pleased to take orders from his wife. When he finished, he retrieved two brandy glasses from the cabinet and filled them halfway. He set one on the counter for Monique and sat on a stool at the counter, taking swigs from his drink.

Monique set the steaks in the oven and turned the timer on the oven's broiler to fifteen minutes. She took a pack of brown and serve dinner rolls from the bread box and passed them to Nick, along with a baking sheet to set the rolls on.

"I thought I was through working," Nick said.

"Would you like to entertain Sharmain?"

"No," Nick said, setting his glass down and opening the bread package.

Twenty minutes later, Monique, Nick and Sharmain sat down in the dining room and ate Monique's delicious meal.

"So, Monique, are you ready for the holidays?" Sharmain asked, laying her fork on the corner of her plate.

"I'm about as ready as I'm going to get," Monique said.

"Well, we don't have to worry about you, Nick." Sharmain lifted her fork and knife and cut into her steak. "You received your gift when Granny gave you that land . . . uh?"

Nick didn't comment. He stared at Sharmain for a short time. For the remainder of the evening, they ate their meal in silence.

While Nick helped Monique stack the dishes in the dishwasher, he realized he'd had no idea that she was a good cook. He stole a glance at her before he complimented her on the dinner.

"You're a pretty good cook," Nick said as he rinsed the last glass.

"Thank you," Monique said, filling the plastic container with the leftover salad. Her mother had been responsible for her cooking skills.

Nick chuckled.

"Don't get used to it," she added.

"I think I already have." Nick replied, wanting to cradle her in his arms and kiss her until she wanted him as much as he wanted her.

While they were in Paris, they had broken the rules. He had lost control and made love to her. Tonight, he was worried. He would keep his emotions intact. Sleeping in the same room with Monique was not going to be easy.

"Nick. Monique." Nick heard Sharmain calling out to them from the stairway. Nick reached out and folded his arms around Monique. It was another opportunity to kiss her. He lowered his head and captured Monique's lips with his kiss. The small gasp that slipped from her throat made him want her more.

"Oh, please!" Sharmain said as she stood in the kitchen door. "I forgot what I came for."

Nick held Monique, not wanting to let her go.

In Monique's bedroom, Nick lay on the sofa bed and inhaled the powder and perfume that reached out from the bathroom's open door, circulating through the bedroom.

From the sofa, he watched Monique go into her closet. It wasn't long before she walked out wearing a long sexy nylon gown. He felt his uncontrolled power coil inside him. For the first time in his life, he felt helpless.

Monique dozed in and out of sleep, tossing and turning until she was finally wide awake. She sat up in bed. The lights from the streetlamps shone through the thin lines in the vertical blinds.

A distant bark of a small puppy filled the night as Monique sat in her bed, unable to dismiss the question that nagged at her. *How was she going to get out of this predicament with a sound mind, unwounded heart, and her soul still intact?*

Unfortunately, no answers came to mind.

Just as she was about to slip beneath the blanket and make an attempt to fall asleep again, she heard Sharmain outside the bedroom door.

"Nick. Monique."

"What?" Monique heard Nick's husky drowsy murmur.

Monique raised up and saw Nick turn on his stomach. Sharmain knocked on the door.

"What?" Nick called out to his cousin.

"I need a blanket," Sharmain called back.

"Damn!" Monique heard Nick curse under his breath

while he got out of bed and immediately began taking the covers off and folding the bed back into a sofa.

"What're you doing?"

"Sharmain is not going to leave us alone," Nick said, motioning for Monique to turn the covers back on the empty side of her bed. "I know my cousin."

Monique pushed the covers back, while Nick went to the closet, put his blanket away and took a fresh blanket from the shelf for Sharmain.

He opened the door and gave Sharmain a fresh blanket from the closet. "Do you need anything else?"

Monique watched Nick stand in the doorway of her bedroom, wearing black pj's and his bare chest.

"I guess not, but if I do, I'll be back."

Nick seemed annoyed to Monique. He stepped back and closed the door with a quick, firm snap.

Monique felt her breath catch in her throat when Nick slid into bed beside her. She felt the warm heat from his body. The scent of soap mingled with cologne. She felt her pulse pound. Her urge to sleep disappeared.

"I can't sleep," Monique finally said.

"Me neither," Nick replied. "But I think I have a remedy." He got out of bed, and left the bedroom.

Minutes later, Nick was back carrying two brandy glasses.

"This usually works for me." He set the bottle of brandy and the glasses on the nightstand before filling their glasses with the alcoholic beverage.

Monique took the drink that Nick held out to her and sipped. The liquid warmed her insides. She took another small sip and set the goblet down on her nightstand.

"Maybe we should get a hotel room for Sharmain," Monique suggested.

"As long as she behaves herself, she can stay here," Nick said, setting his glass on the table.

"She's determined to find out about us," Monique said, almost to herself.

"Maybe we should give her what she's looking for." Nick pulled Monique to him, cupping her face with his broad hands. He touched his lips to hers.

Unable to resist, Monique sank against him, enjoying Nick's caresses, as his lips trailed to the hollow of her throat, making a fiery trail to her breast.

Monique was glad the only light in the room was the glow from the street light that beamed rays through the blinds. The semi-darkness served one purpose. Nick couldn't see the tortured expression on her face as he stroked her, building a blazing fire. His hands moved under her gown, exploring her thighs. Slowly and gently, Nick moved downward. His lips touched the center of her stomach, and made a trail to her pleasure points.

Monique felt as if she was swirling, her heart pounded, fluttering against her breast. Her body tingled with shivering delight. She tried to think. Her thoughts were blurred, and her emotions skidded out of control.

Her body trembled from their close contact, and soft moans escaped her. She felt Nick's broad steady hand slipping the strap of her gown off her shoulder. He cupped her breasts in his wide, broad hands and slowly kissed them until they peaked to hard mounds.

Soft murmurs slipped from Monique's throat, as Nick slid further down, slowly dragging her gown with him exploring every inch of her body, until her blood felt as if it was on the verge of boiling. As her blood reached the boiling point, Nick proceeded to the point of satisfaction, like hot iron against soft cushions. Lost in a deep lagoon, they swam into a sea of pure unabashed lovemaking, rising to a peak of no return. They trekked to the edge of a steep mountain, then slid wildly back to the bottom.

The knocking sound on their bedroom door was like a hammer somewhere in the middle of the night. Monique heard what sounded like a growl coming from Nick as he rolled over pulling her with him.

"What?" Nick said, his breathing fast and hard.

"Where is the thermostat?" Sharmain called back.

"At the end of the hall," Nick said after a long pause. He gathered Monique closer.

She held on to him. She made no excuses. Being with Nick was like quicksand. The more she struggled, the deeper she sank in a world of sizzling pleasure.

The next morning, Monique woke to find Nick out of bed.

When she had finished her shower and dressed, she took her purse and black leather gloves and headed downstairs. From the top of the stairs, she heard Sharmain's voice.

"You can tell that lie to Granny, Aunt Clara and Uncle Mark, but you can't lie to me."

"Sharmain, you are entitled to your opinion." Nick paused. "Matter of fact, your opinion doesn't matter to me."

"Nick, I am going to prove that you and Monique's marriage is the biggest fraud ever."

"What you do with your time is your business, Sharmain," Monique heard Nick say in an angry voice.

"I know people from your office that saw Jacqueline there with you."

Monique listened to this conversation, unable to control the jealousy that raked at her heart. She calmed herself and walked downstairs to join Nick and Sharmain in the kitchen.

"Good morning," Monique said, breaking up the argument.

Monique didn't miss Sharmain's cynical smile.

"Are you ready?" Nick turned his attention to Monique.

"Yes," Monique said, pulling on a pair of black leather gloves as she walked past Sharmain.

Monique had an appointment to service her car. Nick was driving her to work.

On their way out of the house, Nick reached out and covered her hand, leading her over chips of ice that were scattered on the steps to their house and driveway.

"Monique, I don't know how much you heard of that conversation. But Sharmain will accuse me of just about anything, right now." Nick unlocked and opened the door to his BMW, and waited until Monique was inside the car.

Monique leaned over and unlocked the door for Nick, while searching for a reasonable explanation to Nick's comment. By the time he slid behind the wheel, she realized that to wrestle with knowledge that she had no control over was meaningless.

"It doesn't matter," Monique said, reaching into her purse and taking her sunglasses out. She put them on to shade her eyes against the brilliant winter's morning sun.

Monique glanced at Nick from the corner of her eye. She hadn't expected him to live like a monk. But this information was too much.

"I'm not seeing anyone." He started the engine and backed out of the driveway.

"There's no need for an explanation." Monique settled down in her seat. Once more, she had allowed her good sense to take flight. The proof was simple. She allowed herself the pleasure of passion.

"Are you mad at me?" Nick asked, wheeling the car near the curb by the diner.

Monique didn't respond. From the corner of her eye, she saw Nick give her a quick easy glance.

"Are you mad at me about last night?"

"Why should I be mad at you?"

"You're not talking to me."

Monique was quiet. Discussing his affair was off limits. She planned to never make love to him again.

"Monique, talk to me," Nick said again when they were

seated at their table in the diner, waiting for their breakfast.

Monique ignored Nick. She took some change from her
purse and dropped it in the small jukebox on the wall near
their table. She punched in the numbers to her favorite
song from the seventies. While the song played on the
jukebox, Monique drank her coffee.

Life was too sweet to worry about things she had no
control over.

NINETEEN

Christmas Day at the Parkers was about the same. The six-foot Christmas tree stood in the living room, trimmed with gold and red bulbs and clear twinkling lights. Small and large gifts sat underneath the long healthy green branches.

At the dinner table, the usual argument took place, with Sharmain leading the heated discussion.

"Aunt Clara, I guess you're satisfied," Sharmain said, pushing away from the table as if she had lost her appetite.

"What is it, Sharmain?" Clara said.

"I guess you're satisfied. Nick has his wife, and from the way things look, he's going to receive that gift of land Granny promised him after all."

"Sharmain, is that all you have to talk about?" Mark said, seemingly annoyed at his niece.

"I wish you wouldn't talk about me as if I weren't here," Nick added.

Sharmain looked at her relatives, one at a time. "I'm sorry, but I don't think it's fair."

"Sharmain, this is Christmas, and we are going to have peace in this house," Clara said, ending the discussion.

Most of the dinner conversation turned to Daniella and Brant and their coming addition to the Parker family.

"I think it's a boy," Daniella said, mentioning that the

doctor was not sure. "So don't go out and buy girl things," she smiled.

Monique noticed Nick watching her from across the table. She and Nick had never discussed having a family. There was no need for that type of discussion, since their marriage promised to be a short one. As she watched him, she wondered if the thought had crossed his mind.

After dinner, Monique and Nick, along with the others, went to the living room and opened their gifts.

Monique opened her gift from Clara and Mark. The gold brooch was perfect. "Thank you," Monique said, smiling and giving her mother-in-law and father-in-law a hug.

"You're welcome, Monique" Clara said, beaming.

Nick, Brant and Sharmain received stock certificates from the family.

Just as Clara and Lucy Morgan were marveling over the silk scarves and the one-year gift certificate they received from Monique, the doorbell rang.

Clara's sister, Sharmain's stepmother Kate walked in, carrying a shopping bag filled with gifts.

Kate was an elegant woman, dressed in an off-white wool pants suit and gold heels. Her long silver hair was pulled back in a ponytail and clipped with a gold-beaded band. Large round gold earrings and a matching brooch completed her outfit. When she entered the room behind the maid, the subtle scent of her expensive perfume filled the room.

"Merry Christmas, everybody." She bent down and gave her mother Lucy Morgan a kiss, before she hugged Clara and gave her the shopping bag.

"Mother," Sharmain said to her stepmother.

Kate gave Sharmain a kiss.

"I hope I'm not too late for my gift, because I know it's good," She laughed.

Before Kate sat and joined the family for eggnog, she

opened her purse and gave Sharmain a thin envelope. "I thought about giving you nothing. I heard how you've been carrying on around here. You should be ashamed of yourself."

Kate had been in the islands, taking care of her export business.

"But mother—" Sharmain started.

"I don't want to hear about it no more," Kate said, holding up her hand. She poured herself a glass of eggnog and sat beside Monique and Nick. "You must be the newest Mrs. Parker," Kate said, extending her hand to Monique.

"Yes, I am." Monique smiled.

"Son, you know how to pick a wife," Kate said to Nick.

Monique watched Nick grin at his aunt as he encircled his arms around Monique, giving her a tender squeeze.

"Mother, that was exactly what I was talking about," Sharmain said. "If you heard anything about me, it was because those two are married for reasons other than love."

Kate inched to the end of the sofa, holding her drink in midair.

"Sharmain, you were a nosy little girl." Loud chuckles filled the living room as Kate continued. "And now, you're a nosy woman."

Sharmain shrugged her shoulders and went to sit beside her grandmother.

"I heard that the two of you celebrated your marriage in Paris," Kate said, turning her attention back to Monique and Nick. "The honeymoon must've been romantic."

"Yes," Monique said, recalling the passionate night she and Nick had had while they were in the romantic city.

Monique leaned closer into Nick, her memories returning to the sizzling love they had shared. A shiver raced through her. Monique dismissed her reflections.

Kate soon turned her attention to Brant and Daniella, congratulating them on the baby they were expecting.

In the meantime, Nick planted a kiss on Monique's lips. "Are you ready to go?"

"Not really," Monique said, enjoying Kate's high spirit. "But, I'm ready if you are."

Nick stood, pulling Monique up with him. They thanked the family for their gifts and left the room with Lucy rolling in her wheelchair beside them, wishing Monique and Nick a happy New Year.

When they reached the door and were standing under the mistletoe, Nick cradled Monique in his arms and gave her a burning kiss that left her weak and wanting him.

When he released her, Monique noticed a smile on her grandmother-in-law's lips.

By the end of January, Monique was seriously considering going to the doctor for the flu-like symptoms that were making her weak and draining her energy. She had doubled her intake of vitamin C, but she still wasn't feeling well. One day she called Colleen and asked her to keep an eye on the salons. She didn't feel like going in. All day she stayed in bed and slept. She woke only to talk to Nick, who was in Washington on a business trip, and later to take a shower.

The phone woke her around five o'clock.

"It's me," Colleen said. "How're you feeling?"

"Rotten," Monique said, positioning herself up in bed so she could talk to her girlfriend.

"If Nick is still out of town, I can come over and make dinner for you," Colleen offered.

"Thanks Colleen, I'll appreciate that."

Monique hung up, glad to have a friend like Colleen.

Since the second week in January, Nick had been attending to business out of town. At first Monique had thought Nick was avoiding her, until she saw his work schedule.

Regardless, Monique had kept her distance from Nick, especially with Sharmain back in Atlanta. Monique could breathe in peace again.

Monique made her way to the bathroom. While she showered, she heard the phone ring.

After the third ring it stopped. Monique checked the caller ID. It was a call from out of town. She wondered if it was Nick who had called her, since the number didn't register on the ID window.

By the time Colleen arrived carrying grocery bags filled with the evening's dinner, Monique was downstairs.

"Girl, I got some of that hearty chicken soup and dinner rolls." Colleen named off each item as she took them from the bag. "I got some butter for the bread and I got some of your favorite herb tea from the health food store."

"Thanks, Colleen," Monique said, taking a pot from the hanger over the counter and directing Colleen to the electric can opener.

"I don't know what you're coming down with, but I hope I don't get it." Colleen poured the soup in the pot and turned on the burner.

The phone rang. "Hello," Monique's voice sounded weak as she spoke into the receiver. "Mrs. Wakefield," Monique said, looking in Colleen's direction.

"Elaine told me that you weren't feeling well," Amelia Wakefield said. "I hope you don't mind that I called to check on you."

"No. I don't mind."

"I hope you feel better soon," Amelia said, sounding concerned.

"If I'm feeling better, I'll be in before the end of the week," Monique assured her.

"I'll see you soon," Amelia said.

"Good-bye, Mrs. Wakefield."

Colleen laughed. "Tamika told me that Mrs. Wakefield asked for your phone number. When she didn't give it to her, Mrs. Wakefield found the number in the telephone book."

Monique managed a weak smile. "She would do that."

"Well, she likes you," Colleen said, stirring the soup.

It wasn't long before the scent of chicken soup filled the kitchen.

"Oh, my gosh," Monique bolted off the stool, making a dash for the washroom by the garage. The scent from the soup made her sick.

"Monique, are you okay in there?" Colleen ran behind her.

"What kind of chicken soup is that?" Monique asked once she had composed herself, and was sitting on her barstool.

"It's chicken soup," Colleen said, eyeing her friend closely. "Monique, are you pregnant?"

"No, why do you ask that?" Monique crossed her ankles and allowed them to swing nervously. True, she and Nick had made love. But she was taking the pill. Even if the pill was for regulation. Monique looked away from Colleen. She had been late.

At the end of the month an extra pill was in the pack. She remembered then that she'd missed taking the pill the night Sharmain had stayed with her and Nick. Monique wasn't sure if taking the extra pill would help her. But to be safe she had taken the pill anyway.

"You're pregnant. Did you tell Nick?"

It was as if a cyclone had hit her and knocked the wind out of her.

"No, Colleen."

"Uh, weak, sick, can't stand the smell of food. Sounds like a little Parker is on her way," Colleen said, letting out a chuckle. "And I am going to be the godmother."

"I'm sure it's nothing. I'll be fine."

Monique felt a tear spark at the brim of her eyes. Her problems had compounded. To make matters worse,

Roger hadn't completed his findings and her world was slowly crumbling into tiny miserable pieces.

"Colleen, don't get excited. I haven't seen my doctor," Monique said, referring to her new discovery.

"The soup is ready," Colleen said, taking two bowls from the cabinet.

"I can't eat," Monique said, realizing that she hadn't eaten since last night. She had forced the food down because she had no appetite. It never crossed her mind that she may be pregnant.

"Well, let's see. Do you and Mr. Parker have a box of saltine crackers around here?" Colleen went through one cabinet after another, searching for crackers. She found them.

"Ah, ha!" Colleen said, taking a box of crackers from the cabinet. "Eat one of these." She gave Monique the pack.

"For a woman who doesn't have children, you know quite a bit on this subject." Monique opened the pack and took out a cracker.

"Oh yeah, one year half my clientele was expecting bundles of joy." Colleen smiled. "It got so bad that we decided to add saltine crackers to the salon's snack bar list."

Shortly after the dinner that Monique couldn't eat, Colleen left, leaving Monique to bask in her worries. Of all the things in the world for her and Nick to do, she suspected that they had created a life. This type of thing was supposed to be planned, Monique pondered, as one worried thought after another winged its away across her mind. But at the top of her list of worries, she realized that her child would be fatherless. There was no way she would have Nick think that she had trapped him into staying married to her.

After considering the fact that her child was going to be fatherless, Monique called her doctor's answering service to set up an appointment.

"The earliest appointment I can give you will be in two weeks," the woman on the other end of the line told Monique.

"Oh my Lord . . . Are you sure you can't squeeze me in?"

"I'm sorry, Mrs. Parker."

"Thanks," Monique said, and hung up.

Monique decided that if she felt better by morning, she would go to the drugstore and buy a pregnancy test. She had to know.

The next morning, Monique felt better. She showered and dressed in a pair of jeans and a sweatshirt. She drove to the drug store and purchased a pregnancy test.

After listening to Colleen's evaluation last night, she was sure she had more than the flu, Monique mused as she drove home to find out the results.

Minutes later, she was home and in her bathroom. A sick feeling swept over her while she observed the pink line on the tester.

TWENTY

Nick sat in his hotel room with the sound of the television playing in the background of his thoughts. He had called Monique the night before, hoping to talk to her. After several rings, the answering machine answered his call.

"We're unable to take your call at this time. Please leave a message and we'll return your call." Nick listened to Monique's recorded voice. He hung up, he wanted to tell her how he really felt about her. Monique had been polite but cool to him since the morning she had overheard Sharmain tell him that he was still seeing Jacqueline.

Not to mention the fact that he had broken the contract. He had broken it more than once. He had tried, but he couldn't keep his hands off her. He loved Monique, it was as simple as that.

Nick lay back on his bed and tried to sleep. When he did, he dreamed. His dream turned into a nightmare, as Monique repeated her hate for him. *I hate you . . . I hate you!* He woke up, drenched with sweat from Monique's angry voice ringing in his dream.

Nick dialed his home number. After the tenth ring and no answer, he hung up.

* * *

In the meantime, Monique stood the great room, holding the papers that Roger had just given her, and letting the phone ring.

Her hands trembled as she read the heart-wrenching information that Roger had found regarding her parents.

"Roger, this can't be true," Monique said between the tears she tried to swallow.

"It's all there, Monique. I'm sorry." Roger reached out and pulled her into his arms, while she sobbed gut-wrenching tears. A surge of apprehension coursed through her. Anger knotted her insides. Fate had dealt her a game in life to play, a game that she was sure to lose. Icy fear gnawed at her heart, and she knew she could never stay married to Nick.

Monique recalled her pregnancy test she had taken earlier. A fresh batch of tears replaced the old ones.

Finally, Monique pulled away from the comforts of Roger's embrace. "I want to be alone," she said, going to open the door for Roger. This was her chance to get out while Nick wasn't around to try to stop her. And before Nick could learn the horrible information Roger had found on both her parents.

Monique was certain that Nick would think she was a robber and a thief like her biological parents. If not her, their baby would join the ranks of the long line of thieves that, according to Roger's report, hung on the Taylors' family tree.

Monique wasn't sure what she was going to do about her salons. All she knew was that Nick could never know she was carrying his child. He would never let her go.

Monique sank down on the couch when she heard Roger's car drive out of the driveway and, for the second time, she read the report.

Her mother was a kleptomaniac who had spent time in jail on several occasions. Her father was a dope addict, and was also a thief. The family, who's last name was Taylor, were slow learners and mental retardation was common.

Finally she went upstairs and packed as many of her summer clothes as she could get into her luggage. She added a couple of sweaters, knowing that the weather sometimes got a little chilled in Miami, especially near the ocean. She was going to her mother's condo in Florida. Yvonne was usually on her winter cruise by now or had traveled off to a European country. Monique would be alone, where she could think.

She took a pad and pen from her nightstand and scribbled a note to Nick. She took the note to his room and laid it on his bed. Even though she was leaving Nick for a short time, she didn't want him to worry unnecessarily.

While Monique packed, she wasn't worried. Her child would probably be a ward of the juvenile system by the time she or he was seven years old.

Unable to discard the thoughts about her unborn child, Monique called the airport. Considering that the weather was getting worse, threatening snow storms, she was lucky to get a flight out of New Jersey to Miami.

Afterwards, Monique drove to Shagreen II and met with Elaine. She left her phone number where she could be reached in Miami.

Monique made Elaine promise that she wouldn't give Nick the phone number, or any information on where she would be staying.

Last, Monique met with Tamika. She had no choice but to give Tamika her phone number, assuring her that if the problem wasn't urgent, she could always call Colleen or Elaine.

"Tamika, no one is to know that I'm in Miami."

"Mr. Parker called this morning. He wanted to speak to you."

Monique was determined that her secret was not to be

revealed. "Don't mention to anyone that I am in Florida, and I mean no one."

"What about Mr. Parker?"

"Don't tell him, either." *Especially Nick,* the thought sailed across her mind.

On her way to the airport, Monique stopped by Colleen's salon. In the privacy of her best friend's office, Monique allowed hot salty tears to roll down her face as she told Colleen the results of Roger's findings. She told Colleen that her pregnancy test results were positive.

"That's wonderful." Colleen hugged Monique.

"It would be wonderful if I hadn't read Roger's report." Monique couldn't control her tears. Together, she and Colleen cried.

Finally, Monique composed herself. "Colleen, please check on Tamika," she said, explaining to Colleen the instructions she had left with Tamika. "Will you call this number and make an appointment with the doctor for me. If I'm pregnant, I'm going to need her services."

"Monique, that goes without asking. I'll call the doctor and I'll check on the salons every day."

If there were any problems with her salons that Colleen, Tamika or Elaine couldn't handle, she would handle them over the phone.

"While you were giving Tamika instructions, I hope you instructed her not to tell Nick that you're in Florida," Colleen said.

"I warned her," Monique said, realizing that Nick could call the airlines if he was interested in what city she had flown to.

A month was the longest that Monique planned to stay in Miami. She needed time to sort through her life. When she returned, she planned to file for an annulment and move into a hotel. The lawyer that had rented her house had a lease that did not expire for a few more months.

* * *

Tall buildings rose up over the ocean, silhouetted against the dark Miami sky. A tropical warmth swelled though the air. Honking horns and the screaming sound of a fire engine sent cars pulling over to the side of the road.

Somewhere in the distance of summery sounds, Monique heard laughter mingled with the sound of rhythm and blues.

While the cab drove Monique to her mother's home, her mind wavered to Nick. He was strong-willed, persistent and loving. He seemed to know what he wanted and Monique knew that Nick never began a task he didn't complete.

If it was at all possible, she would stay with him forever. Under the circumstances, she knew she couldn't.

The cab stopped in front of the condo building. Monique got out and walked inside the tall white building. She would sort through her life, and she hoped she would make the right decisions.

"Monique," Yvonne reached out, circling her arms around her daughter. "I'm surprised."

"No, Mother, I'm surprised. I thought you were going on a cruise."

Yvonne smiled. "I'm leaving this week." Yvonne's tone was filled with excitement.

"I hope you're going someplace exotic," Monique said, keeping the conversation light.

"Yes, the ship is going to make several stops," Yvonne replied. "But, young lady, what brings you back to Miami, another seminar?"

"No, I just needed to get away," Monique said, not divulging any information her mother hadn't asked for.

"How's Nick?"

"He's fine," Monique replied in a low voice.

"What happened?" Yvonne asked, seeming to study Monique's face closely.

Reluctant to divulge the details, Monique told her mother about Roger's findings.

"Nick will understand," Yvonne said, assuring her daughter that Nick was a reasonable man. "Anyway, you should be thankful that you weren't raised in a family as dysfunctional as your biological parents were raised in." Yvonne drew in a breath and let it out slowly. "There's more, isn't there?"

The time for truth had finally arrived. Monique could no longer deny her mother the truth about her and Nick's marriage and how her ex-fiancé's parents had scorned her because of her past. As she disclosed her fears to the woman that lifted her from the jaws of poverty to a world that she hadn't known existed, Monique cried. When she mustered more control, she told her mother about the baby.

Yvonne seemed undisturbed by her daughter's fears. Monique noticed what seemed like a concerned frown crease her mother's smooth forehead.

"Monique, Nick is an intelligent man. I'm sure he'll understand."

"Anyway, when we adopted you, your parents' records were closed. It was a court order. But there was no indication that we were adopting an unhealthy, disturbed child."

Monique took a tissue from the box on the coffee table. Her mother may have been right, but it could have been that the retardation skipped a generation and her child would be unhealthy.

"Monique, if that was the case, we would've known." Yvonne leaned forward. "I knew those employees that worked at the orphanage. And believe me, if there was anything out of the ordinary that concerned your parents or you, I would have known."

Monique calmed herself after listening to the information. It still didn't cease the battle that she fought within her. She was sure that Nick would have some concerns, the same as she was concerned for their unborn child.

"So, did the doctor give you and the baby a clean bill of health?" Yvonne asked.

"I couldn't get an appointment as soon as I wanted to. So I used a tester. I'm planning to see a doctor while I'm here," Monique said.

"I know a wonderful doctor," Yvonne said, getting up and leaving the room. When she returned, she gave Monique the name of a gynecologist. "Just to make sure," she said, sitting down again.

"But if you are pregnant, honey, that baby is going to be just fine." Yvonne smiled. "I can hardly wait to hear what the doctor has to say."

Monique forced herself to smile. Exhausted from her trip and her frazzled nerves, she got up and went to the bedroom.

"Good night," she said over her shoulder.

Nick unlocked the front door to his house. The house was dark, and quiet. He turned on the light in the great room, and went upstairs.

"Monique," Nick called out to her. When she didn't answer, he knocked on her bedroom door. Usually, he could hear contemporary jazz playing on her radio. Nick opened the door to the dark room and turned on the light.

It wasn't like Monique to leave her closet door open. Nick walked over and closed the door. Monique was out or working late, he mused, going to his room.

Nick sat on the edge of his bed and pulled off his shoes. He picked up the note behind him and stood up.

Nick,
    I had to get away for awhile. I'll be seeing you soon.
                                      Monique.

Nick stood frozen. It seemed as if he was rooted to the floor. He headed back to her room when he could move. He checked the closet again and found her luggage gone.

Nick felt as if his heart would break as he stood gazing out her bedroom window. His eyes brimmed with tears.

Finally, he walked over and sat on her bed. Nick took a tissue from the box to wipe his tears. As he reached for another tissue, he saw a brown manila envelope. He lifted the envelope from the nightstand. He turned on the lamp light and read the information.

Nick should have been shocked at what he read, but he wasn't, for the simple reason that Roger Cumming's signature was scrawled at the end of the report.

He read the letterhead.

Roger Cummings, private detective agency. Roger's office address was written underneath the name of his agency.

Nick always suspected that Roger was in love with Monique. And if Nick was right, he knew Roger would do anything to break them up.

Nick had a terrible feeling the night he had found Roger in his house. It wasn't that he didn't trust Monique, but he didn't trust Roger. Nick wasn't sure, but he believed that Roger had used his search for Monique's parents to destroy their marriage. In his gut, he knew it was true.

Nick paced back to the window. Snow had begun to fall, sprinkling the oak tree at the edge of the street like white powdered sugar.

The sweet thought brought to mind his love for Monique. He didn't care if Monique had lived in an orphanage until she was ten years old. He could care less that she had been adopted.

Nick had an inkling that Monique had broken off their love affair for fear that he would reject her. *Or had she?* He wasn't sure.

Nick walked back to the window and gazed out at the snow that had thickened.

"Oh, no," Nick said aloud. What if Monique went to look for her family? Nick covered his face with his hands. "Dope addicts. Oh God, please, let her be anywhere except with those people." Nick prayed and cried. He had to find her. For the first time in his adult life, Nick felt helpless and afraid.

Roger would know, Nick considered. He went back to the nightstand and looked at the report again. There was no address for Monique's family listed.

Nick dropped the report on the bed. He glanced around the room, as if hoping Monique had written Roger's phone number on the wall.

Think, Nick mused. She has to have Roger's home number here, someplace in this house. Nick went to the nightstand and opened the top drawer. He fished around inside the drawer, pulling out a pen, a pad and a pack of envelopes. The second drawer was empty. Nick checked the second nightstand. Nothing.

He went to the closet. He had never looked among Monique's personals before. Tonight was different. Nick started with the chest. He opened the top drawer. Lace panties. "Oh, gosh." He swallowed hard. When he had composed himself, he went back to his hunting, lifting the contents in the second drawer. More bras, panties and panty hose. He didn't find an address in the chest. The dresser was the same.

He reached behind the pillows and blankets on the top shelf in the closest. His hand came in contact with three boxes, two small and one medium sized.

Nick took the first box off the closet shelf, sat on the foot ladder and start flipping through the index file. He started with the C's, looking for Cummings. He was unsuccessful. He got up, put the box back and took the second box. "Cummings, Cummings," he repeated aloud while he thumbed through the index cards. "Yes," Nick said to himself. He took the index card with Roger's home phone number and address and went to the bedroom. Nick picked up the phone and punched in the number.

On the third ring, Roger picked up.

"Roger, this is Nick."

"Is Monique all right?"

"I don't know, you tell me."

"Look, man, I don't want to fight with you."

Nick calmed himself. He couldn't afford to have Roger hang up on him. He might not answer the phone when he called him back.

"Listen, Roger, Monique is gone. Do you know where she is?"

"No."

"Roger, don't play games."

"Games? Man, I'm not playing a game."

Nick paused and took a deep breath. "I read the report."

"And?"

"When I got home, Monique was gone. She left a note. If she has gone to look for those people that are her family, I want their address."

"I . . . I . . . I don't understand," Roger said.

"I don't care if they are living in the state prison, I want the address," Nick said, yelling into the receiver.

"Nick, I don't have an address."

"What do you mean, you don't have an address?"

"I don't. I wooo—"

"Roger."

"Nick, listen to me. You're saying that you can't find her?"

"If I knew where she was, I wouldn't have called you."

Nick felt his voice raise once more, louder than before. "Roger, if you don't tell me what's going on, I am not going to think about what I am going to do to you."

"All right," Roger said. "Calm down, brother."

"I'm listening."

"There is no address for her parents, because I . . . I made it up."

"You didn't find her parents?"

"Yes, I found them."

"You're playing with me," Nick said.

"No, I did."

"Who are they, Roger, and where do they live?"

"Monique's mother is Amelia Wakefield."

Shocked, Nick eased down on the bed. "Okay."

"Her father is dead."

"All right."

"That's it."

Nick knew his gut feeling had been right. He felt hot all over. If he had been near Roger, he didn't know what he would have done. Nick clenched his teeth and spoke.

"Roger, if anything happens to Monique, you'll be sorry."

"Nick, I don't know," Roger said in a worried voice.

"You better find her, and you better start looking to-night!"

"I'll call you if I find her."

"Roger, tell me one more thing."

"Anything man," Roger said.

"Why did you tell Monique that lie?"

Roger was quiet. When he didn't speak, Nick called out to him. "Roger?"

"I . . . ah . . . Nick, I really thought that you didn't love her. And there's a special place in my heart for her."

"If you don't find my wife—"

"I will, first thing in the morning," Roger cut in.

"Call me, anytime and anywhere," Nick said, giving Roger his cellular and his pager numbers.

"I'm sorry, Nick."

Nick slammed the phone down.

Suddenly, Nick remembered that Monique might have visited her mother. Yvonne usually went to Florida this time of the year. He dialed the number.

On the fifth ring, the answering machine answered.

"Leave a message at the sound of the beep."

"Mrs. McRay, give me a call." Nick didn't want to alarm Monique's mother. If Monique wasn't visiting with her, he didn't want her to worry.

He checked his watch. It was late. Nick let that thought register, and he continued to worry.

Nick went back to the closet to make sure he had replaced the boxes in order on the shelf, when his hand touched the medium-sized box. Out of curiosity, Nick lifted the box from the shelf and opened it. He sat on the footstool and removed the top. A pair of small black shoes with worn-down heels was inside the box. Nick held them in his hand, then set them back in on the floor. He slipped his fingers around the slender light blue ribbon. "Uh," Nick grunted. He laid the ribbon back inside the box. He picked up a card and read the message.

Monique, we wish you the best, and hope you find happiness and love with your new parents.
From the staff
Pine State Ophanage

Nick's eyes watered. He was glad that he wasn't near Roger. How could Roger use Monique's past to try to intimidate her? He had to know that she feared rejection.

Nick put the contents back in the box and set it back on the shelf, and went downstairs to his study.

Just as he settled on the couch, the doorbell rang. Nick went to open the door. On the other side of his peephole, he saw Stone.

"What's going on, man?" Stone walked in, took off his long thick black coat and laid it on the chair. He took his hat off and set it on top of his coat.

Nick tried to mask the inner anxiety that made a slow rippling trail through him as he and Stone walked to the study. He found it useless to attempt to disguise his feelings from his best friend.

"Monique is gone," Nick finally said as he opened a bottle of brandy at the bar and poured himself a drink.

"You mean she left you?" Stone took a glass from the rack and poured himself a shot of brandy. He held the glass under his nose and inhaled the aroma. "What happened?"

Nick sank down on the hunter green leather sofa and drank more of the brandy before he answered Stone.

"Stone, it's a long story." Nick took another sip of the drink. "But Roger Cummings is at the bottom of this."

Stone sat in the matching chair across from Nick. "The guy that worked for Jerry Mack a few years ago?"

"The one and only." Nick cupped his drink in his hand and crossed one leg over his thigh.

"Monique knows Roger?"

"Yeah," Nick said. "She hired him to find her parents."

Stone took another drink and looked out at Nick over the top of his glass. "What do you mean, find her parents?"

"She's adopted," Nick said, explaining the problem to Stone.

Stone chuckled softly. "That sounds like a stunt Roger would pull."

Nick set his drink down and locked his fingers behind his head.

The phone rang. Nick grabbed the cordless phone on the first ring, hoping that Monique or Roger was calling him.

"Yeah." Nick said, listening quietly. "Did they take anything?" Nick stood up and paced the floor. "No, don't lock them up." Nick cursed under his breath. "I'm on my way." Nick set the phone back on the cradle.

"Don't tell me that one of our clients is in trouble," Stone said.

"No, but we've got to get to the office," Nick said, going to get his coat and hat. "Sharmain and Debra broke into my office."

Ten minutes later, Nick and Stone walked into Nick's law office.

Files and papers from Nick's desk were scattered on the floor. The sofa's cushions were on the floor amid the papers, and the computer was on.

"I was checking the grounds when I saw the light from a flashlight," the guard said. "I came up here and found two women. They told me their names and begged me not to call the police."

"You did the right thing," Nick said.

"Are you sure you don't want to press charges?" the security guard asked Nick.

"No." Nick said while he and Stone gathered papers from the floor and put them on his desk. "Are they in the building?"

"They're in the office with another guard."

When Nick and Stone finished picking up scattered files, they took the elevator to the security office on the first floor.

"What're you looking for?" Nick asked Sharmain, while ignoring Debra.

"I was looking for your marriage contract."

"What makes you think I have a contract?"

"It would take all night to tell you why I suspect there's a piece of paper somewhere that explains in detail your marriage to Miss Monique."

"The next time you break into my office, you're spending all night in jail." He looked at Debra. "You too."

"I can release them, Mr. Parker?" The guard asked.

"Let 'em go." Nick walked out of the office with Stone following close behind.

The next day around noon, Roger walked into Nick's office.

"I can't find her."

"You got to have better news than that." Nick looked up from the paper he was reading.

"I'm serious. I contacted her mother at the address in Atlanta. She's out of the state and left no forwarding address."

"Roger, find Monique." Nick placed one hand on his narrow hip, while clutching the phone in the other. *Roger was all trouble and no help,* Nick pondered, deciding that Roger might not have known about Yvonne's condo in Florida, and every year this time, she left Atlanta for a few months.

"I'm doing the best that I can."

Black fear stabbed at Nick. What if Monique had had an accident. He hadn't watched the news last night. Nonetheless, he hadn't heard of any plane crashes. Nick reached for the phone and called the airport.

On the first ring, Nick hung up. He didn't have a flight number and he didn't have the slightest idea what state she had traveled to.

Nick got up and brushed past Roger. He put on his coat and beckoned for Roger. "If you find her, call me."

"I will," Roger said, following Nick out into the corridor and onto the elevator.

Nick walked through the lobby, passing by the receptionist. "Tell my secretary that I'm out for the day."

He waited for the woman to answer. Nick pushed aside the glass door and headed out to his car.

Ten minutes later, he was walking into the Clip and Bob salon.

"Ump, ump, ump, the handsome hunk has returned," Nick heard a woman say as he walked through Colleen's lobby. He ignored the woman, and walked back into the work area. He stood for a moment, looking around the salon for Colleen. He saw her in the back talking to a man that looked as if he were her employee.

Nick stood beside Colleen and waited for her to finish talking to him.

"Nick."

Colleen didn't look surprised, Nick noticed.

"Where is she?"

Colleen opened the door she was standing next to and ushered Nick inside. "Nick."

"Colleen, if you know, tell me." Nick gazed into Colleen's eyes, hoping that she would tell him where Monique had gone.

"I promised."

"But you know."

Colleen was quiet. She walked around to her desk and sank down in the chair. She nodded. "I know I don't want to break my promise to Monique again."

Nick pressed one hand against the wall and crossed his ankles. "Is she all right?"

"As far as I know, she's fine."

Nick straightened from his stance and pushed his hands in his pockets. It felt as if a heavy weight had lifted off his chest. "I need to talk to her."

Colleen positioned her hands as if she was about to pray. She looked at Nick, then looked away. "Oooh, Nick."

"Come on, Colleen, you won't regret it."

Colleen picked up the receiver and dialed Monique's number.

"If she wants you to know where she is, she'll have to tell you herself." Colleen waited for Monique to pick up the phone. "I'm sick and tired of getting in the middle of yours and Monique's business."

"Monique, Nick is at the salon. He wants to know—"

Colleen stopped. "I didn't tell him where you were. But Monique, he looks so pitiful," Colleen turned her back to Nick and whispered.

Colleen listened. "You're not. Okay."

Nick reached for the phone.

Colleen snatched it away. "Stop," she said to Nick, picking up a pencil and cracking the top of his hand.

"Will you talk to this man before I hurt him."

Colleen talked to Monique for another minute, assuring her that her Shagreens were running smoothly. "I'll talk to you soon."

Colleen gave Nick the phone and walked out.

Nick perched himself on the edge of Colleen's desk. He wished that Monique was beside him. In the meantime, he had to settle for a phone conversation.

"Where are you?"

"I'm in Miami."

"Where were you when I called last night?"

"I was out," Monique said.

"With who?"

"I was out with friends," Monique answered.

Visions of Jeremy circulated across Nick's mind, laced with green jealousy. It was as if he was standing on red-hot coals. "I have been going crazy worrying about you, and you're out with friends?"

"Nick, I had to get away."

Nick closed his eyes and breathed a sigh of relief. "When are you coming home?"

"I'll see you soon," Monique said.

They said good-bye and reluctantly, Nick hung up, with plans to get the next flight to Miami.

Nick called the airport and booked a flight for Friday night. If he didn't have to be in court for the next few days, he would have left earlier.

TWENTY-ONE

The cab driver sat the luggage on the narrow porch. Monique gave him a generous tip, unlocked the door and dragged her luggage into the great room. She opened the closet door and pushed the suitcases inside. She planned to ask Nick to bring them upstairs when he came home.

For the first time in days, she felt wonderful. Monique went upstairs and headed for the shower.

She kicked off her heels and discarded the black pants suit she wore from Florida, along with her other clothes. She turned on the shower and stepped in.

While she enjoyed the hot water spraying against her, Monique recalled her telephone conversation with Nick the day before. As usual, the sound of Nick's voice made her heart warm and flutter. She had detected his worry, yet her body vibrated at the sound of his voice.

Knowing that she was going to be all right seemed to have made her fully alive. She felt relieved just knowing her problems were over.

Monique stepped out of the shower and wrapped a huge thick white towel around her. She went to her bedroom humming "Almost Doesn't Count."

She put on lotion, sprayed cologne and slipped into a short yellow tent-style lounge that stopped at the knee. She didn't bother to put on the matching slippers. It felt good and free padding around in her room shoeless.

Still humming, Monique went to the bathroom and brushed her hair. For no reason at all, she took out her red lipstick and applied the cream strawberry flavor to her lips.

Just as she was blotting her lips with tissue, she looked into the mirror and noticed Nick's reflection. His arms were folded across his bare muscular chest. His mouth was set in a hard line.

"Nick." Monique jumped.

Nick moved into the bathroom and rested his back against the doorjamb. "Do you know that I almost lost my mind?"

"Nick, I left the note so that you wouldn't worry."

"You didn't think I would worry after reading Roger's report?"

Monique remembered being in a rush to get away. She had left the report. However, she hadn't forgotten the information that Roger had presented to her.

Monique leaned against the vanity. "I thought about it. And I was upset. I wanted to know who my parents were, and now I know." She blinked back a tear. "I'm not proud of them, but that's life." Monique went back to the mirror and continued brushing her hair.

"Those are not your parents," Nick corrected her.

"What?"

"Your mother lives in this town."

"How do you know that?"

"Roger finally told the truth."

Monique swirled around to face Nick in the flesh, instead of his reflection in the mirror.

"Who is my mother?"

"Amelia Wakefield."

Monique was shocked. Was this the reason why she got that strange feeling around Amelia Wakefield? It certainly explained Amelia's actions toward her. The woman was attentive, as if she was her mother or at least a friend.

Monique had to admit that part of her was relieved. She would rather have Amelia for her mother any day than the parents Roger had concocted. She had waited so long for the truth.

"He has his reasons," Nick said, not telling Monique what Roger's reasons were.

Monique walked past Nick and into the bedroom. "I wonder why Mrs. Wakefield didn't tell me."

Nick shrugged. "Maybe she feared you would reject her."

Monique glanced at Nick. She could imagine the woman's fear. Hadn't she been afraid that Nick would reject her?

"It's possible."

"Weren't you afraid if I learned your past?"

"That's different."

"How?"

"Well."

"Right, there's not much difference, Monique."

"Nick, maybe she doesn't want me to know that she's my mother. She could be embarrassed at having had a child . . . I don't know."

"Maybe."

"The only way you're going to know how she feels is to talk to her."

"I can hardly believe it," Monique said, as if she was thinking aloud.

Nick smiled. "Amelia is a nice woman."

"How do you know?" Monique paused. "Oh, okay . . . you're her lawyer." Monique remembered Amelia Wakefield telling her that Nick was her lawyer while they were having lunch before her wedding.

It was clear that the woman who was her mother was not going to confront her. Amelia Wakefield had been receiving services for months in her salon, and had not introduced herself. Monique decided that she would break the ice. She herself knew the kind of fear that lurks at the bottom of one's soul when fearing rejection.

"I'll meet with her," Monique said to Nick as he followed her to the sofa and sat on the arm.

"Are you sure you want to do that?" Nick asked Monique, who had stopped pacing.

"I think it would clear things up for me." Monique propped her elbow on her arm that she had rested across her waist. She fingered her chin in deep thought.

"Nick, what if she has other children? A husband?"

"Her husband died months ago," Nick assured Monique. "As far as I know, she doesn't have children."

"Maybe she doesn't want me to know," Monique contemplated, worrying out loud. "What do you think?"

"I think that you should sleep on it. If you still feel the need by morning to meet with Amelia, do it." Nick moved over and stood before her.

"Maybe that'll work," Monique replied, considering Nick's suggestion.

Monique suddenly became aware of Nick's closeness. He towered over her.

She looked up at him.

"What?"

"Don't you have something to tell me?" Nick sat on the edge of the sofa's arm, holding on to Monique's wrist.

Monique thought for a moment. She couldn't think of any urgent message she had to tell him.

"I don't think so," she replied after a few seconds of thoughtfulness.

Nick reached out and pulled Monique to the edge of the sofa where he was still sitting on the arm.

"Are you pregnant?"

The only person who knew she thought she was pregnant was Colleen. However, the pregnancy had been a false alarm. She hadn't gotten around to telling Colleen since she had just returned home.

"I'm not pregnant."

"If that's true, why did Colleen have a message on her desk from your doctor?"

"It was a false alarm," Monique said, hoping to soothe Nick's worries.

Still holding Monique's wrist, Nick stood up and gazed down at her, as if he dared her to avoid him. "Tell me about it."

"I thought that I was . . ." She let the words fade. "Anyway, I bought a pregnancy test from the drugstore. It turned out that it was defective."

"How do you know?"

"I went to the doctor while I was in Miami." Monique touched Nick's arm. "I wanted to make sure."

Nick continued to hold Monique's gaze.

"The test was negative," Nick stated flatly.

"Um, hum."

He didn't relent.

"Are you sure about that?" Nick's voice was low and, to Monique, it was as if he spoke with an icy tone.

A horrible realization crept across Monique's mind.

"Oh . . . no. I wouldn't—" Monique stopped herself. Nick couldn't be thinking that she wouldn't want their baby. But considering their reasons for marrying, she could understand his suspicion.

"I should've told you," Monique stated, pulling Nick with her to the sofa to sit. "But after reading Roger's report, I figured it was best that I didn't." She smiled. "I don't know how I was going to keep you from finding out." She turned to Nick again, studying his handsome face. "I didn't know what I was going to do. But if I was pregnant, I had planned to raise the child."

"No, we would've raised our child together."

Monique didn't say anything. Being with Nick just to raise their child was even more frightening.

"Nick, a baby is not a reason for us to stay married,"

Monique said. "There's no reason for you to feel trapped just because you feel obligated to be a full-time father."

"I wouldn't feel trapped." Nick propped one foot on the sofa and rested the other on the floor. "Would you?" He rested his arm on his propped knee.

"Nick, we married for our own gain. And I think that babies are supposed to be planned." Monique frowned. "If I had been pregnant, I expected that we would divorce as planned, and I would raise my child."

"No, that would've never worked."

"You don't have to worry. It just happened that I had a bad case of the flu," Monique said.

Nick leaned over and pulled her to him. His lips captured hers, burning and making Monique swirl, just so. He held up, his eyes sweeping over her seductively. "We can plan that kid right now."

In spite of herself, Monique laughed. "I don't think so."

Nick leaned into her again. His mouth covered hers in a drugging kiss.

Monique clung to him, feeling her desire rise along with her temperature.

Nick raised up again. "Your project is complete. There's nothing stopping us."

Monique circled her arms around Nick's neck and hugged him. As she felt him fold her in his arms, she allowed herself to nestle against his strong, hard body. She wanted to stay in his embrace forever. She couldn't. The time for their marriage would soon end.

"No, there's nothing stopping us, except that maybe you need time."

"For what?" he asked. His lips brushed hers as he spoke.

"I don't share."

"Neither do I."

Monique untangled herself from Nick's embrace, at least they would part as friends.

"Nick, these last months have been hard. Every time we made love, it was because we were pushed together."

"I know, we didn't follow the contract, but I'm not complaining."

"I think we should take our time and see what will happen."

"If that's what you want," Nick said, pulling her back to him.

"We can go out and become good friends, like we were before."

"Sounds good to me."

"If by the end of the six months, we're still friends, we'll stay together."

Nick kissed her lightly, tapping his fingers against her spine.

Monique swayed and spun. Her blood inched through her veins. Her mind was not willing, but her body disobeyed.

Nick lay in his bed, awake and unable to sleep. The months had rolled in like tides in the night. Soon his and Monique's marriage would end. If only Monique loved him. Their marriage would work. Nick made up his mind that he would stay out of her bedroom. Monique seemed to enjoy their lovemaking. After that, it was as if he didn't exist.

Monique needed time. He intended to give her as much as she needed.

TWENTY-TWO

The next morning, Monique sat behind her desk in her office and dialed Amelia Wakefield's phone number that she retrieved from her salon files.

While Monique waited for Amelia to answer her telephone call, she hoped she wasn't making a mistake.

"Hello." Amelia's voice came across the line and out to Monique.

"Mrs. Wakefield, this is Monique from—"

"Shagreens," Amelia said, finishing Monique's sentence. "What can I do for you, dear?"

"I would like to invite you to have lunch with me today."

"I would love it."

Monique noticed that Amelia Wakefield didn't ask her what the occasion for their lunch was. "Will one o'clock be too late?"

"No, the timing is perfect."

Monique chose a quiet restaurant on the outskirts of town.

"I'll be there," Amelia said, sounding as if she was smiling.

"Thank you, Mrs. Wakefield."

Monique hung up. Before she could register her conversation with Amelia, her phone rang.

"Monique, let's do lunch," Colleen said.

"I can't, I have a lunch date."

"It's about time you and Nick started acting like husband and wife."

Monique listened to her girlfriend, who had hoped that her and Nick's wedding really meant living happily ever after.

"I'm not lunching with Nick. I'll fill you in later."

"Monique, who're you going to lunch with?"

"I'm not telling."

"Ahh, Monique, you're not cheating on my boy."

"Colleen, stop saying that. Some of your nosy customers might hear you."

"Tell me you're not."

"I'm not cheating, but you're really going to be surprised."

"Monique."

"Good-bye, Colleen." Monique hung up and went to assist the clients.

Cheating? Monique reflected on Colleen's suspicious statement. *Never.*

Monique pushed open the smoked glass door to the restaurant and walked inside across the black and gray marble floor. She checked her coat and waited for the maitre d' to seat her.

The pianist sat at the glossy black piano striking the keys softly, playing the tune, "Rain Drops," as the elegant lunch crowd gathered.

"Enjoy your lunch." The maitre d' pulled back a chair near the wide window that showed a view of a flowing fountain.

"Thanks," Monique said, smiling up at the tall elderly sophisticated gentleman.

"As soon as your guest arrives, I will walk her over." The man spoke with a Parisian accent. He laid two long, thin brown leather-bound menus on the table, one in front of

Monique, and the other where he intended to seat
Monique's lunch guest.

It had been several months since Monique had dined
in the restaurant. However, nothing had changed except
for the fresh flowers that usually decorated the dining
room and bar area in the summer months, along with the
tall green trees.

Monique reached out and touched the tree that was
standing slightly behind her chair. The leaves were silky
and green. If she didn't know any better, she would have
thought the trees in the restaurant were authentic.

Monique settled back in her soft, cushioned chair and
observed the flowing fountain. She was determined to banish the small apprehension that coursed through her.
What if Amelia Wakefield had put her in an ophanage
because she didn't want her? What if she had no other
choice? What if . . . Monique pushed the scary pondering
out of her mind.

"Hello, Monique," Amelia said, allowing the maitre d'
to seat her.

"Hi," Monique smiled, admiring Amelia's burnt orange
calf-length suit. Her makeup was impeccably applied. Her
neck and wrists were circled and sparkling with expensive
jewelry.

Seated and smiling at Monique, Amelia sat straight in
her chair. "So, tell me, how is married life treating you?"

"It . . . it's fine." Monique almost choked on her words.
Her and Nick's marriage was about as good as expected,
under the circumstances.

Not wanting to waste time, Monique opened the menu
and chose her lunch. Amelia joined her as they flipped
through the menu. Monique chose her favorite dish,
shrimp-spinach crepe stack and a strawberry-peach cooler.

She closed the menu, noticing that Amelia hadn't made
a choice in selecting her lunch from the menu. But she

thought it would be an excellent idea to get down to business concerning the subject of biological parenthood.

"Mrs. Wakefield, I recently became aware of some news that I would like very much to discuss with you."

"Sure, how can I help you?" Amelia looked up from her menu and closed the book.

"In the process of searching for my biological parents, I learned that you were my mother," Monique said, getting to the point of the issue.

Amelia pressed her hand against her chest, her jewelry dangling just so from her wrist. She opened her mouth to speak, but no words came out.

"I didn't mean to upset you," Monique said, sorry that she had confronted the woman, who probably wanted nothing to do with the fact that she had an adult daughter.

"No," Amelia finally said. "I'm shocked that you know, and I am so ashamed."

"Ashamed?"

Amelia blinked her long lashes as if blinking back the tears that Monique recognized in her clear eyes.

"Yes. I should've told you. But I thought that if I introduced myself as your mother . . ." Her voice faded.

Monique leaned forward. Amelia seemed emotionally distressed.

"Listen, I didn't mean to upset you. I needed to know for my own satisfaction who my natural parents were. I'm not angry at you."

Amelia opened her purse that lay in her lap and took out an embroidered white handkerchief. She dabbed her eyes.

"Let me explain, please," Amelia said, eyeing Monique closely. "I was sixteen . . . fast . . . fresh, and I loved the ground that Marshall Taylor walked on." She looked out at the fountain, as if she was remembering yesterday.

"My father was the head of many organizations in the church. My mother was head nurse at the local hospital."

Amelia turned to look at Monique, as if checking Monique's reactions. "When they forbade me to see Marshall, I disobeyed my parents, and I sneaked out of more windows in our house that I care to mention." She lowered her gaze. "Marshall was twenty years old."

"Marshall worked on his father's farm for two years before he went to college. He told me one Sunday night that he was leaving for college the next day. I purposely left my mother's potted plants outside in the cold that evening."

Amelia smiled at her daughter. She wiped another tear. "I told my mother that I was going out to bring the plants inside. Instead, I met Marshall. We made love, and you were conceived."

"I see." Monique didn't know what to say. She wanted to ask more questions about her father, but seeing how emotional the conversation had made Amelia, Monique decided not to pry further.

The waiter set their salads before them. Amelia smiled at the young man and waited for him to leave before she continued.

"When I learned that I was pregnant, I thought my parents, especially my dad, were going to drag Marshall out of college and give us one of those shotgun weddings." Amelia laughed in spite of the tears that settled in her eyes.

Monique smiled at her.

"Instead, my parents shipped me off to Vermont to my dad's older sister. I stayed there until you were born. My aunt sent me home telling me that she was going to raise you and take care of you. I trusted her." Amelia could not control the tears that rolled slowly down her cheeks.

Monique reached for her napkin and dabbed her eyes. "You don't have to continue. I get the picture."

"No. I need to do this. I was never allowed to speak about you to anyone, until after I finished college."

"Why? I don't understand." Monique was curious.

"It wasn't proper for young ladies to conceive children before marriage in those days. So it wasn't proper for my aunt to bring the child that she was supposed to be looking after to my parents home on holidays when I was home."

"I was young and stupid!" Amelia almost shouted the whisper. "When I asked my aunt or parents how you were doing, they all lied and agreed that you were fine."

"Did your aunt put me in the ophanage?"

"No, my parents did."

"Oh."

"I learned all of this when I graduated college."

Monique actually felt sorry for Amelia.

"When I tried to retrieve records through the courts, the records were sealed."

"I know. The same happened to me when I began my search for you."

"Did you hire a detective?"

"I did," Monique said.

"I did too. But when I learned that you had lived and probably suffered in that . . . that horrible place . . ." Amelia finally ate a small piece of the lettuce. "And then I found you . . . I knew you would blame me."

"I don't blame you."

"I could hardly blame you if you did."

"I probably never would've searched for you if it hadn't been for an incident that took place in my life," Monique said, spearing a slice of carrot with her fork and eating it.

"A bad experience?" Amelia inquired with a worried expression.

"It's over, and it's nothing to worry about," Monique assured her.

The women ate mostly in silence after Amelia's confession.

When they had finished their meal, Amelia offered to pay.

"No, lunch is on me," Monique promised her.

"But I do have one request," Monique said. "After learning that you're my mother, I can't possibly go around calling you Mrs. Wakefield. So, I would like to call you Amelia."

"That's perfect," Amelia said, laughing.

"Do you know what happened to my father?"

"Oh, God rest his soul. He passed on."

"I'm sorry to hear that."

"He knew that my parents didn't approve of him. So, he worked hard and he became a very wealthy man. After our spouses died, I . . . we met and I told him that I had found you and that I was too afraid to tell you."

"He was alive?"

"Yes, but very ill."

"In his will he left you property." Amelia smiled. "I've been trying to decide for the longest time how I was going to tell you about the apartment complexes he left you in Piscataway, New Jersey." Amelia took a slip of paper from a small note pad in her purse and wrote the property address. Underneath that she wrote the name, address, and phone number of Monique's father's lawyer. She gave the information to Monique and pushed away from the table.

"He never knew me."

Amelia lowered her lids. "He saw you one day . . . at work."

Monique's mouth fell open. Not a word came out. She remembered the tall, light skinned man with a thick stock of curly hair in her lobby at Shagreen II. He had smiled at her. She, being polite, had returned his smile.

"Shortly after that he had another stroke," Amelia said.

Monique didn't know what to say.

"Listen, I have a meeting in about twenty minutes. So, I will see you tomorrow, young lady."

Monique smiled as she watched Amelia walk swiftly across the marble floors.

On her way to the coat checkout station, Monique

glanced across the room. Her heart felt as if it had flip-flopped. Nick was having lunch with an attractive woman that looked to be in her late thirties or early forties.

Monique moved to the coat station and positioned her-self so that she could see Nick without looking obvious. She knew that Nick often had lunch with his clients. And many times he took his secretary or colleague to lunch.

As much as Monique wanted to believe that this woman was a secretary or a client she couldn't. The woman was attentive to him, hanging on to his every word. The woman turned her face slightly toward Monique, before she turned back to Nick. Monique realized that Nick was hav-ing lunch with Jacqueline.

"Your coat," the young man working the coat station interrupted her gazing. Just before she gave the man her ticket for the coat, she noticed Stone joining Nick and Jacqueline. She turned her attention back to the young man who was holding her coat out to her.

"Thanks," Monique forced a smile, and tipped the gen-tleman.

The green-eyed monster that Monique thought had died sprang to life, clawing at her heart.

Monique went straight to her office after she returned from having lunch with Amelia and called Nick. She told the receptionist her name and waited for Nick to answer her call.

"Monique, are you all right?" Nick asked, as if he was surprised to hear from her.

"Yes, and no. Mostly yes." Monique said careful not to mention to Nick that she had seen him at the restaurant with Jacqueline.

"What happened?"

"I met with Amelia, and the woman had me almost in tears."

Nick chuckled. "Everything went well."

"Great, to be exact. My father left me property in Piscataway, New Jersey."

"Get out of here."

"I'm not kidding you." Monique laughed lightly at the turn of events the day had produced.

Monique and Nick said their good-byes after making plans to go out dancing after work. She set the receiver down. She might as well enjoy herself. She and Nick would be divorced soon. Monique studied the thought. Maybe, maybe not.

That evening, Monique dressed in a low-cut, tight black dress and black heels. She twisted her hair up on her head, pinning it with a gold comb.

She was putting on her earrings when Nick knocked on her bedroom door.

"Let's go, Monique. A man will starve to death waiting on you."

"I'm coming. Gracious!" Monique pushed and clamped the last earring back in her pierced ear. Hurrying so that Nick wouldn't starve, she grabbed her purse and walked out into the hallway.

Dressed in his charcoal gray suit, Nick greeted her with a low, slow whistle.

"Ah, cut out the wolf whistle."

Nick laughed as they took the stairs down to the foyer.

Monique took her and Nick's coats from the closet near the door.

"Stone and his new woman friend are having dinner with us tonight." Nick took the coat Monique was handing him and put it on.

"Do we know her?" Monique asked while Nick helped her with her coat.

"I've met her," Nick said, opening the front door, holding it so Monique could step outside.

Monique didn't see much of Stone. When he came over to visit with Nick and she was downstairs, Stone was always pleasant to her.

The reception dinner was the first time she had been in his company socially.

Nick held the car door open for Monique and she sank down into the soft leather seat and waited for him to take his place behind the steering wheel.

"You didn't tell me where we were going," Monique said when they were driving out on the main highway.

"There's this new little restaurant right outside of town." Nick gave her a sidelong glance. "I think you'll like it."

Monique wasn't sure. Most restaurants were romantic that fit that description.

"How do you know about that restaurant?"

"I had lunch there."

"Lunch, with who?"

Again, Nick gave Monique a quick glance, before turning his attention back to the road.

When Nick turned away, Monique was still looking at him. She noticed his thick mustache tip curl into a smile.

"A smile is not the answer to my question," she said.

"I had lunch with colleagues."

All Monique could see now was the woman from the paralegal department, wearing one of her five-inch dresses or suits, smiling and grinning up at Nick. Monique had gone to Nick's office once and she couldn't help but notice the woman smiling at Nick and watching every move he made.

"Do I have to give you names?" Nick chuckled softly.

"I am waiting patiently."

Nick laughed. "You sound like a jealous wife."

"I am not jealous."

Nick's laughter filled the car as he drove into the parking lot.

"Stone and I had lunch."

"Oh," Monique said, getting out of the car, not waiting for Nick to assist her, and bracing herself to keep from asking about the woman she had seen him with earlier in the day.

The restaurant was small and intimate. Dim lights lighted the small establishment. Round tables were covered with pale pink tablecloths and centered with white candles, glowing from silver candle holders.

Shortly after they were seated, Stone and his woman friend joined them.

Nick rose from his chair and extended his hand, while Stone helped her get seated.

"Felita, this is Monique, Nick's wife. Monique. Felita Mincey."

Felita was about the size of Monique. She was attractive, with a warm light brown complexion and shoulder-length hair. She owned three restaurants. Her most recent purchase was in Cherry Hill, New Jersey.

Monique hadn't remembered seeing Felita around town. She didn't want to make assumptions as to where she lived, so she asked Felita.

"Felita, do you live in town?"

"Yes," she said. "My family lives here."

Monique tilted her head, trying to place her.

"My uncle just opened the newest newspaper in town a short time ago."

"Oh, I see," Monique said. She turned her attention to the waiter, who was prepared to take their drink orders.

After the wine was ordered, Monique stole a glance at Nick. She wondered if Felita Mincey was related to Jacqueline. Monique wanted to inquire into this matter without Nick hearing her.

"Excuse me," Monique said to the men as she got up

from the table. "Would you like to come with me?" she asked Felita.

"Sure." Felita got up and walked with Monique to the ladies room.

While Monique fumbled with her pantyhose that were perfect, she posed the question.

"Are you related to a woman named Jacqueline that works for your uncle's newspaper?"

Felita smiled. "Yes, she's my cousin."

Jealousy crawled through Monique's stomach and clawed at her throat. *I bet Nick did have lunch here last week, with that Jacqueline woman again.* She let the thought grab her and hold her, unleashing the monster that had turned a darker shade of green.

"I'm ready if you are," Monique smiled at Felita.

Back at the table with Nick, Stone and Felita, Monique was quiet. She sipped her wine and stole glances at her husband, while they waited to be served.

Nick leaned over to Monique. "Are you all right?"

"I'll let you know when we get home."

Nick let out a low groan. He turned back to Stone and they continued their conversation.

Monique was polite, talking to Felita and Stone. She barely said much to Nick during dinner.

When they had finished eating, Nick took Monique by her hand and led her out onto the small dance floor. He drew her in his arms.

Monique slipped her arms around Nick's neck as they moved to the beat of the slow music.

"What's wrong?" Nick asked her as they danced.

Monique leaned back and looked at him. To speak her thoughts out loud to him might produce a scene. She had no intentions of making a public spectacle of herself tonight. So instead of talking, Monique rested her head against his strong hard chest and enjoyed being in his arms.

The evening ended with the foursome promising to go out again soon. Nick slipped his arms around Monique's waist and they walked to the car.

Once inside, Nick started the engine. "I'm still waiting for you to talk to me."

"I told you that we'll talk when we get home."

Nick put the car in drive and drove out into the street.

Monique sat quietly, looking straight ahead. Nick would be free to date soon. He was probably as anxious as she was to get this marriage over with. He could have all the intimate lunches he wanted with that woman.

Before long, Nick had parked inside the garage. Monique got out of the car and took swift steps inside. She waited in the kitchen for Nick.

"All right, Monique, tell me."

"If you would've told me that we were going to have dinner with your girlfriend's cousin, I would've stayed home and you could've taken Jacqueline to dinner."

"You did not go there." Nick reached out to Monique as she walked past him on her way upstairs.

"Don't you touch me."

"Monique, I have no control over who Stone dates."

"I'm not saying you do. But to have lunch at a romantic restaurant in the middle of the day . . . I have a pot of gold to give you."

Nick dragged Monique to him as she started to leave the kitchen again. He pressed her hard against him.

"Listen to me. Even with the way our marriage is, I will never cheat on you." Nick tried to explain to Monique why he and Stone had eaten at the restaurant. It was for the sole purpose of seeing if the food and service were good, since it was a new restaurant. "Jacqueline joined us later."

Monique's temper throbbed from anger, as she listened to Nick's explanation.

She and Colleen had done the same thing, once or

twice. It was always better to check first, before inviting another person to join you. But still, she couldn't get the vision of Nick and Jacqueline out of her mind. She swallowed hard, as if by doing so she would swallow her anger.

"Even if I were cheating, I wouldn't be bold about it. You didn't stop until you gave Jeremy our phone number."

Monique wrestled her way out of Nick's grip. "Don't you talk to me about a man named Jeremy." Monique hurried upstairs, went to her bedroom and slammed the door.

Ooh, Lord, don't let me lose my mind.

Nick stood at the top of the stairs and watched Monique's bedroom door. He was in more trouble than he thought. He had to convince Monique that he was faithful. *Maybe I should wait until tomorrow,* Nick mused, trying to make up his mind whether or not he should knock on her bedroom door.

What the heck, Nick pondered, and tapped his fist against the door.

"Go away!"

Nick shrugged. The next time he had a question as to what he should do, he'd follow his first thoughts. Nick went to his room. Some things weren't meant to be. One thing he was sure wasn't meant to happen was his and Monique's relationship. He had run out of ways to make her happy. He had been sadly mistaken if he thought Monique would understand him. The dreadful truth was that she was seriously married in name only. The more he tried to show Monique that he loved her, the more she seemed not to want him around. He had fought battles of restraint, staying out of her bedroom. He had worked late at the office. He had worked on cars with Stone until all hours of the night. He had tried and nothing had worked. Nick knew it was time to give up. His efforts had been useless.

He vowed never to place himself in a situation like that again.

TWENTY-THREE

Six months finally rolled around. Monique McRay Parker sat on the stool behind the reception desk, sipped warm coffee and waited for Tamika to arrive.

While she waited, she summed up her life. Everything changed with seasons. April showers watered the earth, turning leaves on trees green. Flowers blossomed, and the world seemed at peace.

Except for her world. She had money, two successful businesses, and was in the process of buying a day spa. She even owned apartments in Piscataway, New Jersey. Life was strange. With all her semi-wealth, she didn't have the man that she had fallen in love with. Since their last fight, all they had done was avoid each other, as if both had the black plague.

She had distanced herself from Nick, and he had stayed out of her way. This frightened her. But as long as she could remember, she had been afraid all of her life.

She had run to escape from pain and rejection as if she was a fragile woman made of glass, and would shatter at the slightest conflict. She was exhausted from running and she intended to do something about it.

The door opened, drawing Monique out of her deliberations.

"Hi," Colleen said, walking to the reception desk and leaning on the counter.

"Morning," Monique said dryly.

"Aren't we in a bad mood," Colleen lamented, fingering a facial advertisement that was standing up in a tray with about twenty other flyers.

"Colleen, if you were in a situation like I am in, what would you do?"

"Girl, are you referring to your marriage to Nick?"

"I am."

Colleen put her hands on her hips and took a T-stance. "I would be so married to that man . . ." She stopped talking and looked at her friend. "It's time for the divorce."

"Yes."

Colleen looked away, as if she was contemplating Monique's question. "Monique, you know I think that you need to figure this one out for yourself."

"No advice?"

"You can handle it."

"It's just that I'm so afraid sometimes, I don't know what to do."

"Well, I do have one piece of advice. Walk up to your fear, girl."

Monique smiled. "I might just do that."

"That's what I would do." Colleen spread her fingers.

"I do have a few ideas," Monique stated. If she was going to say good-bye to Nick, she might as well do it in style. A style that he would never forget.

"All right, devil, don't write no checks that you can't cash." Colleen laughed.

Tamika walked in. "Good morning. You guys are in a good mood. What're you laughing about?"

"Nothing," Monique and Colleen said in unison.

"Tamika, I have some errands to run. I'll be back to help you close." Monique got off the stool and got her purse from the shelf underneath the counter. It was time. She hoped that she wasn't too late.

* * *

Nick's law office lobby was quiet. Brown shiny leather sofa, love seat and chair were empty of waiting clients. The room was neat and clean. A red, pink and yellow abstract picture that hung on the wall behind the leather sofa shone like new.

Live green plants that appeared to be artificial sat in the corners.

Monique walked up to the white smoky window where she knew the receptionist was perched on her high swivel chair.

She tapped the bell that sat on the counter, alerting the receptionist.

"I'm here to see Nick," Monique said, waiting for the woman to buzz her inside.

"He's in the conference room, in a meeting," the receptionist informed her.

"I'll wait in his office," Monique said, moving toward the door.

"Yes, Mrs. Parker."

Monique remembered the receptionist from her and Nick's wedding and reception. "Thank you," Monique said. She walked through the door that buzzed open for her, down the hallway to Nick's office and entered.

The room was cool and smelled like fresh flowers. Monique noticed a bouquet on the end table near the leather sofa. Awards that Nick had received for mentoring the children from the Community Center hung on the wall. There were large photos of Nick and Stone and another man that Monique had never seen before posing near a red and white '57 Ford automobile.

Young Men's Club awards for Lawyer of the Year and many other plaques decorated Nick's law office. Monique went over to the window and took in the view of the lovely tulips that surrounded the flowing fountain.

She walked away from the window and sat on the sofa while she waited for Nick. She wondered if Nick was serious about his feelings for her. Or if he were being polite. Monique intended to find out.

"Monique." Nick's thick black mustache tipped into a smile. "What brings you here?"

Monique stood. "It's time to annul the marriage. I need to know, have you filed the papers for our divorce."

"I won't file if you don't want it."

"What about you . . . the agreement?"

Nick walked to his desk and dropped the folder down. "You know how I feel about you."

"Do I?"

"Monique, I won't beg you to stay with me." Nick moved back to her.

Her impish considerations made Monique consider carrying out her plan." I'm not asking you to beg me to stay. It's not like we didn't know this day was coming."

"It's up to you," Nick said. "I can't continue like this."

"What do you want from me, Nick?"

"Show me that you care."

"Are you serious?"

"Yes, I'm serious. You mean more to me than a contract."

Monique walked to the door and opened it. "I'll see you later."

The mall was quiet. Mothers were pushing happy babies in strollers. Senior citizens enjoyed mingling and conversing with each other, sitting on benches, surrounded by flowers and plants.

Monique walked into the lingerie shop. The minute she walked in she saw several outfits she liked. Monique decided to browse first, noticing more beautiful negligees.

"Can I help you?" a saleswoman offered.

"No, thank you," Monique said, reaching for a long black nylon gown with thin straps, designed to expose both sides of the waist.

"It's beautiful," the woman said, as if she were complimenting Monique's good taste.

"Yes, it is," Monique said, moving further across the room where there were more sexy night gowns, and negligees. She moved over to the laced teddy and held it out in front of her. Monique draped the tiny lace teddy over her arm. It was too bad she didn't have a marriage that allowed her to show off her sexy new lingerie.

With that thought in mind, the conversation that she'd had with Nick earlier crossed her mind. *Show me that you care.* Monique smothered the thought.

Finally, she paid for her purchases, walked out of the mall and headed out to her car. Monique didn't realize that she had spent so much time in the shop. The sun had sank low in the sky and it was almost dark. She stood on the curb looking out over the parking lot for her car. More cars had filled the empty parking spaces since she arrived at the mall.

Slowly, Monique began to walk in the direction she thought she may have parked. She didn't have all evening to look for her car in a crowded parking lot.

Several minutes later, she found her car. She loaded her packages in the back seat and got in.

As she drove through the thick traffic, Monique allowed herself to think about her and Nick's situation. If they hadn't married for selfish reasons, they could've had a wonderful relationship. But greed knows no boundaries, Monique reminded herself. Nick wanted land, she wanted her business. They had schemed like immature adults to get what they both wanted, and they had been successful.

A car horn honked, drawing Monique out of thoughts, she slammed on the brakes, almost hitting the car in front of her, making her feel as if her heart had flown to her throat.

For a moment, Monique sat in her car not moving, while angry drivers blew their horns for to her move through the green traffic light. Finally, she composed herself and drove home, with tears burning her eyes.

Instead of going inside, Monique sat in the car and cried regretful tears. When she and Nick had dated, she had been too concerned about Nick rejecting her because of her adoption. Later she had learned that he thought it was wonderful that she had been adopted by people who loved her.

Her worries had been in vain. She had made matters worse when she went to him and asked for his assistance. Even worse was that she had married him. Added to the top of that list, she really did love him.

Monique reached back into the back seat and grabbed her packages along with a box of tissues that she kept on the back seat. She pulled a soft white tissue from the box and wiped her eyes, before going inside the house.

Now it was too late for her and Nick. She'd had many chances to show and tell him that she loved him. But she hadn't. Instead, she had been afraid of being hurt. Added to those feelings were jealousy. She could barely stand to see another woman look at him.

Monique got out of the car. She had to show Nick that she cared. She couldn't walk away without a fight.

Monique carried her packages to her bedroom and spread the black lingerie on the bed. She smiled to herself at the short sheer negligee that barely covered her bottom, designed to mesmerize and conceal nothing. It was time to move forward.

Monique went to her closet and began taking her winter clothes off the rack. She put the clothes in garment bags and packed the shoes she wanted to keep.

Monique went downstairs for boxes. On her way to the

garage, she stopped in the kitchen. "Would you make dinner tonight?" Monique asked the maid.

"Of course, Mrs. Parker," the maid said.

Monique told the maid what she wanted on the menu. She was taking daring steps. What if Nick didn't come home? The thought trekked across her mind. Monique banished her musing and continued to help the maid plan the menu.

When she had finished helping the maid with the menu, she took the boxes she had taken from the garage and carried them upstairs.

Upstairs in her closet, Monique packed away the shoes and clothes that she was donating to the Salvation Army. She made a call to the establishment, took the shoes downstairs and set them near the front door.

She had made up her mind. Looking back, she knew that Nick had truly loved her for herself and not for property that he wanted.

Monique ran a hot tub and filled it with strawberry bubbles. She discarded her clothes and slowly sank down into warm water. She sank deeper, humming "Baby, I'm Yours."

For several minutes, Nick observed the boxes near the front door.

Early that day, when Monique had surprised him with a visit, he'd had hope. Now, looking at the boxes on the floor, he knew it was the end for them. He couldn't force her to stay, and he wouldn't.

Nick walked upstairs to his room instead of going to the study, which was usually his first stop when he came home from work.

As he moved through the house, he could smell the dinner he was sure the maid was preparing.

The maid only cooked when he asked her to, when he was living alone. He didn't have an appetite tonight. He was exhausted from work, worry and his relationship with Monique.

In his room, Nick undressed and showered. When he finished, he pulled on a pair of charcoal gray silk pj bottoms and attempted to relax in his recliner. He stretched his long legs out, resting them on the ottoman and savoring the snuggling passion that he and Monique had shared in the short time that they were together.

If he thought it would have done any good, he would get on his knees and beg her to stay. He knew better. Monique was a stubborn, determined woman. Once she made up her mind, she did exactly what she wanted to do.

Nick was going to let her leave, but he couldn't watch her go. He lay back, resting his head against the chair's soft leather. He hadn't made many mistakes in his life. But marrying Monique and losing control almost every time he was within two feet of her were the biggest mistakes he had ever made.

Monique had her businesses, and he had his land. They had both achieved their goals. She wanted nothing to do with him now.

He lay on his bed and closed his eyes. He felt as if his heart was going to shatter into a million tiny pieces.

The knock on his door drew him out of his chagrin. Nick rose. It was probably the maid, wanting him to come down for his dinner.

"I'm not hungry," he said, lying back and rolling his head from side to side. It was as if the rotating motion would somehow roll all the memories he had about Monique out of his head. But he couldn't dismiss the strong passion and true love that he felt for her.

The door to his bedroom opened. Monique stood in his room wearing a white terry bathrobe, black fur top heels and carrying a small basket.

Nick raised himself up on his elbows. "Are you leaving soon?"

"When I'm finished here," she said.

Nick noticed her moving closer to him. "I'm tired," he said, knowing if she moved too close to him, he wouldn't be able to keep his promise.

"I think a nice massage will untighten those muscles," Monique said. "All you have to do is lay back and relax."

"Why're you doing this?" Nick asked. He wanted to be alone in his misery. What was Monique trying to do, make him crazy?

Nick watched through half-opened lids as she reached into the basket. She took out a bottle of lotion, held it up over his chest, and squeezed out the creamy liquid. It dropped slowly on his chest and stomach. Nick groaned from the cool strawberry-scented sensation.

With the soft stroke of her fingers, Monique massaged the lotion into his skin. He let out another lamenting groan as she slipped his pj's down his long strong legs and off his body. Nick watched as she flung them over her head and onto the floor.

Suddenly, he could feel her weight shift. Nick opened his eyes just long enough to see Monique remove the white bathrobe. He let out another groan as he marveled at the black sheer short negligee that showed every inch of her.

Nick drew in a deep breath. He was going to stay in control, even if it caused him serious damage. "Monique, if you came here to torture me and leave, you can go now."

"No," was her sexy reply.

Nick closed his eyes. He refused to look at her. If she wanted to give him a well-needed massage, he would gladly accept. But he wouldn't touch her.

He felt Monique sit on the bed again. She leaned over and instead of massaging his body, she blew lightly on his chest, making a burning trail down to the edge of his stomach. Nick gripped the headboard, straining to stay in control.

Monique repeated the process, this time lower. Nick tried to speak, but instead of words, he heard himself growl. Finally, he found his intelligent voice. "You were supposed to massage me."

"I am," he heard her say as his skin sizzled with a slow fiery burn.

When Monique reached the point of no return, Nick tried to tell her to stop in the English language. Instead, a low snarl trekked and inched its way to his throat and finally escaped from his lips. "Ahhhhhh."

"Stop it," he said when he could finally speak, breathing almost out of control from waves of electricity that raged through his body and shocked him out of his good sound masculine senses.

Monique stopped.

He watched her stand and gather her basket. Out of control, he raised up and pulled her down underneath him, making her squeal delightfully.

"Are you going to stay with me?" Nick asked her in a low husky voice, before he captured her lips in a smoldering kiss.

"Yes," Monique said.

"You like to play?" He gazed into her eyes, easing the straps down off her shoulders and off her arms.

"I'm not playing," he heard her say, as if she was breathless.

"Neither am I," Nick's seductive gaze held hers. "I love you . . . too much." His voice sounded as if loving her had been a guarded secret. "I want more than our lovemaking. I want a true loving relationship with you." He spoke to Monique in a low husky whisper.

"I love you, Nick," Monique confessed, meeting his intense gaze.

"I'm serious, baby." Nick lowered his head, touching her ear with his lips. "If we can't have real love, I don't want anything from you."

As she melted in the sweetness of her and Nick's love, they became one heart, one body and one soul. All was well in her and Nick's world.